I0680943

Pride Publishing books by M.C. Roth

Single Books
The Drumbeat of His Heart
A Song for His Heart
Karma's Kiss
Greedy Boy
Feral Woods

It's a Kink Thing
Kinked Up
Unkinked
Kinks and Crosshairs
Dupli-Kinked

Collections
Secret Santa: Daddy's Secret

It's a Kink Thing

DUPLI-KINKED

M.C. ROTH

Dupli-Kinked
ISBN # 978-1-80250-513-9
©Copyright M.C. Roth 2023
Cover Art by Kelly Martin ©Copyright February 2023
Interior text design by Claire Siemaszkiewicz
Pride Publishing

DUPLI-KINKED

Dedication

For Q

Chapter One

Copley

The ring burned a hole through the pocket of his jeans, drawing his attention with every step. It was supposed to be a symbol of his love, which had simmered for three years and burned bright for another two. Instead, it was the sole representation of his humiliation.

He'd been so excited when he'd strolled into the jewelry store while wearing his best dress shirt and a pair of slacks that had fit him just right. He dressed well for his work, but he'd never really worn something truly expensive before.

He'd kept his jaw sewn tight as he looked at the price tags on every ring, going from glass case to glass case until he'd finally found the dismal selection targeted for men. A simple gold band had barely been within his budget, but he'd needed something. He hadn't been able to go another moment without telling Spencer how he felt about him.

They'd hardly spoken during the whispered moments at night when they had lain together in the most intimate embrace. But what was he supposed to say to someone who had started as his roommate but had stolen his heart instead?

It had all begun so innocently as a way to blow off steam. The tension had seemed to build as soon as they'd settled in as roommates, even though they'd been strangers at the time. Outside the apartment, they'd become friends who were perhaps more affectionate than most, but as soon as the apartment door had closed behind them, their walls had come down.

Spencer had been *his*. He would slip into Copley's bed and lie with him until the sun peeked through his bedroom curtains when he had to roll out and go to work with his ass aching and his lips still bruised from their kisses.

"Copley, come back to bed."

How many times had he fallen for that? How many sick days had passed with them in bed as they kissed and made love until they simply couldn't anymore?

That was why the ring had been so important, and why he'd purchased the simple gold band from the clerk, who had given him a slightly disappointed look, as if he should have spent thousands instead of hundreds.

He was in love, but he still had to eat.

His heart had been ready to pound out of his chest by the time he'd arrived home, pulling the ring from the tiny box and clutching it in his hand. He had bitten his tongue, pushing himself through the door before he could chicken out.

And everything had come crashing down.

He'd grabbed his packed bag from his side of the bed, wiping the tears from his cheeks before he'd fled the apartment with Spencer staring after him looking so confused and concerned that it had nearly broken his heart a second time.

The bag was heavy on his shoulder, thumping against his back as he took practiced steps toward the main street. He'd packed light for the second part of his would-be surprise—a camping trip just for the two of them.

The bag contained a single change of clothes with one tent and an extra-large sleeping bag that would have zipped around them just right. It was the perfect way to celebrate a new engagement.

Only he'd been wrong from the very beginning. While Copley had been falling in love for five wonderful years, Spencer hadn't felt a thing. Their stress relief had been just that and nothing more to him—which was why Spencer had introduced him to his girlfriend while Copley had clutched the ring in his hand like some clueless idiot.

Wiping his cheeks with the back of his hand, Copley looked out onto the street and the zooming traffic that was slowly starting to thin. For a gloomy fall Saturday, the road was surprisingly busy, with people rushing here and there as they prepared for winter.

It would have been near freezing in the tent on their impromptu trip, and they would have had to snuggle so close to share their bodily warmth, fogging the air as they breathed each other in.

Copley sobbed, cupping his hand over his mouth as he stumbled to the nearest bench. He sagged onto the slatted wood frame, dropping his pack as he pressed his face into his hands. A wail seeped past his lips as his chest pulled so tight that he wondered how he could still breathe.

"You okay?"

Sniffing, Copley turned to the man next to him, who looked rather startled at his new bench mate. His hair was gray, a few age spots peeking from under his waterproof cap that matched the poncho around his shoulders.

"Yeah." Copley sniffed, wiping his hands over his face to try to squish the sobs at the source. It didn't quite work, but the stranger's eyes on him stalled his tears where they were. He'd already humiliated himself enough for one day.

"I get like that on rainy days, too, sometimes." The stranger tipped his cap as he gazed up at the cloudy sky. "Not sure if it's the best weather for camping, though, son." He eyed Copley's bag and the sleeping bag nearly bursting from its packaging. "It's going to be a mighty cold one tonight, and you don't look like you're dressed for it. I can feel a storm brewing in my bones."

Copley's lips twitched in the briefest of smiles as he let out a breath. "You sound just like my mother. *'Don't forget your sweater, Copley.'*" He shook his head, pulling his arms around himself as a gust of wind stripped him of warmth. The guy was right, though. In his haste, he hadn't grabbed a jacket, and with the nightfall only a short time away, it was already starting to get chilly.

"Sounds like a wise woman, like my Nancy. I would forget my pants if my wife didn't remind me every morning." He smiled, rubbing his hand over his knobby knee and grimacing. "I'm surprised she even lets me take the bus anymore. Some days it's just nice to meet new people, but she's more of a homebody. Always was."

Smiling through the last of his tears, Copley leaned against the bench and shuddered as another wind gust swept over him. The blue and yellow bus sign blared above his head, but there were no vehicles in sight. The routes went every fifteen minutes in the city, and he could hop from one to the next with his eyes closed. He'd never even thought of having his own car before.

"Where are you headed, son? Up toward Forrest Lake? Or maybe down by the flats? We used to party there in my day. Don't tell my Nancy, but there were quite a few ladies that liked to tag along, if you know what I mean. I played football back then. Nothing like a bit of pigskin to get the fire started."

Copley blinked, chuckling awkwardly as he looked around for an escape. Listening to an old man talk about his young and straight escapades was slightly awkward, if he were honest. He didn't want to be rude, but that generation tended to be a tad…ungentlemanly to him when they found out he was attracted to men.

"I wouldn't know, actually. And as for where I'm headed…? I haven't figured that out yet." *I couldn't catch a football if it was covered in glue.*

He looked to the bus sign. Route fifteen looped around the north side of town before it hit low-income housing and some spots that he didn't dare step into while he was dressed the way he was. As much as he tried to be open-minded and non-judgmental, he clutched his keys tighter when he passed by graffiti or a few gang members on a corner.

"Well, this bus will take you to some of the best spots," said the old man, tugging his cap back over his brow as the sun peeked out one final time before clouds consumed it again. It was starting to get low in the sky, bronze blushing to pinks and reds as a few lamplights buzzed to life.

"My Nancy was raised on South Street, just next to the old inn. Not much to it now, but in its glory, it was a beautiful place. Do you know it?" He looked to Copley, his bushy eyebrows scrunching as he slowly blinked.

"I do. I was raised up that way, actually," said Copley, tugging his shirt tighter around his belly as a raindrop landed on his knee. The rain was cold, sinking straight to his skin as a second drop landed on the bench next to him.

He had been raised near Highbury Street, which was only two blocks from South, and he knew exactly why he shouldn't travel there. He remembered the noises in the night and the shouts that had kept him awake. His mother and pop had done their best to raise him and his brother and keep them safe in that neighborhood, but sometimes he wondered how he'd ever made it out.

When he'd been old enough, he'd left the neighborhood behind, and his parents had followed shortly after, only they had moved so far south that he rarely saw them in person anymore.

"My brother is still down that way, actually. He's in the old apartment building near the corner of Highbury…the one with the yellow brick and the steeples," said Copley. The brick had been all but crumbling the last time Copley had seen it, the shingles on the peaked roof barely hanging on.

"That's the old McGuire place. He used to own the old bus line in town before it went out of business. Committed suicide not long after that, and his wife went into a nunnery."

"Oh dear," said Copley, trying to keep his face blank. *Do nunneries still exist?* He used to watch *The Sound of Music* with his mother all the time, and he still knew the songs by heart. The man nodded, his mouth set into a grim line.

"We lost a lot of good men to things like that back then. Not so much now with people my age, but then, half of them aren't alive anymore, anyway. There are only two people left from my high school graduating class." He let out a long sigh, finally stilling his hand where he rubbed at his knee. "But I should be going before Nancy sends the search party out for me. I hope you find your way, son."

The old man stood with a groan, his shoulders stooped as he grabbed the cane that was sitting next to the bench. "And be careful in that part of town. There are a lot of sons of bitches out there." He walked off, slowly shuffling his feet against the sidewalk.

Copley looked to his pocket where he could still feel the ring like a blazing halo of misfortune. He wasn't close to feeling any better, but at least he had a touch of perspective.

"Well, I guess I know where I'm headed."

He grabbed his bag as the bus pulled up to the stop and parked with a burst of air brakes before the doors swung wide. Stepping inside, he clutched the strap of his pack as he paid and slipped into a seat near the front. He hadn't seen his brother in years, so he was woefully overdue. Hopefully, he had a couch that still had its cushions where Copley could sleep.

He let out a sigh as his eyes began to burn again, his tears budding afresh as he looked back to the bench and his neighborhood. *It's going to be a long night.*

Chapter Two

Copley

Copley stepped off the bus, swallowing hard before he immediately ducked his head and shied right. There were people milling around the darkening street corner and some of them were wearing even fewer clothes than he was. Blue eyes and red lipstick caught his gaze as he pointedly tried to look away.

"You lost, honey?" someone called out to him, but he shook his head, clutching his pack and sleeping bag as he scurried away from the corner to where he remembered his brother living. It was within sight of the bus station, but there was a dark alley between him and where he needed to be.

Someone touched his arm and he flinched, whirling on them with a startled yelp. He shrank away as he eyed the woman who had touched him before looking over her shoulder at the crowd who all seemed to be watching.

Her red hair was twisted into tight curls that hung over her naked shoulders, her silver tube-top the only thing that was keeping her nipples from making an appearance. Copley wasn't sure how she managed to walk in heels that were nearly as high as her feet were long, or how she stayed warm when her skirt stopped an inch or two past where her underwear should have ended. He did not want to find out if she was wearing any.

"You okay, honey?" she asked, reaching for him and wiping a fresh tear from his cheek. Her long red nails dragged over his skin in a motion that was almost comforting. Her lashes touched her cheeks as she blinked slowly before dropping her hand.

He shook his head, swallowing the lump in his throat as he looked to the others and back to her. "I don't want any trouble. I'm just trying to get to my brother's place."

In his long list of recent terrible ideas, this was one of his worst, but he had no place else to go. His friends were few and far between, and they had families to look after. His brother was his only family member left in the city. He just wasn't certain if he was going to make it to his apartment without getting stabbed or mugged.

"Just because I suck dicks for money doesn't mean I'm a bad chick, honey," she said, waving her hand at the spectators as he looked at them again. "Don't worry about them. We stick together, especially on nights like tonight when the boss is on the prowl." She gave him a wink before she licked the line of lipstick from her teeth.

"Sorry." He looked at the sidewalk as his face flamed. Her shoes caught his eye again, the black straps crisscrossing her calves in a way that was almost explicit. "I like your shoes."

She gave him a wicked smile before patting his arm. "Let me walk you home, baby. Free of charge this time. Can't have a treat like you out on the street right now without protection."

He bit his lip as he gripped his things, guilt surging through him at his earlier thoughts. He had grown up in the neighborhood, and as much as he'd come to love his new place in life, the old parts were still in his blood.

He didn't know any of his neighbors in his latest apartment building, and he'd been there for five years. But back *home*, he'd known everyone and everything about them…at least, as much as a child could understand. How many of them were still here?

"Thank you, but you don't have to. It's not far." He forced himself to stand straighter, wiping his tears from his other cheek and sniffing. The building was maybe two hundred feet away, looking ominous in the darkness where no streetlights were posted on watch.

"Call me Sweetie, baby. All the boys do. You ever need someone to walk you home, you just ask for me." She turned, heading to her group that murmured as she rejoined them. A few of them shifted as a silver truck pulled up to the corner. A blonde stepped up to the truck, leaning through the passenger window before the driver popped the locks.

Turning away, Copley walked as fast as he could without breaking into a run. Things were *slightly* different than he remembered. The neighborhood had never been the safest, but he couldn't recall prostitutes waiting around for their next john. Perhaps that was why his curfew had been so early, though. When he'd gone to college, he'd seen eleven p.m. for the first time in his life, and it had been as exhausting as it was thrilling.

It was only a minute later that he stepped up to his brother's apartment building, swallowing his fresh terror as he looked from the crumbled brick to the actual hole in the roof where the jagged shingles gave way to a bleak attic that was probably full of raccoons.

In its day, it had probably been a nice place, with a white picket fence and a huge lawn for cookouts and block parties. But the roof looked like it hadn't been maintained in the last thirty years or so, and the lawn was overgrown with rusted trash strewn all over it. In one corner, there was a kiddy pool that was cracked down the middle and almost hidden beneath the overgrowth, with a sapling bursting through the fissure.

There were two cars in the makeshift parking lot, neither looking like they would start. Calling it a parking lot was perhaps a bit of an exaggeration. The gravel had given way to rutted mud with only a few scarce stones mixed in.

The wooden porch creaked under his feet as he stepped up, pushing through the exterior door that was too big for its frame. It stood ajar, the smell of weed and piss wafting toward him. There was a fist-sized hole through the door where the doorknob should have been, and the frosted glass window was cracked.

Stained blue carpet and peeling walls greeted him as soon as he stepped inside, the sounds and scents instantly clinging to him. He wasn't sure about the last time he'd smelled *that* much weed without getting high himself, and the walls literally vibrated in rhythmic beats of a raging song.

"Oh, God, where the hell am I?" A wave of fresh tears streaked down his cheeks as a sob escaped his throat. It was his own stupidity that had ended him up in the place that was probably going to kill him. If a drug addict didn't, the black mold on the ceiling would.

The fact that his brother had been here all along gave him more grief than thinking about his ex-roommate.

Their parents had done their best, and although their house hadn't been nice, it hadn't been falling to pieces with the walls dripping something yellow and a pile of what looked like dog shit in the corner. The last he had checked, his brother worked for a mechanic, so he should have been able to afford a better place.

Why didn't you ask for help? Why didn't I reach out to you? The guilt soaked into him, dragging him down even further.

He knocked on the first apartment, holding his breath as he heard footsteps on the other side. He self-consciously clasped his hands as the knob turned and the door swung wide, the music blasting into him with full force.

Swallowing, he took a step back as he eyed up six feet of solid muscle and rage. *I'm gonna die.*

"What the fuck do you want?" the man snarled at him, and Copley yelped, taking another step until his back pressed against the wall. He glanced to the exit, wondering if he would make it if he ran. The door was still open, giving him a peek of freedom.

"I'm...I'm just looking for my brother, Sauble. Do you know which apartment he's in?" His voice came out as a terrified squeak, and he had to curse himself for sounding so pathetic. It was survival of the fittest out here, and he was doing a good act of the baby deer with a broken leg.

The man stepped into the hall, looming over Copley as he furrowed his forehead and clenched his fist. After a moment of contemplation, he slammed his fist into the wall above Copley's head, leaning close until Copley could smell the reek of alcohol on his breath.

"That asshole still owes me. Who says I shouldn't just take it out on his brother?" There was more than just alcohol on his breath. His orange teeth were covered in bits of Cheetos that made Copley want to gag. He was never eating them again.

Sweat dripped down his neck and into the collar of his shirt as Copley started to tremble. He dropped his pack to the ground as he lost control over his limbs, hoping he didn't piss himself to top it all off.

"What you got there?" The man looked to his bag, before reaching for it and pulling the zipper open. He snapped off the small keychain that Copley had always kept there so he could tell his bag apart when he traveled. It was a tiny unicorn figurine no longer.

"I-It's just clothes. That's all, I swear." Copley held up his hands as the man turned the bag upside down, dumping the sleeping bag and everything else onto the filthy carpet. His rolled socks made it the farthest as they attempted to escape, one pair catching on a silver pair of boxers. The lube that he'd packed for the trip thunked against the floor as it flopped out, adding insult to injury.

"What are you, some kind of queer?" the man asked as he eyed up the lube before his upper lip pulled back in a sneer.

"Hey, what's going on here?"

Copley turned to the new voice, almost shouting with joy when he spotted his brother standing at the entrance with a paper bag in his hands. He'd changed since Copley had last seen him, but he'd recognize those eyes anywhere.

He remembered Sauble as the cute kid who loved doting on him and going swimming on stormy Sunday afternoons. He'd loved bracelets and pizza and always passed out at the sight of a needle. Even as he'd matured, Copley had clung to that image with everything he had.

But the years between them had obviously cured Sauble of his fear of needles, if nothing else. He was wearing a black tank top and every inch of his exposed arms and shoulders were covered in ink. He had gained fifty pounds of muscle, and although he'd always been tall, he somehow seemed to have grown an inch or two. *Maybe it's his shoes?*

"Bernie, get your fucking hands off him before I break them. Copley, what the hell are you doing here?" Sauble set his bag on the ground. It shifted, the pointed head of a pineapple peeking out as an apple broke free from a tear in the side and rolled away.

"You owe me two Gs, asshole. And if you aren't gonna pay, your brother sure will." Bernie turned to Sauble as he approached, poking a meaty finger into his chest. Sauble didn't react except for one raised eyebrow.

"I paid you on the second, Bernie—or were you so drunk that you don't remember? You're drunk now, too, aren't you? Come on, man. You were doing so well. You were on the sixth step and everything." Sauble slapped Bernie's hand off him. "Don't touch my brother or you'll regret it," he said, his glare softening as Bernie slumped. "But if you need someone to talk to, I'm your man. I'll give you the name of my sponsor, too. He's a badass bitch, but he's always helped me." He patted Bernie on the shoulder as he retreated with a nod, slamming the door to his apartment.

Sponsor? Copley had only heard that term in movies before when someone was a recovering alcoholic. The Sauble he knew had hated the taste of alcohol, drinking pink coolers instead, despite the jeering of his friends.

"You're an alcoholic?" asked Copley, his voice cracking as he stared at his brother. His blue eyes were still the same, but everything else had changed. When had he gotten so lost?

"Nah." Sauble waved him off before ducking down and scooping Copley's sleeping bag and clothes from the ground and stuffing what he could back in his bag. Copley scrambled to help, shoving the bottle of lube to the deepest, darkest corner.

Although he'd always been comfortable with his sexuality, he'd had his fair share of haters in his life. Usually, he ignored them, with the rare circumstance that he stood up for himself if he was at the edge of his patience. He'd come out long after he'd left home, though, and had never mentioned anything to Sauble before.

He looked to Bernie's door and the light that streamed under the crack. The music had gotten louder somehow, the doorknob vibrating with a metallic clink.

"What are you doing here, Copley?" asked Sauble again as he led them to the next door, which looked exactly the same as Bernie's. Turning the knob, Sauble held it open for him. "Not that I don't miss you, little brother, but I haven't seen you in six years. I didn't think you even remembered where I lived."

"I remembered." He set his bag next to the shoe tray, toeing off his runners as Sauble did the same. The door helped with the noise some, but he could still catch the thump of the beat that had been so strong in the hall.

The space before him was gray and tired, with sagging ceiling tiles and a yellow stain dripping down the wall. It smelled clean, though, with only a faint wisp of smoke and cat litter, and no clutter to speak of. Besides the simple kitchen, couch and television, there wasn't much at all.

"I was afraid to come to see you," said Copley, looking to his feet. His toes were sweaty from being trapped in his dress shoes for so long, his arches starting to ache. He flexed his toes into the thin carpet that only had a few stains.

It was strange seeing his brother for the first time in years. He hoped they would still be able to talk like no time had passed at all.

"I know the neighborhood has gotten rougher since you left, but it's still home. There are a few assholes, but the rest are family." Sauble shrugged, setting his bag on the counter and pulling the pineapple from within. "That still didn't answer my question, though, Cope."

"I couldn't stay at my place tonight." He sniffed, rubbing his hand over his face as he thought of Spencer looking at him with his hand on his *girlfriend's* shoulder. How long had they been together? And was she even the first? The thought made him want to puke.

"Girlfriend kick you out?" asked Sauble, wincing sympathetically as he gathered a few apples as they tried to roll away again.

Copley huffed. The last thing he needed was shit from his brother too. It would make his day so much better. "Guy, actually. My roommate. I thought he was my boyfriend, but he brought a woman home today to introduce me to her. She'd already met his parents, and I guess I was the last stop."

He touched his pocket, plucking the ring and setting it on the counter. "Just happened to be on the same day I brought this home for *him*." The ring wobbled in the light until it slowly stilled, its gleaming surface the only new thing in the apartment.

"Ouch." Sauble threw an arm over his shoulders before pulling him close. "I didn't even know you were gay. What a dick. I can kick his ass for you if you'd like. Nobody treats my little bro like that."

Copley cracked, unable to hold himself together for another second. Turning into his brother's chest, he let his sobs out as Sauble held him, eventually leading him to the couch where he slowly wound down. His face radiated heat, and his eyes were so swollen that they ached by the time he'd shed his last tear.

"Just like old times," said Copley, shaking his head as he pulled away from Sauble, grabbing another tissue from the box he'd almost drained. "I get beat up, and you come to my rescue. The only thing missing is the spray paint for our revenge." He let out a wet chuckle.

The last time he'd cried in front of Sauble, he'd been a gangly fifteen-year-old who hadn't owned an ounce of muscle. One of the jocks on the football team had thought it would be funny to shove Copley's head into a toilet. After choking out nearly a pint of water, he'd run to Sauble. Sauble had spraypainted the inside the jock's locker — along with all his gear — a bright pink in retaliation.

"I gave up the spray paint a while ago," said Sauble, patting him on the shoulder and shooting him a smile that didn't reach his eyes. "I don't have a second bedroom, but you can crash on the couch until you find a place of your own. It's lumpy, but it's bedbug-free, I swear."

"It's perfect." Copley rubbed his nose, wincing at the sensitive sting before he grabbed his bag and started sorting through it. The sleeping bag would drape over the edge of the couch but it would work. "Some of these clothes might just fit you if you want them. Spence isn't getting them back, even if he begs." He pulled out a pair of jeans that were way too wide and long for him.

He'd packed for both of them so they could leave right away on their impromptu trip. It was lucky he had, or he would have been without a shirt to his name. Unfortunately, the one he'd packed was worn and plaid—the best thing to wear when there was no shower in sight. His boss would just have to deal with it until his next paycheck.

"I don't have a lot of money, but I can help pay for rent and food. I can clean and cook too, and just let me know if there's anything else I can do." He tossed Spencer's shirt to the side, tempted to tear it in half. "Do you want this? Because I will not be needing it." He held out the lube, snickering when Sauble's eyes went wide, and he held up his hands.

"I'm more of a hand cream kind of guy. If I'm having a night in, I want to smell like coconut," said Sauble, snickering as he went to grab a glass from the kitchen.

"I did *not* need to know that," said Copley, setting the lube on the table before tossing his clothes back in the bag. With the way his day was going, he was surprised that the lube hadn't exploded.

"And I don't need to know the brand of lube my brother uses, but here we are." Sauble cracked a smile before he disappeared through a door that presumably led to his bedroom. He returned with a pillow a minute later, laying it out on the couch. "You can have the shower first, but keep it under three minutes. After that, it gets cold enough to shrivel your bits."

Copley grabbed his hand as Sauble tried to turn away, giving it a squeeze. "Thank you, Sauble. I'm so glad to see you. I should have come sooner — "

He swallowed. There were a lot of things he should have done differently… Like not turning away from his past just because he was afraid.

"You're here now. Try to get some sleep tonight. I start work early, so I'll walk you to the bus stop then."

Copley rushed through his lukewarm shower, borrowing a toothbrush and coating it with a tiny bead of paste to complete his nightly routine. With the lights off, he settled on the couch, casting an eye to Sauble's bedroom door as a snore shook the room. *Some things never change – and some things do.*

The front door rattled as a particularly loud beat of music sounded, the entire building vibrating with the thrum of a bass guitar. The couch smelled faintly of old cheese, and he could already feel the ache in his shoulder starting to set in. A bit of light from the kitchen kept him completely aware that he was not at home.

Chapter Three

Nikita

Tapping his key card to the sensor, Nikita let himself into Unkinked. The kink club had been part of his life for more than a dozen years, and the curtains guarding the entryway had yet to change. The bouncer was new, though, and gave him a startled look as he stepped through the doorway before letting it slam shut behind him.

He'd always managed to fill a room to capacity. But the curtained space that kept the inner workings of the club from prying eyes on the street was no larger than an elevator, putting the bouncer on edge as Nikita stared at him.

With a quick second look, he pushed through the curtain into the main bar area, the bar itself on his left and booths along his right. The space was mostly empty, with a few faraway voices coming from the open play area where he was headed.

The owner and founder, Clint, had uncharacteristically closed the bar for a few hours and had called on the Dungeon Masters for a meeting. Nikita couldn't remember the last time there had been one. With the community so tight knit that everyone knew each other, and in extension, knew every tad of gossip, there hadn't been a need.

Unkinked was perhaps a bit different than most kink clubs, with few munches or planned get-togethers. Instead, everyone gathered when they were able, seeking open arms and support from within the community on a sometimes-nightly basis.

He strolled past the booths, heading to the back where the main stage and open play area were, along with the private kink rooms down the hall. Pushing through a second curtain, he paused just inside the open play area, taking a headcount of every Dom and sub who were present.

He was only mildly surprised to see Maverick and his sub there, since Maverick had had his membership temporarily suspended. He'd been working hard with his sub to earn his way back into the ranks with Clint's guidance. Derreck was there, too, a gravedigger who had come in handy on one or two occasions, along with his sub Maddy, who worked at the club as Clint's assistant.

He skimmed over a few others, nodding at one of the Dommes as she made eye contact. She knew her way around a whip better than most, and her subs were some of the most loyal he'd ever seen. One of them was at her feet, sitting cross-legged on a pillow. He would have been kneeling, if not for his knee injury that made it impossible.

Clint looked up from the card tables he must've erected for their meeting. There were three end-to-end with Maddy between Clint and Derreck at the head. Nikita slid into the only remaining seat, resting his elbows on the table and leaning forward. The table gave a squeak of protest at the weight and the Dom next to him shifted uncomfortably.

"Thanks for coming, guys and gals. We have a few new rollouts coming in the next few months, and I wanted you to be the first to know. Some are up for discussion and others aren't." He glanced at Maddy, who flushed and tucked himself closer to Derreck.

Nikita stared at the back wall as Clint began, his eyes on the St. Andrew's cross that blended in perfectly with the rest of the décor. It had never been his favorite device to use, but there were few Doms like him and even fewer subs who were fearless enough to trust him with anything more than a public scene. That was why he usually found himself doing rounds as a Dungeon Master, patrolling the open play area to make sure that couples were being safe and safewords were respected.

"One thing that we will be instating is criminal background checks," said Clint, tugging at the collar of his dress shirt. Nikita couldn't remember the last time he'd seen him in anything but a faded T-shirt or pajamas. "It came to my attention that one of our members was a sex offender and lied about it on his initial application. Every existing and new member will have a background check to make sure that doesn't happen again."

Nikita huffed, crossing his arms as he leaned back in his chair. Tracing over the tattoos on his wrists, he waited for Clint's gaze to settle on him. Most of the Doms at the table were the very few on a list of people that weren't afraid of him. Outside of the safety of the club, he was fear itself. It was his job, after all.

"You know who I am and my profession. Will it be a problem?" Nikita asked, every gaze turning to him.

Maddy gulped, sinking farther into Derreck's side, even as Derreck looked completely unflustered.

"Not unless your six-year prison sentence was for rape," said Clint. "There is a gray area here, and we all have to be aware of it. If someone has a criminal background due to theft or similar charges, then I don't think they should be barred unless they have poor behavior in the club or don't follow the rules. What I don't want is a rapist taking advantage of an unsuspecting sub within these walls on my watch. I can't do anything out *there*, but I can make sure we have a safe place here for everyone."

Nikita nodded, urging himself to relax. He had never forced someone in his life. Even the thought of it made him want to reach for a knife and get the castration over with. He wasn't that kind of Dom or person, but he wasn't a good man, either. If other things became part of that pool, then he would be barred from one of the only places he called home.

"Good?" Clint looked to each of them again, nodding. "Next stop is an open house or open kink night—call it what you want. The one last month went really well overall. There were fourteen new sign-ups and only one incident that was taken care of quickly." He sent a smile to Nikita.

Nikita huffed, his chair creaking as he shifted. One bratty asshole had tried taking pictures of unsuspecting couples during play and had nearly ruined the night for him. He'd taken care of the brat, along with his phone, which had ended up beyond recognition after Nikita had checked the man's accounts for any pictures he had tried to upload.

"We are hoping to make it a bi-monthly thing starting at the beginning of next month. That gives us two weeks to prepare and for people to bring their concerns to me," said Clint.

Nikita's phone vibrated in his pocket, his boss's number going through his 'do not disturb' setting. He slid it from his pocket, glancing at the screen before he excused himself and stepped away from the table before bringing it to his ear.

"Yeah, boss?" He pushed through the curtains, heading outside so no one would overhear his conversation. He trusted his fellow Doms, but only to a certain extent. Anyone in his position would have done the same.

"I need you to take care of a debt collection for me," said Nestor, his low voice thick with accented English.

Nikita grunted, rubbing a hand over his face before he stepped onto the street, letting the nondescript door fall shut behind him. There was one person at the Office Depot across the street, but otherwise, every vehicle was accounted for by those inside the club.

"Get someone else to do it." He leaned against his car. "You know I don't do that kind of dirty work anymore." After his prison sentence, he'd left some of the harsher parts of being an enforcer behind, not wanting to tangle with the law too directly, lest he get thrown back inside.

Beating the shit out of someone when they didn't pay their debt had never been his jam to begin with, but being Nestor's personal bodyguard suited him much better. He could almost call his boss a friend, and he wasn't afraid to lay things out the way he saw them.

"I could send your brother instead."

Nikita grumbled. The last thing he needed was for his hothead twin Maxim to get word of a beatdown. At one time, they had worked together, the infamous Twin Tigers who were feared across the country. Maxim was still the tiger, with the temper to boot, whereas Nikita honestly preferred to take a back seat unless he had to dodge a bullet.

"Only if you want to try to get your money from a dead man. What about Pete or Tony? They're young, but they've never let you down." The fact that Nikita had trained them helped, too.

The door slammed open behind him, and Nikita shot a look over his shoulder, moving away as the other members filed after him. He nodded to Clint, who gave him a concerned look before he disappeared back inside.

"I need you for this one. It's down on Highbury Street…apartment two. I think you know which building." Nestor let out a sigh. "You know I wouldn't ask you if I thought someone else could handle it. Take a piece if you need it, and I'll take care of the rest." The line went dead as Nestor ended the call.

Unfortunately, Nikita knew exactly what building Nestor was talking about. There was one man who had the strange inkling that he was some kind of son of the neighborhood, never calling in an owed favor or using a heavy hand. No one seemed inclined to oppose him, and people loved his charisma and kindness. But most of them didn't know that he owed close to a hundred thousand dollars for all his *kindness.*

A gambling debt and an addiction to boot could be the fall of anyone.

Chapter Four

Copley

"Hey, Sweetie!" called Copley as he stepped off the bus and onto the corner that was getting more welcoming with every passing day. After Sauble had walked him to and from the bus stop a few times, introducing him to every person they passed by, people had started looking at Copley differently.

Sauble had been right, of course. The neighborhood was rougher than it used to be, but the people were still family. He'd never had so many friends in his life.

"Hey, yourself," said Sweetie, curling a red strand of hair around her finger and walking toward him as he hit the sidewalk. She looped her arm in his, pulling him off-balance as she placed a kiss on his cheek. "Nice night tonight. Should be busy, but I'll walk you home."

Smiling, Copley pulled his jacket from his shoulders before tossing it over Sweetie's. They'd made fast friends after Sweetie had offered to walk him home when Sauble hadn't made it to the bus stop on time one day. His brother was anything but prompt, which was something Copley was learning quickly. Dinner was anywhere from seven at night to one the next morning.

"Any sexy guys last night?" asked Copley, zipping Sweetie into his jacket and very carefully pulling her hair free. They were the same height, and luckily, he was slim, so his jacket fit her almost perfectly. Their love of pretty men was another thing they had in common.

"You should have seen him, Cope." She closed her eyes, tilting her face into the light of a nearby streetlamp. "Six-two, arms like boulders and six-and-a-half inches of glory." She snickered, pushing his shoulder when he let out a disappointed sigh.

Kicking a few leaves out of their path, Copley chuckled. "I would have preferred eight-and-a-half, but that's why I'm the size queen."

She snorted. "You aren't the one choking on it. I think your ass is a little more flexible than my gag reflex. I like them small so they fit in my mouth and don't ruin my voice for the next john."

When he'd first met Sweetie and learned what her profession was, he hadn't known that sex was off-limits for her. It had taken them three conversations before Copley had scrounged up the courage to ask her prices, purely for curiosity's sake.

She had given him a long look before she'd told him that he was too willing for sex work, and he would give away the prize for free if a handsome man flexed his biceps once. Her limits were strict—a hand job or a blow job but nothing more than that. If they wanted a fuck, they could go fuck themselves. And anyone who tried to push ended up with a taser to their dick.

"This is me," said Copley unnecessarily as they approached the front steps to his building. The lawn was a touch tidier after Copley had spent a Saturday picking up trash and empty bottles. He'd carted the bottles all down to the liquor store for a return and had ended up with almost forty bucks, which he'd used to get new numbers for the building and the apartment doors. Since he was getting his mail forwarded, he needed the postman to be able to find him.

Sweetie was looking away from him, her gaze locked on a dark sedan that had no business in being in front of his building. He had yet to meet the actual owner of the place, but he would have thought that their car would be just as beat up as the rest in the lot.

"You be careful, hon. Looks like one of Nestor's guys is here, and that always spells trouble." She motioned to the sedan, her lips set in a grim line.

Copley scratched his head as he tried to place the name. There had been so many new faces and names that he couldn't remember them all, but it did sound a bit familiar. "Who's Nestor?"

The license plate gave nothing away, and there was nothing on the dash of the vehicle either.

"My boss. He runs this neighborhood and most of this city. You best watch yourself." She pulled the coat from her shoulders before passing it to him.

Well, that was why the name was a tad familiar. Nestor was the leader of the biggest and most notorious gang in the city. Some people called him a mob boss because he liked to wear suits and had a criminal background. If you ended up on his bad side, you didn't last long. His father had run the city when Copley had been younger, and Nestor had followed in his footsteps.

Copley shrugged as he grabbed the coat from Sweetie, waving her off with a final goodbye. He had tried and failed every night to get her to keep his coat so she'd be warmer.

Pounding music greeted him as he opened the door and grabbed his mail from the box that was barely holding together. Sighing at the overdue utility notice, he shook his head.

Just another bill that Sauble had forgotten to pay on time. He seemed to lose things left, right and center, including bills and invoices, along with Copley's ring, which had mysteriously disappeared from the counter. Copley was still convinced that it had been sucked up by the vacuum, but he'd combed through the trash four times and hadn't found a thing.

He jiggled the door, twisting it open and pushing into the apartment. The lock didn't work and apparently never had, but if he jiggled it just right, it made it harder for people to break in.

His jacket and mail hit the floor as something cold and hard pressed against the back of his head. His mind stumbled to catch up as he reached for whatever it was.

"Don't move."

The emotionless, deep voice cut through the last of his calm and sent him straight into panic, his hand frozen in the air halfway to his head. Sweat prickled on his skin as his gut turned to ice.

"Please don't hurt me." He choked as he realized it was a gun against the back of his head. He'd never even held one before. *This is why we need a working lock.* "My wallet's in my back pocket. There's not much in there but take it. I have…"

In his old place he'd had a safe with a few watches along with his passport and certificates, but he hadn't gotten the nerve to face Spencer to retrieve them. He would rather replace them than step foot in his old apartment ever again.

A hand slid into his back pocket, plucking his wallet free with a tug. Shuddering, he tried to clamp down on his squeak as the cold barrel of the gun was pulled away from his head. At least when it had been there, he had known where it was.

"Hmm, Copley, it's your lucky day," he said, obviously flicking through Copley's wallet. "You tell me where Sauble is and you get to pretend this conversation never happened." He slapped the wallet shut, sliding it back into Copley's pocket.

His heart pounded as he bit his lip, trying to hold back the sudden tears that threatened. "Is he in trouble?"

He had kept his questions to himself when it came to his brother's addiction. He hadn't thought it was something as serious as drugs, but Sauble had proved to be exceedingly efficient at hiding things.

"He owes my boss a lot of money." The deep voice sent another shiver over his skin.

"I can pay you," Copley shouted, his body trembling even as he tried to stay still. "In my wallet. I have money."

"You have twenty-five dollars."

He was so close to his ear that Copley could feel the breath against him. He shuddered, a few tears creeping from his eyes. Heart pounding, he clenched his fists tight.

"I have more in the bank. Let me just go to the bank. I got paid today so there's two thousand dollars there. I can get it for you." He struggled not to hyperventilate as the man stepped from behind him, the floor creaking as moved. Copley slammed his eyes shut. The only thing more terrifying than not seeing an attacker was seeing their face.

A touch on his chin had him shooting his eyes back open. He stumbled, reaching for the wall as he lost his footing. A steady hand on his shoulder saved him from his fall, and he got the first real look at the man who threatened him.

He was huge—bigger than any man Copley had ever had the pleasure of seeing. His arms looked thicker than Copley's thighs, and his hands could probably cup the meat of his ass easily. Tattoos scrolled over every inch of his arms, disappearing under the cuffs of his plain black T-shirt.

It was his eyes that really caught Copley's attention. Beneath the warm brown, there was something almost feral as he raked his gaze up and down Copley's body, leaving him more off-center than the gun had.

The gun. He looked to the man's hands, but they were both empty. The man smiled, tugging something from his pocket before showing it to Copley. It was a thick black Sharpie, the silver casing almost as large as the barrel of a gun.

"A little trick, Copley," he said, a small smile on his lips as he placed the marker in Copley's trembling hand. "You don't need to be afraid of me. I just want to talk to Sauble." He lifted Copley's chin as he tried to duck his head. "My name is Nikita, but you can call me Niki. Tell me where Sauble is."

Niki stepped closer until Copley could smell the rich cologne on his skin mixed with laundry detergent and a touch of sweat. It made his mouth water as he eyed the spot on Niki's neck where an inked tiger peeked above the collar of his shirt.

"I can't tell you... I don't know." The lie came out flat and strained, and Copley gulped in another breath. He flinched as Niki raised his hand, placing it on the wall beside his head. The heat from him was thick and absolute.

"It's okay, Copley. You can tell me. I know you want to protect him, but this is his only chance to come clean. Sauble owes my boss a lot of money, and Nestor is a man who expects results. I can't go back to him without it, or it will be my ass on the line. You wouldn't want that, right?"

Copley shook his head, his throat clicking as he swallowed. Niki's voice was so soft and calm, wrapping him in a warm blanket, that he wasn't sure if he wanted to leave or not. He could scarcely believe it was the same person who had pretended to hold a gun to the back of his head.

"I can give you everything I have, but just leave him alone," said Copley. After everything Sauble had done for him in the last few days, he couldn't betray him. "I can...my old apartment. I have some watches I can get for you, too." The offer rolled off his tongue, and he blinked in surprise. He wasn't sure why he was still talking when he should have been running.

Niki clicked his tongue, turning to survey the apartment. He paused at the couch, staring at the neatly rolled sleeping bag where Copley slept. His bag was on the table, with his dirty laundry in a small basket tucked underneath.

"I'm sorry for the mess," said Copley, his cheeks flushing. He wasn't sure why he was even apologizing, but Niki's gaze seemed to pick up every little detail.

Chuckling, Niki grabbed the bottle of lube that was still sitting on the table. Copley hadn't wanted to throw it out—it was a perfectly good bottle of lube after all—but he didn't have a dresser to store it in, either.

"Should I ask, Copley? Should I wonder why a beautiful boy like you is sleeping on your brother's couch with a bottle of lube at the ready? If he's forcing you, it won't be a fake gun to the back of *his* head." Niki stalked closer, dropping the lube into Copley's palm. The seal was still on, the little label on the front that declared it was great for anal sex, making him flush warmer. But anyone thinking of Sauble like that made him sick.

"No! My brother is a good man, even if he forgets to pay his bills on time. I'm sure he just forgot, and this is all a misunderstanding." Copley paused, but Niki only stared at him, his gaze piercing and unwavering. "But the lube? Uh, I bought it for my ex-roommate… Well, I thought we were more than that, but I guess not? So I left, but it was already packed. I'm just not sure what to do with it now. Seems like a waste to throw it out."

"It would be," said Niki, his grin going wide as he plucked the lube from Copley's hands. "Something like this lasts a long time. It would give me plenty of time to cherish and make someone come apart over and over. I wouldn't throw that away."

After ripping the seal open and popping the cap, Niki tipped a drop onto his fingertip, swirling it around the pad of his finger until it glistened. Copley's breath caught as he watched, completely mesmerized.

"Tell me where he is, Copley."

Copley licked his lips, unable to look away as he shook his head. What would that lube feel like on his own fingers or somewhere else? Niki's hands were so big that his breath caught at the mere idea of it. "Work."

Niki's lips curled. "Now I know you can't believe that. His shift finishes at five every day, and he's not at the casino, either. So, likely he's found a new spot to spend my boss's money, or he split town."

"I...uh." Copley's brain went offline as Niki dribbled another line of lube over his fingers, slicking them until they were ready for action. It was bad enough that Niki checked every box for his ideal man in the physical appearance department, but his voice made him want to close his eyes and open his legs, just to see what would happen.

"I don't know." Copley whimpered as Niki touched him, skimming his clean hand over his cheek. He leaned into him, so touched-starved that he longed for more. He had always been a physical person, and he'd gone far too long with only platonic touches.

"I believe you, Copley, but I need you to do something for me." Niki was close, his breath whispering over the shell of his ear and making him shudder. His fear had run for the hills, leaving only simmering desire behind.

"I need you to give your brother a message. He has one month to get Nestor his money or my brother Maxim will be coming next time. Trust me when I say that would not be in his best interest. Until next time, Copley. Be safe."

Niki pushed away, setting the lube back on the table before slipping through the door and shutting it softly behind him. His presence stayed in the room, thicker than the music that pounded against the walls.

Copley pressed his hand against his groin, hissing from the contact. *Had Niki noticed?* He couldn't remember the last time he had been so terrified and so turned on, his body throbbing in time with his arousal even as fear for his brother crept in.

He shook his head, pushing away from the wall before grabbing his cell and sending a text to his brother.

Nestor's men are looking for their money. What did you do, Sauble?

Niki's cologne was still thick in the room. Breathing deep, he tried to commit it to memory. He'd never thought he would think of another man like he had Spencer. He'd assumed that he'd been ruined after his heart had shattered completely. The pain was still with him every day, slowly knitting as his new friends took him in.

But when Niki had looked at him like *that* and had called him beautiful, he'd felt better than he had in weeks. His phone buzzed as Sauble replied.

Shit! I'm on my way. Give them whatever they want, Copley. Don't get hurt!

Copley touched his chest to where his heart still pounded. He needed answers.

He moved to the couch, waiting until the door opened and Sauble pushed his way through, slamming the door into the opposite wall as he frantically looked around. When his gaze settled on Copley, his concern disappeared into confusion.

"Are you hurt?" asked Sauble, slowly closing the door before he approached. Copley patted the empty spot beside him, scooting down so his brother had room.

"No…he left." Copley looked at his hands. They were steady with only the memory of Niki behind him. Was it strange that he wanted Niki to come back, so he could push him just a tad further? *I'm insane.*

"He didn't hurt me." *No, he did the opposite.* "He gave me a message for you, but I have a question first. I know it's not my place and I've only been here for a little while, but please answer." Sauble winced as Copley turned to him. "How much money do you owe the Bratva?"

Copley wasn't really sure what to call the criminal underground who had existed in the city since before he was born. Mafia brought to mind machine guns and enough cocaine to build a sandcastle, but that was so far from his image of the city that it just didn't sit right. They were dangerous, even if Niki had been almost kind to him.

Sauble let out a sigh, tugging his arm free and running his hand through his hair. It was the first time Copley had seen him concerned. "A hundred grand."

Copley choked, thumping his chest until he could breathe past his disbelief. "A hundred thousand dollars?" He looked around the apartment that had a total of about five hundred dollars' worth of furniture. "How? Are you on drugs? Oh my God, what are we going to do? He said you had a month to pay up or he'd send some guy named Maxim instead, but there's no way we can make that much money that quick. I only make about fifty thousand a year, and that's before taxes."

Grabbing for the couch cushion, he held on as his head began to swim and his breathing picked up.

"It's not your problem, Copley. You should have a new place by then, and I can take care of myself."

Sauble stood, stepping away as Copley reached for him.

"You're my brother," said Copley. "I'm *not* going to let you get beaten or worse, over money. I can't stand by and do nothing."

"It's not your problem," Sauble hissed through his teeth, his arms flexing as he gripped his hands into fists. "Get yourself out of here, baby brother, and when you do, don't come back."

Chapter Five

Nikita

The moment he stepped into his apartment he opened his pants. Plunging his hand inside, he brought himself off with three quick pulls and a drawn-out moan. He thudded his head against the door as he released all over his knuckles, his seed drooling over his palm and onto the floor by the time he went empty.

That's why I don't do this shit anymore. He bit his lip before going limp against the frame as the images ran through his mind again. Pink lips, soft blue eyes and the cutest ass he'd ever seen had followed him out of Sauble's apartment and straight back to his, making his cock throb with every step.

Copley had been afraid of him at first, but Nikita had been shocked with how quickly that fear had become interest. Most men would have frozen with a gun to the back of their heads. But Copley had spent the entire time trying to protect his brother, only starting to slip when Nikita had poured lube all over his hand.

A little 'good gangster', 'bad gangster' usually went a long way, but Copley looked like he had fallen for both, his lips parted as he'd blushed and leaned his cheek into Nikita's hand.

If people didn't judge Nikita by his size first, they fled the moment they discovered his profession. They didn't just give in, no matter how hard they tried to convince him that they loved a bad boy.

"Niki, what the hell?" Maxim shouted as he rounded the corner to the hall, his eyes going wide as he spotted the cooling cum on his twin's hand. "I know blue balls are a bitch, but could you wait until you're in the bedroom next time? Boss is here for you."

Shaking his head, Nikita grabbed a nearby tissue, wiping the cum from his hand before stuffing himself back in his jeans as Maxim snickered. His orgasm had been dismal at best, and would have been so much better if he'd just asked Copley the question that had been on his tongue since he'd caught his first glimpse.

"Missed a spot," said Maxim, scooping up a dollop that had landed on the bottom hem of his shirt before shoving it into Nikita's mouth. Niki spluttered, slapping his brother's side.

The few subs that had ever mustered up the courage to scene with Nikita had fled the moment they'd met Maxim. His twin was chaos and anger with the same face and body as his own, with a side of sadism that made most people cringe.

"You're an asshole," Nikita snarled, looking down at himself to make sure he was semi-presentable.

"And you're not satisfied. Admit it. I know you, Niki."

He nodded, knowing there was no use denying it. Maxim knew him better than anyone else, and he trusted his brother in all things, even if he was gross sometimes. Eating cum was something he usually left for his subs to do. It was an acquired taste.

"Couldn't do anything about it when he was the target," said Niki, keeping his voice low enough so only Maxim would hear. Maxim's eyes went wide, and Niki pushed past him, nodding at Nestor as he rounded the corner. Ivan was at Nestor's shoulder, standing guard over him, even in the safety of the apartment.

"Nikita, have a seat," said Nestor, waving to the chair opposite. "Do you have my money?"

Nikita shook his head, crossing his arms when Nestor frowned. "Your money is gone, and the only person I could find was Sauble's brother. I gave him a month to get the hundred grand to you before Maxim goes in." Grabbing a napkin from the table, he dabbed at a spot on his belly that looked like he might've missed. "Don't know why you gave that kid any money in the first place. That place was a fucking pigpen." It had been tidy, but the walls were literally crumbling. He wasn't sure who owned the hellhole, but he was going to find out.

Nestor shrugged, a small smile on his lips. Every hair on his head was in place, and his suit fit perfectly. The speckle of gray in his hair made him look much older than he actually was. "What can I say? I like the kid. He's lucky, just not where it counts. But a month is way too long."

"Then send Maxim there now. Just leave Sauble's kid brother out of it." He gripped the edge of the table, letting out a huff as Nestor tilted his head. "I told you I don't like doing that shit anymore. The kid was fucking terrified." *But that wasn't all. He wanted me, too. I'm certain.*

"Smart kid." Nestor looked to Ivan before he nodded once. "Fine, a month it is. After that, the neighborhood's son is going to be a neighborhood ghost."

Chapter Six

Copley

"I'm really not sure if this is my kind of thing," said Copley, clutching his jacket closer before rubbing his tired eyes. He hadn't slept well in two weeks, and every day things got a touch bleaker. The inside of Sauble's apartment had gone from semi-comfortable and welcoming to stressful from the not-so-subtle questions about when Copley was going to leave.

Work had been no better. His boss had been on his case near-constantly when Copley had arrived with next-to-no sleep and drifted his way through the day, making more mistakes in weeks than he had in his entire career. A helpful co-worker had even slid him a business card for a good therapist.

Therapy? Him? It just made him want to start crying all over again.

The real kicker had been when Spencer had texted him on his way home from work, wondering if he wanted to hook up *'like old times'*. Copley had run to

Sweetie, who had been stepping out of a car when he'd rounded the corner to her usual spot.

"I got what you need, honey. You'll be my date tomorrow. You keep me company, and I'll find you a man that will make you forget your troubles."

He had expected a gay bar or maybe an evening of karaoke. Sweetie had given him a strange look when he'd guessed that one.

"The people here are some of the nicest around, and no one looks twice at you because of what you do for a living," said Sweetie as they stepped off the bus and started down one of the back streets that Copley didn't think he had ever been on. He'd lived in the city all his life, but sometimes he surprised himself when he realized how little he'd actually seen.

"But like ropes and stuff?" he asked, looking over his shoulder and lowering his voice. "I don't think I want to get tied up and *spanked.* That's not really my thing." His thing *had* been whatever Spencer had wanted, until that ship had sailed, and Niki had taken over his dreams. Since then, death threats and expensive cologne had been his thing.

"Don't diss it until you try it," she said, her red curls swaying as she shook her head. "It's not really about the rope, anyway. When someone ties you up, you're so secure that you can't move an inch and so helpless that you feel like you could never take care of yourself again." She let out a wistful sigh. "That's when you let go and realize that you don't have to. Someone else has got you, and for as long as you're with them, you don't have to care about anything else in the world. Just their hands on your body and the rope against your skin matter. I've never had freedom like that until I kneeled at the feet of my Domme."

Oh, wow. "I never thought about it like that." He bit his lip, hurrying to catch up with her as she strolled away with long strides. Sometimes being short was the worst, and compared to Sweetie, his legs felt like they belonged to a hamster.

"How many people are going to be there, though? And what if I see someone I know?" He pulled at the collar of his too-tight shirt — something that sweetie had insisted on when he'd tried to wear plaid and jeans instead.

"You can say hi if you want." She shot him a smile. "Just enjoy yourself. This is only the second open kink night they've had in the last three years, so it will probably be packed. No one will touch you if you don't want it, and if they do? Well, they better watch out for the Dungeon Master."

The street was bursting with cars, and he watched a few people disappear through a white door. There was no name at all, only white against the brick. Sweetie tugged the door wide, motioning for Copley to step inside.

One step forward and Copley immediately wished he could take two steps back. There wasn't much — only a curtain and a bouncer who looked like he was getting another couple to sign a bunch of paperwork. But curtains always started the most terrible things…like a high school play where he'd accidentally puked all over the stage or haunted houses where he'd scream like a little kid three seconds in.

"Sign these papers, honey, then we can get to the good stuff."

He squiggled his signature on the non-disclosure agreements and waivers, trying to get a peek through the curtain as it moved aside and the other couple stepped through. When he handed the papers back and took Sweetie's hand, his trepidation was morphing into excitement.

Leather. So much leather. There were so many beautiful people, some fully clothed and others barely wearing more than a G-string and collar. The booths on one side were packed to capacity along with the bar, and the floor space was thick with groups of chatting people.

Copley looked to a collared man who was kneeling at the feet of a woman and leaning against her leg. He looked happy, although his knees must've been killing him on the hardwood floor. Another was wearing a corset that looked so tight he wondered how she could breathe. She laughed, tilting back her head as the noise filled the air.

"I thought people would be angry," he said, leaning close to Sweetie's ear so she could hear him over the music and conversation. She just gave him a smile and shook her head.

"The first rule of kink, baby. Don't scene when you're angry." She looked around the space, her smile going wide as she spotted someone. "Let me introduce you to my Domme."

She grabbed Copley's hand, her grip harder than before as she led him through the crowd. She lowered her eyes as they approached a slim brunette who was speaking with a group of men. Copley skimmed the crowd, trying to find someone he knew before letting out a sigh of relief when he didn't.

When they reached the lady, Sweetie just stopped, squeezing Copley's hand hard when he turned to her in question. *Why the hell are we just standing here?* The brunette hadn't acknowledged them, and neither had any of the others. It made Copley want to flush in embarrassment and hide, for some reason.

"My love." Sweetie's Domme turned, sliding her hand over Sweetie's neck before cupping her chin.

Sweetie turned, placing a kiss on the inside of her Domme's wrist. "Madame."

"Introduce me to your friend. I've been dying to meet him." She looked to Copley briefly before she dragged her gaze back to Sweetie.

"Madame, this is Copley. His pronouns are he and him. Copley, this is my Domme. Her pronouns are she and her."

Copley had to blink with the complete change to Sweetie. She had always been a spitfire with a loud laugh and a tongue that could make anyone blush, but she also walked with the weight of three lifetimes on her shoulders. Now she was relaxed, her eyes only half-open as she placed another kiss to the inside her Domme's wrist.

"You may call me Bethany, Copley. Please, join us." She turned away from her sub, motioning for Copley to step in beside her to complete the circle again. There was only space for the two of them, but Sweetie made no effort to move, standing just behind her Domme with her head lowered.

"So, Copley, are you enjoying yourself?" Bethany asked with a small smile on her lips. She had short dark hair and two delicate silver loops through her ears. If Copley had seen her on the street, he would've had no idea that he'd find her in a kink club.

"There's a lot of leather."

A few men in the group chuckled, and he caught Sweetie's snicker over the music. There was one man who looked to be close to his age, but the others were either older or younger than him. It was a more diverse crowd than he'd expected.

"I had a leather couch once," he blurted as his mind went blank, staring at his shoes as his face flushed. "The cats scratched it to all hell." He trailed off until his voice was barely a whisper. He reached for Sweetie's hand, meeting empty air. Bethany was looking at him like he was only slightly insane, which was a relief.

Something caught his eye and he jolted, nearly getting whiplash from the violence of the movement. It was barely a whisper of *something*, but it pulled his gaze and demanded his attention. His breath was dragged from his lungs as his body throbbed.

"Niki?"

Niki paused his trek in the direction of the bar, whipping his head to the side and catching his gaze. There was no way he could have heard Copley through the lull of music, but he prowled closer with purpose, the group making a space for him without even having to be asked. Copley gulped when Niki moved right next to him, their arms brushing just the smallest amount. That touch alone was enough to bring back every dream.

So maybe he had a fantasy that popped up from time to time. Usually, it featured someone pushing him against the wall or a desk and taking what they wanted. The fantasy had almost fizzled away over the last few years, but Niki had brought it back in full force.

Every night on Sauble's couch he'd dreamed of those large hands that could take what they wanted but were so gentle instead. The deep timbre of Niki's voice threaded through his dreams, so he woke up aching every morning.

The same thing was happening now, even though he was wide awake and in front of a group of strangers who could probably bind, beat and make him come with a snap of their fingers.

He expected Niki to at least say something to him, but instead, he turned to another in the group, his voice carrying across the space.

"Your sub is busy, Derreck?" asked Niki.

Copley stared at his shoes, somehow throbbing harder as his heart fell. Maybe Niki didn't even remember him. He wasn't exactly worth remembering, and he didn't have the same assets as most of the other people in the club. He couldn't imagine that he'd ever look so good nearly naked or that a collar would suit him at all.

Derreck grunted in response before he nodded to the bar. Biting his tongue was the only thing that stopped Copley from gasping at the sight of the man behind the bar who was filling drink orders faster than should have been possible. He was shirtless, his skin so mottled with healed marks that he didn't even look real.

"Can you watch things for me? I found something that caught my eye," said Niki. "I'll owe you." Derreck nodded before melting away from the group.

Something caught his eye? What does that even mean? Niki may have been dark and mysterious, but he wasn't a crow who got distracted at the sight of something shiny. A tap on his shoulder pulled Copley from his thoughts, and he looked to Niki, who was staring at him with an unreadable expression.

"Come with me."

Such a terribly good idea. Swallowing hard, Copley followed Niki as he turned away, gazing at the movement of his back through the tight fabric of his shirt. Niki moved with fluid motion that was too easy for a man of his build. People parted around him without question, giving way to the beast of a man who was as dark as his voice.

And I'm following him.

Pulling a second curtain aside at the back of the room, Niki ushered him through. Copley stopped just inside the curtain, widening his eyes as he took in the sights and sounds before him. His heart picked up, but he didn't want to run.

He flushed as he caught sight of someone strapped to a dark cross, their naked body gleaming with sweat as their Dom touched them with some kind of glove that made them writhe. There was no pain on their face — only pure bliss. His mouth went dry at the sight.

There were others...so many others in varying positions and every state of undress. In the corner, someone was getting fucked from behind while choking on a second man's cock. He didn't know if he was supposed to keep watching or look away.

"Can I touch you?" asked Niki, his rumbling voice dragging Copley's attention back like a black hole that he couldn't resist. The tattooed manacles on Niki's wrist caught his gaze and he reached out, touching the ink with his trembling fingertip.

Niki tugged his arm away with the shake of his head and the click of his tongue. "I didn't say you could touch *me*, Copley. That's something you have to earn." He flexed his hand, muscles rippling along his forearm.

"But you don't have to earn it from me?" Copley asked softly, tilting his head in confusion. He wanted to touch *so* badly, but his urge to feel Niki's hands on him was even fiercer. Niki chuckled before shaking his head.

"There are other things I'd like to earn from you, but first I need your consent. Did you come to this club looking for someone to dominate you? Or are you just here for a free show?" Niki leaned close, his breath coasting over Copley's ear.

Copley leaned in, seeking more as his arousal approached a boiling point, but Niki just drew back, avoiding his touch.

"You can touch me. *Please* touch me," said Copley. *Am I insane?* He was asking the man who had threatened him and his brother and had put a deadline on his brother's life? Thinking about it just made him hotter for some reason. Maybe it was the late nights and tormenting dreams, but he wanted to know what Niki would really feel like against him.

"Good boy." Niki raised his hand, stroking Copley's cheek with his knuckles. This time, when Copley leaned in, Niki didn't pull away, but swept his thumb over Copley's lips instead.

"Did you want to be mine for tonight, Copley? Will you submit to me and let me show you things that you've never dreamed of?"

His lips were so close that Copley could have turned his head and they would've kissed. But he didn't want to make the same mistake twice. If he hadn't earned a touch, then he definitely hadn't earned a kiss.

"Please."

Lips curling into a smile, Niki led him to a free spot in the room, motioning to a table that looked like something out of a massage therapist's office. Copley touched it, tracing the padded surface as he trembled. *What am I doing?*

"Do you know what a safeword is, Copley?" Niki circled the table, trailing his hand over the leather.

Copley shook his head, gnawing at his lower lip. He didn't know anything about kink, which was becoming abundantly clear. It was *not* just a few people trying to spice up their sex life.

"I'll give them to you tonight, but you might want to use something different in the future. Some subs use words that have a special meaning to them. If you say 'red' then everything stops, and we start aftercare. If you say 'yellow', I'll pause the scene and give you a chance to ask questions or adjust what's going on."

"Why can't I just say 'stop'?" asked Copley, staring straight into Niki's eyes, even though he longed to look away. He had a touch of scruff on his chin that gave him a look of pure sin. How many more tattoos were hidden from view? Would he ever find out?

Niki chuckled, the sound raising the hairs on Copley's skin.

"I can guarantee that you will tell me to stop more than once tonight, but inside, you'll want me to keep going and push you until you can't take another thing without breaking."

Trembles racked his body as he stared at the tiger on Niki's neck, its open jaws ready to swallow him whole. "Please don't hurt me. I-I don't like pain...not like that." He looked across the room to where a man was being beaten with a whip that had too many tails.

"Copley, look at me." Niki touched his chin, guiding him back despite his fear. "I will never hurt you. That's not the kind of Dom I am, and it's one of my limits. If you're looking for impact or pain play, you'd have to go see someone else. My style is a touch different."

"Okay." The fear fluttered away as he took one last look at Niki's eyes before dropping his gaze away. "I trust you." *It's official. I'm insane.*

"Don't trust so easily, Copley. Someone might take advantage."

Chapter Seven

Nikita

He'd never been quite so hard during discussions, but then again, he'd never met anyone like Copley, who was willing, despite his fear. It was almost as if he fed on it.

Niki explained limits to Copley, laying his out in the open and walking Copley through a few other things. With most subs, he had to figure out where to start before he could make them tick, but with Copley, it felt like they were already halfway through the scene.

"What kinds of things do you like?" asked Niki as he slowly pressed Copley down on the bench. Anyone else he would have stripped naked, but he didn't want another Dom to see his prize at the moment. There were always ones who were looking for a new sub, and they could piss off.

"Um…I like bottoming if that's what you mean. But really just whatever." Copley shrugged, looking from side to side as he settled on the bench. Niki cupped his cheek, soothing him with a single touch. Copley leaned into him before closing his eyes.

"Dominance and submission aren't about me doing what I want and you taking it. This is for us both. I'm the type of Dom who *needs* you to enjoy yourself. Have you ever been restrained and brought to the edge over and over? Have you ever worn a cock ring or played with a vibrator after you've come, until you're so sensitive that you can hardly take it?"

Copley's eyes went wide, the flush on his cheeks more endearing with each passing moment. Niki longed for his home with his own bedroom where he could lay Copley out naked and inspect every inch. But he didn't touch kink outside the walls of the club. Out there he was who he had to be, but inside Unkinked, he was the man who he always ought to have been.

"I...no. I've never really been adventurous before. With Spenc—I mean, my ex—it was usually doggy style from behind with the occasional reach-around. Don't get me wrong, I liked it, but looking back, it was a touch monotonous. Don't know why I didn't figure out that was doomed from the start." Copley gave a self-deprecating laugh that had Niki frowning. *Something I can fix.*

He loved emotionally lifting his sub until they were on top of the world and making sure nothing or no one could drag them back down. It sounded like Copley had a long way to go.

"Then we'll start slow," said Niki, biting back his growl at the mention of another man's name. "Right now, you're mine."

Copley swallowed, his throat bobbing. "What happens if I mess up? Everything is so new to me, and I don't even really know what I'm doing here—"

"You'll be a good boy for me. I have a feeling." He touched Copley's cheek again as he flushed, dragging his fingers until he settled on Copley's throat. Some people were drawn to big arms or delicate hands, but he had always been a neck guy.

One touch and he could feel a pulse under his fingers, the smooth skin so vulnerable and soft. Copley was slender in every way, but his pale neck was the best part of him by far. A few stray hairs scratched his skin where Copley had missed them with a shaving razor, but the rest was butter soft.

The only problem was that the table had been made for a shorter guy, and Niki's back was already starting to protest. He hadn't turned forty yet, and he wasn't exactly looking forward to it.

"I've changed my mind. Stand up for me and face the wall. I'll guide you where I want you to go." He couldn't stand another moment without getting his lips on Copley, and he didn't want to break his back. It really was too bad that there were no private rooms available, because he would have loved to have Copley facing him instead of hiding him from the crowd that they were sure to gather.

Copley scrambled to comply, following the direction of every simple touch. He was so responsive, gasping and shivering as Niki trailed his fingertips over every bit of covered flesh. He was mouth-wateringly soft, with only down instead of coarse hair on his arms. A siren in every sense of the word.

"Good. Very good." He touched Copley's waist as he stood, guiding him until they were within arm's reach of the wall. The height difference was enough that Niki's thighs were in for a workout, but hopefully, the burn would just be a reminder for when he was alone later. *Nothing like jerking off to the memory of a scene.*

Breathing against Copley's ear, he pulled him close, pressing his chest to Copley's back so he could feel the shudder go through him. His skin was molten through his tight shirt and goosebumps prickled on his flesh as a line of sweat made its way along the dip of his neck. Niki wanted nothing more than to lick it away.

"There's only one thing I want you to do for me tonight, Copley, and that's to promise me that you won't hold back." *So simple, yet so intimidating.*

Copley nodded, and Niki inhaled before he leaned down and placed the first kiss just below Copley's ear. Sucking the lobe into his mouth, he teased it with his tongue before tracing the shell. Copley trembled, letting out a soft whine that had him aching.

Fuck he smelled good and tasted better, with a hint of salt and citrus body wash. He was so responsive, too, arching when Niki finally put his hands on his chest and circled his nipples through his shirt.

"How are you feeling?" he asked against Copley's neck, licking a stripe up the column and reveling in the scratch against his tongue. He scraped with his teeth when Copley didn't respond right away, as both a warning and a threat.

"G-Good." Copley closed his eyes, going lax in Niki's hold. He licked his lips, his tongue glistening in the club lights. There were moans all around them, adding to the low soundtrack that thrummed through the air. "I'm already so close, though. I don't want to make a mess."

So much better than I thought. Niki had to bite his lip to keep from groaning aloud as he caught sight of the tent in Copley's pants. He'd had responsive subs before, but no one who had been ready to please him from a few simple touches.

"You can come in your underwear or against the wall where everyone can see. I'll leave it up to you, baby." He trailed a finger down Copley's belly, pausing at the waistband of his pants.

"I-I'm not... Sweetie said I shouldn't wear underwear, so I didn't."

Well, that was probably one reason that his bulge looked so prevalent. Without anything to hold him in place, his cock had put up a *'hand wanted'* sign.

"Where, then?" Niki nuzzled his throat, biting down gently as Copley let out a long moan.

"The wall." Copley shuddered. "I can't hold back."

"Don't, baby. Be good for me." Plucking his nipples once, Niki ducked beneath Copley's shirt with one hand, getting his first real touch of warm skin. With his other hand, he freed Copley from his jeans, tugging them down his thighs so his cock was bared to the room.

What a pretty thing. Uncut and average, Copley's cock was better than Niki could have imagined. He wrapped his hand around it, tugging once and nearly coming himself as Copley trembled out his release.

There was no build to it. One moment Copley was trembling and the next he shouted against Niki's ear, his body going tight as he painted the wall with cum.

Niki eased him through it, finally releasing him once his cock went soft. He brought his hand to Copley's lips, pressing a coated finger just inside. Copley parted for him, sucking him as if he'd read Niki's thoughts. He throbbed harder, barely able to keep himself from grinding against Copley's ass.

"That was good, Copley. So fucking good for me. How long is your recovery time?" He offered him another finger and Copley stripped it clean in seconds, groaning as if it were candy and not cum.

"I don't know. I've never really tried to come more than once. I usually just take care of myself and pass out after." His orgasm seemed to have loosened his tongue, his heavy eyelids barely open.

"There is so much I want to show you," said Niki, pulling his cleaned hand away before moving it beneath Copley's shirt so he could pinch both nipples at the same time. "Are you okay if we continue or did you need a break?"

"I'm good. So, so good."

"Say 'yellow' if you need to." Niki mapped out every inch of skin, sweeping down Copley's sides before curving his nails in to drag all the way back up. Sucking a bruise along Copley's neck, he teased at the edge of his groin, trailing his fingers lightly through the hair before touching between his thighs and petting him softly. There were so many spots that could make someone come undone and so many more that people often ignored.

It didn't take long for Copley to fill out again, his cock dripping and already wet. Niki took him in hand, ringing another orgasm from him with an expert hand. When Copley cried out, Niki caught his mouth with his own, drinking his moans when he didn't let up, even as Copley started to soften.

Breaking the kiss, he gave Copley the option to safeword as he continued to stroke, bringing him back to hardness and beyond in only a few minutes. His cock barely dribbled with his third orgasm, but Copley slapped the wall with his hand and let out a shout that dragged a few sets of eyes to them.

His pupils were blown, his lips red and bright as Copley blinked at him, looking as if he could barely stand. *Good.* He was gorgeous, sinful and innocent, all wrapped into the perfect package that had Niki struggling to hold back. He couldn't remember the last time his high had hit him so hard.

There was a crowd behind them, and Niki did everything he could to keep Copley from knowing it. It was one thing to discover that you were kinky, but he didn't know if Copley had an exhibitionist streak as well.

"On the table and close your eyes," Niki growled, so turned on that he had to keep from manhandling Copley into position just to get him there faster. His patience was wearing thin, his boxers so slick with pre-cum that he felt like he'd been leaking for hours.

After grabbing a condom from his pocket, he slid it over Copley's semi-hard cock the moment he settled into position. There was a time to talk about testing, but it wasn't when his sub was laid out before him with his pants barely clinging to his hips and his lower lip between his teeth as he tried to hold back a whimper from the touch.

Pulling Copley's lip from between his teeth, Niki let out a growl. "No holding back."

Copley whined, the beginnings of tears in his eyes.

He crouched over the table, taking Copley's cock to the back of his throat before sucking as hard as he could. He wished it was salty flesh and Copley that he was tasting, but latex and lube would have to do for now. It was worth it to see Copley writhe and buck on the table, barely restrained by Niki's hands on his hips.

"Don't hold back your sounds. Let me hear them," said Niki as he reached to pull Copley's lip from between his teeth a second time. He pinched the swollen flesh until Copley winced.

He *hated* hurting his sub, but sometimes it was for their own good. He sucked the abused spot into his mouth, flicking his tongue deep into Copley's mouth before he eased away.

"I can't." Copley's voice was high, a sob caught in his throat as his shoulders shook. He grabbed the edge of the table, his knuckles going white as Niki dropped back onto his cock, bobbing his head until Copley started to get hard for him again.

It took longer than any of the previous peaks, but Niki didn't pause. His jaw was aching, and his tongue was nearly numb from trying to stroke along the bottom of Copley's shaft in time with each suck. *And so much for not getting a sore back.*

When Copley came, the noise was nearly a scream that was sucked up by the people in the room, so many of them looking his way. Niki grinned as he pulled back, jerking Copley's cock with his hand until he collapsed.

Copley's chest heaved, his eyes fluttering behind his lids as he drifted. Niki touched his face, but he didn't even stir, too lost to the maddening pleasure.

Tossing the condom into a nearby bin, Niki lifted Copley to his chest, cradling him with one hand as he motioned to a service sub who had stepped forward with cleaner and towels. Normally it was something Niki would have taken care of himself, but he wanted to get Copley away from the crowd before he roused.

One pair of eyes caught his gaze over the crowd before he turned away, rushing Copley to the recovery couches beyond the curtain.

What the hell is he doing here?

Chapter Eight

Maxim

He wasn't really sure what all the hubbub was about. His brother was borderline obsessed with his little club and all his kinky friends, but Maxim had never seen the appeal.

Sure, sex was okay, but most nights Niki came home from the club still hard in his pants, jerking off in the shower or his room where he thought Maxim couldn't hear. He'd always claimed to be satisfied, but Maxim wasn't so sure.

So why am I at Unkinked? Maybe because every man he'd slept with had left him wanting? At first, he'd thought that maybe he wasn't gay, but his attempt at sleeping with a woman had been a disaster. He'd paid her well, throwing in a tip when she hadn't laughed at his failed situation. *Not doing that again.*

So, men it was. He'd tried silver foxes, cute twinks and everything in between, researching positions online to try to spice it up a little. When Niki had offered to take him to the club on numerous occasions, Maxim had always scoffed and shaken his head.

He supported his brother, but he didn't need any help with his sex life. He also didn't think that choking someone was likely to get him off. He had enough of that in his daily life, and that had never turned him on.

Slamming the car door, he crossed his arms, leaning against the frame to watch a few people stroll by. Some of them nodded his way and he did the same in return, scratching the back of his neck as others lowered their eyes and practically pissed themselves.

It was interesting to see people's reactions when they thought he was someone he wasn't. Other than his tattoos, his brother was identical to him in every way. His schooling had been a breeze with Niki doing his exams, and Niki had pulled him out of the worst situation of his life by switching places with him.

The latter had cost Niki six years of his life. Six years that Maxim could never repay.

Waiting for the couples on the street to finally drift away, he strolled to the club, swinging the door wide to take his first step inside. He nodded to the doorman, who gave him a quick glance before waving him through the curtain.

Should I make a PSA to explain identical twins to people? Their personalities were like blazing fire and the storm that put it out. But for some reason, people couldn't see it.

He kept up his charade of mild glares and nods as he scoped out the bar area before stepping up to the counter to grab a drink. He paused to enjoy the view as a man passed him dressed in little more than a G-string and some conveniently placed straps. Now *that* was something he could get into. But how many ways could he dress someone before he got bored?

He waved down the bartender, swallowing his surprise at the extensive array of marks on his skin. He seemed to wear it without shame, though, his chest out and his head held high. His gaze zeroed in on Maxim, and he narrowed his eyes.

"Did you sign in?" The bartender moved closer, glaring at Maxim like a chihuahua that was about to bite his ankles.

"Maddy, that's Niki. I thought you'd met him." A blond on the other side of the bar called, giving Maxim a little wave. He was cute, too, with bedhead and arms to die for. It helped that there was currently a dribble of Coca-Cola sliding over his biceps. *I'd lick that off for him.*

Maxim licked his lips, giving Maddy a smirk as he leaned against the bar top. Maddy scowled, poking Maxim in the chest with one finger.

"Look here, buddy. I don't know who you are or what you're doing here, but you need to sign in if you'd like to stay." Maddy poked him again, his touch fierce.

"I'm Niki, like the other guy said." Maxim looked to the man on the stool next to him—a smoking-hot redhead with long, straight hair and a thick collar around his neck. The place was like a gold mine.

"Niki has manacles tattooed around his wrists and you don't. Niki doesn't smile like that either, because he's not a douche," said Maddy, reaching below the bar and pulling a baseball bat out. It looked huge in his petite hands. "And that '*other guy*' is one of Niki's good friends, so you would definitely know his name if you were him."

Maxim swallowed, eyeing up the bat. There was no way that Maddy would ever land a hit, but there were enough guys in the club that would probably come to his aide.

"Shit, sorry." Maxim gave him a weak smile before giving in. "Almost worked though, eh? My brother has asked me to come here a dozen times, so I invited myself when I heard there was some kind of open house. I'm Maxim." He held out his hand, his smile faltering when Maddy ignored it. *I can play that way, too.* "I'll sign in, as long as you give me your phone number," said Maxim, lowering his voice and leaning close. There was something untamed and wild about Maddy that made his gut thrum.

Maddy's scowl deepened before he pointed off to the crowd that was gathered on what could have been a dance floor with the right music. "You see that tall guy there…the one who's looking this way and just crossed his arms?"

Maxim looked to where Maddy pointed, trying to keep his shock at bay when he spotted Derreck. Derreck was an enigma, but he did good work, and he was stronger than anyone Maxim had ever met. He was probably one of the only guys who Maxim would lose to in a fight.

"Yeah, that's Derreck. I didn't know he came here, too." He really didn't know much about Derreck at all except for what he did almost every night. Gravedigging was a nasty thing, but Derreck was the best in the business.

"That's him," said Maddy with a little smile. "He's my Dom and my partner, and tonight he's Dungeon Master. That means that if you try to pull another stunt like you just did, you'll be out on your ass before you can say 'safeword'."

Maxim blinked. *I see.* He didn't really feel like dying on the same night he'd finally mustered up the courage to go with his brother to the club... Not that Niki knew he was here.

"Noted. I'll keep my hands to myself." He slid his hands into his pockets to be safe. His jeans pulled tight across his ass, showing off his assets to whoever cared to look.

"And your lies, too," said Maddy, retrieving a stack of papers and a pen from beneath the bar. "I may be oblivious sometimes, but I can usually tell when someone is lying. Unkinked is a place for people to be themselves, no matter who that is. Leave your bullshit at the door, please."

Maxim skimmed the paperwork, signing with a flourish before handing it back to Maddy. "Now where's my brother? I best give him a proper hello."

Maddy nodded to the end of the room where there was a curtain instead of a wall. "He's back there, and he's busy. He won't like it if you interrupt, but he's in the open play area, so you can watch if you like." His cheeks tinted as he lowered his eyes. "If you're into that kind of thing. With your brother, I mean."

Maxim chuckled, shaking his head as he thanked Maddy and moved on. Niki and he didn't have the same boundaries that most siblings did, but it wasn't as if they were a couple. The idea of that seemed a little self-absorbed, even for him.

He weaved his way through the crowd, pausing only once when a woman asked him to join them. "I'm not who you think I am." He gave her a wink before he moved on, dancing a few steps to the low thrum of music. It was something poppy with a good beat that didn't overwhelm the conversation around him too much.

After slipping through the curtain, his breath caught. *Now this is more like it.* It was like every porno he'd ever permanently deleted from his browser history, only better and way more realistic.

To his left was a woman on an actual cross getting her ass flogged with the funkiest whip he'd ever seen. Just beyond that was a man getting fisted, which he'd never seen in real life. He wasn't sure it was exactly *safe* for so much to disappear into a place that was usually a tight squeeze for his cock, but it was eye-catching, all the same. He skimmed over a few more couples and their audiences before he saw something that took his breath away all over again.

His brother looked positively wild as he kissed the neck of a man who Maxim had never seen before. His jaw dropped wider when a moment later, Niki undid the man's pants and cum painted the wall.

It was almost like watching a mirror, only he had no control over the shadow of himself. His cock stirred, but he could hardly feel it. He was too focused on the scene and every twitch and moan from the mystery man.

But he swore he could feel warm skin under his hands as Niki worked over his sub as if he were desperate to make him come as many times as possible. He could certainly hear the yells that built until they drew a crowd of aroused onlookers.

But Niki didn't seem to notice the others as he laid the man out on the bench and went down on him like latex was a new popsicle flavor. When the man collapsed one final time, Niki swept him into his arms, carrying him away from the scene.

He caught Niki's gaze, wondering if his brother would smile or kick him to the curb, but he did neither. He just looked back to his sub, ducking through the curtains and out of the room.

Maxim followed, his mouth dry and his legs like leaden weights. Niki was seated on a leather couch already, cradling the man's head in his lap. Every stress line had been erased from Niki's face as if they didn't spend eighteen hours a day there. Niki brushed his knuckles over the man's cheek and the man turned to him, nuzzling into his palm and gripping his shirt.

What Maxim would give to switch places with his brother and have someone look at him like that.

"I get it now," said Maxim, his voice low. Yes, he was still hard, but he was buzzing in a way he never had before, and he hadn't even lifted a finger. His desire to come was squashed beneath his desire to see more of the mystery man.

But could he do the same thing? Could he give someone pleasure over and over and soak it up like a feast to his soul? He wasn't soft in any definition of the word and that wasn't going to change any time soon.

"If you have questions, they'll have to wait. I'll see you back at the apartment once we've both come down safely." Niki looked to his sub as he spoke, barely sparing Maxim a glance. He lowered his voice, pressing a kiss to the man's forehead. "It's okay, Copley. You did so well for me. We are going to stay here as long as you need."

Maxim took a step back, the dismissal like a punch to the throat. He caught the profile of Copley's face as he blinked and stretched before snuggling deeper into Niki's belly. Heart thudding, he bit his lip. He'd never seen anyone so beautiful.

"At least you have good taste." Maxim tried to smile, but his lips were as heavy as his shoes. "I'll see you later."

"You don't have to leave, Max." Niki sent him a quick concerned glance, probably wondering what the hell was going on with him. *I'd like to know, myself.*

Maxim shook his head, closing his eyes at the scene before him. Another moment and it would be burned into his memory forever. Only it wasn't Niki holding Copley in his imagination, it was him clutching Copley to his chest and running his hands through his hair.

"Fuck."

Chapter Nine

Copley

Copley smiled and looked at his phone as another text from Niki came through. It had been three days since he'd broken his record of most consecutive orgasms, and he hadn't had so much as a morning wood since. He was almost certain that he'd be shooting blanks for a least a week but fuck if that wasn't the best thing ever.

"Before you head out, can you run this to the post office?"

Copley looked at his boss, pushing his thoughts of texting Niki aside. His boss, Cambridge, was an older gentleman who unfortunately had the memory of a goldfish. His gray hair had gone from speckled to silver in the last year, and his eyes were always dark and bleak. Copley couldn't imagine losing a partner to a sudden heart attack, but Cambridge wore every sign of his loss in open view.

Glancing at the clock, he nearly balked when he saw the time. He was surprised that he wasn't starving, as it was already after seven.

"I can take it with me tonight if you'd like, but I'll put it in the mail tomorrow. The post office is already closed for tonight, sir." He took the package, glancing at the scribbled address on the plain white envelope. "Or I can just drop it in the box on my way. It looks like it just needs a stamp." He grabbed one from his desk, lining it up in the upper corner before smoothing it onto the envelope. "Anything else for today, sir?"

His boss was facing away and looking out of the window toward downtown. More often than not, he simply stared off into space. Copley's heart broke a little every time.

"Sir?"

His boss startled, sending a confused look his way before he shook his head. Turning back to his office, he closed the door with a click before drawing his blinds shut.

His phone buzzed again, an insistent purr that indicated a call instead of a text message. Standing from his desk, he accepted it before putting the cell to his ear.

"I found a great place for you, Cope." Sauble's voice cut through the speaker and Copley squinted down at the number. It was a different number than the one Sauble usually texted him from.

"Um, okay?" Copley grabbed his lunch bag, pulling the strap over his shoulder before he headed for the door. "You kicking me out? I was just starting to get the ass-groove in your couch just right." He chuckled. That couch had about thirty ass grooves and none of them were his.

"I should keep you around just for the comedy, but no. You know you can stay until you are back on your feet, but with the Bratva thing going on—"

"I'm working on it," said Copley, scratching at his chin where he'd missed a bit of scruff. His premium shaver was still in his last apartment. "Kind of." He hadn't talked to Niki about it at all, but he figured he could at any point. He just wasn't sure when yet.

"I told you to stay out of it, Cope," said Sauble, a low growl in his voice.

"Uh-huh." Copley pushed through the door and started toward the bus stop. Darkness had fallen, and there was a chill in the dank air. A chill was better than snow, though.

"But about this place. It's with a guy named Brad. I work with him and he's really straight, so you won't have a roommate problem again—and he's a nice guy. He has a second bedroom and he's only looking for about five hundred a month for it."

Five hundred is cheap. Copley bit his lip. But as for the roommate problem... His last roommate had been straight, too...until he wasn't...then apparently was again.

"Sounds good," said Copley, leaning against the post at the bus stop. He smiled at the lady sitting on the bench with a toddler bouncing on her knee. The cute kid was bundled as if it were mid-winter. "I'm thinking January. Do you think something like that would work for him? That way we can do Christmas together for the first time in years."

The silence was near deafening.

"Copley, do you think this is some kind of joke?" Sauble cursed, something smashing in the background.

Copley couldn't remember the last time he'd heard Sauble so upset. Even their first conversation about him leaving paled in comparison.

"I'm not leaving right now, and I told you that I'm working on it. I've been saving everything from work and pulling as many overtime shifts as I can. Between the two of us, we can at least give this Nestor guy a down payment." He was exhausted down to his very soul, but he wasn't going to just abandon his brother.

"We can't make a hundred grand by the end of the month," said Sauble, his voice rising until Copley winced and pulled the phone away from his ear. The mother looked up from the bench, concern etched on her face.

"I said a down payment." Copley lowered his voice, turning away. The last thing he needed was for a stranger to know they were indebted to a gang. That seemed like a fast way to lose friends.

"That's not how these guys work, Copley. A hundred grand or bust."

"Well, how much do you have?" asked Copley, chewing his lip as he spotted the bus down the street at another stop. There was a crowd, so hopefully, he had a minute or two. "You have a good job, and I know you make a lot more than I do. Between the two of us, we should be able to come up with ten or fifteen thousand by the end of the month."

He'd had to sell a few things to make it stretch that far, but he wasn't a miracle worker. He'd talked to Sauble's neighbors and had found out that rent was pennies, and the utilities didn't exactly exist in the traditional sense.

"Nothing. I don't have anything, little bro. If you thought you could ride in on some white horse and fix all my problems for me, then you've got another thing coming. I don't need your fucking money, and I don't need your pity, either. Your welcome has officially expired. You're off the couch by the twenty-ninth of *this* month and that's fucking final."

Copley's breath caught as he gripped the signpost, the tiny circles in the metal digging welts into his palm. "How could you have nothing? You just got paid last week."

"And I spent it," Sauble snarled. "I'll spend fifteen bucks for every ten they pay me, and that's not going to change any time soon. You want to know why I want you gone, Copley? All you're doing is feeding the habit."

"What?" A sob worked its way up his throat. "I'm trying to help out. I'm buying groceries and —"

"No, you gave me *money* for groceries. You wanna know what happened to those hundred bucks? They're fucking gone. And that ring you keep looking for? I pawned that off the night after you moved in. It was an unlucky piece of shit, just like you."

The line went dead, and Copley's vision blurred as tears threatened. The bus arrived with a squeal and a burst of air and Copley blinked them away, paying the fare and moving to the very back.

How could I be so stupid? He'd known his brother's gambling addiction was bad, but he hadn't suspected that Sauble would actually steal from him. Sauble was the only one who stood up for him and the only one that actually seemed to care. *Except Niki.*

He looked to his phone, scrolling through his contacts until he found Niki's name. They'd been texting back and forth since their scene, but Niki had made it clear that their activities would strictly be kept to the club.

He almost dreaded using his Dom for anything more than he was supposed to. Even though their relationship was new, it felt almost sacred. *I don't have a choice.* He couldn't let his brother rot because he wasn't brave enough to do something about it.

He pressed the call button, bringing the phone to his ear. It rang once before it connected, and he heard Niki's voice. The grief in his chest eased at the two syllables of his simple hello.

It had taken him years before he'd really felt anything for Spencer, but he'd already given more of himself to Niki. Maybe that was why his heart rate picked up and his tears were suddenly bits of moisture with no meaning. *Everything is okay now.*

"Hey, it's me... I mean Copley. It's Copley." His voice was thick, and he sniffed to try to clear it.

"I didn't expect to hear from you, baby. Everything okay?"

How could a gang's debt collector be a teddy bear at the same time? Copley had no doubt that every one of Niki's threats were serious, but at the same time, his Dom was one of the sweetest men he'd ever spoken to. He couldn't be afraid of someone who loved *Pride and Prejudice.*

"Um, not really," said Copley, scratching the back of his head. "It's not about anything kinky, but me and my brother had a fight. I wasn't really sure who else to call. Could we meet up for a coffee or something?" He scratched at the seat and the initials someone had carved there.

"No."

Copley inhaled. He hadn't been expecting a rejection that was so complete. Niki hadn't even given him an excuse, but his voice brooked no objections. *It really is just kink for him.*

"Okay, I'm sorry. I shouldn't have asked." He stared at his shoes. One of the toes of his dress shoes was scuffed, the polished black surface looking grayer than it should have. It would be time for winter boots soon.

"*No,* you shouldn't have. I set a limit at meeting outside of the club, and you need to respect that, please." Niki's voice was soft, but he may as well have yelled into the phone.

Well, now I feel even worse. The last thing he wanted to do was push his Dom's limits.

"Then can we meet at the club? If you aren't busy, I mean." There was a bus stop close by, so he could get there easily within the next forty-five minutes.

"I'll be there in an hour. I just have a few things to wrap up."

Chapter Ten

Nikita

He ended the call, sliding his phone into his pocket before shaking his head at himself. Just hearing Copley's voice again had soothed any doubts as to how his sub was feeling. It was one thing to text someone to see how they were after a scene, but text could also be an emotionless lie.

And fuck, did it kill him to have to say no to meeting up for a *date*, even if he wanted to. *It's against the rules.* Nestor tolerated his sexuality with a dismissive disgust that Niki managed to shake off most days. His brother was the only person in his life who was truly supportive of him, but the last few days had felt like there was a wall between them, too.

He'd gained a new sub, but the moment he'd seen his brother in the club staring at him and Copley with open adoration, he had felt something shift between them. The silences that used to be comfortable stretched awkwardly, and there had been no new men in the apartment, which for Maxim was practically sainthood.

Maxim didn't care about Nestor's attitude toward them. But Niki had a feeling that Nestor would hesitate to truly say anything against either of them. No one wanted to fight against the infamous Twin Tigers who had brought down more men than anyone could guess.

Still, Niki wasn't going to take a chance. And one-night stands were a hell of a lot different than a relationship, even if it was between a Dominant and a submissive.

The instant he had seen Copley, he'd known he had to be careful. But the moments in the club had been beyond his imagination, and his careful plan had been blasted to smithereens. But he still had his limits, and his sub had to respect them in the same way that he respected Copley's.

Then why do I feel so bad about it?

He glanced to the side at a man who was tied to a chair, his screams caught behind a gag as Maxim worked him over. Nikita should have been keeping watch, but he knew there was no one coming to the rescue. No one cared about a deadbeat asshole who had fucked up one of their girls and had landed her in the hospital. She would be fine...eventually, but only because she'd managed to get to her phone.

Maxim shot him a look, blood dripping from his hands. He should have worn gloves, but Niki doubted he would ever be able to convince his brother to not get blood on his skin. "You done, Niki?"

Nikita grunted, touching his phone through the layers of his pocket. The blood didn't bother him and neither did the murder that was about to take place.

He'd already done his time in prison…ironically for the one crime that he hadn't committed. "Other business."

"You better watch yourself, bro. Someone might think you're starting to go soft."

The barb stung, probably worse than Maxim had intended, but Nikita kept his face blank. He'd met his fair share of people who thought that because he didn't beat his sub, he wasn't a real Dom at all. He *hated* the term 'soft Dom'.

Was it really soft to make someone come over and over again until their pleasure was so overwhelming that it blew their mind? Was it really soft to edge someone until it was pure torture for them and every word was a plea? It took a lot of control for him to not beat the shit out of someone instead. But that would make him hate himself more than others already did.

"Whatever. Just clean up when you're done." Niki turned away, not looking back, even as his brother called out to him. Stepping outside of the warehouse, he took a breath of fresh air, trying to rid himself of the blood that coated his lungs. It still lingered long after he'd gotten in his car and headed home to shower.

He rinsed the suds from his body, grabbing his brother's body wash and tossing it over the curtain so it landed in the trash. It was nearly a full bottle, but he didn't care. He was too goddamn pissed.

Mostly at himself, but at his brother and Copley, too. His brother had the audacity to taunt him, even when he knew how much it hurt, and Copley crossed a line, even if it had been done innocently. They both needed to be punished, but the worst he could do to his brother was hide his shit.

He chuckled as he finished off the milk, putting the empty carton back in the fridge before hiding every can of Bud Light around the apartment like it was a fucking easter egg hunt. He hadn't counted, and he certainly wasn't going to remember where he hid them all, but he knew Maxim wouldn't touch his Sleeman. They were going to find a can four years from now, and Niki was determined to laugh his ass off when they did.

Jumping back into his car, he sped to the club, arriving with two minutes to spare. Copley was already there and leaning against the wall with his gaze on the sidewalk as a couple passed him on their way inside. Copley gave them a smile, a shine in his eyes that Niki could see from the car.

Letting out a sigh, Niki leaned back against the seat, watching the clock count down as he waited out his anger. Imagining Maxim freaking out as he looked for his post-job beer was enough to make him smile, but watching his sub was even better.

Copley's perky demeanor wasn't diminished by his bloodshot eyes that Niki had noticed as soon as he'd pulled up. Copley obviously wore his pain as easily as he did his pleasure.

Swallowing, Niki turned away for a moment, willing himself not to give in. He had always hated punishments, but over the years he'd found tricky little ways of doling them out with his sub being none the wiser. It was still hard on him, though, but he supposed he deserved that as well. Perhaps he had underestimated their connection and had set Copley up for failure.

Either way, watching Copley's enthusiasm dim and realization set in was like fucking magic. At first, Copley probably wondered if Niki was stuck in traffic or maybe picking up coffees along the way. Eventually he gave up on that hope, maybe wondering if he'd been forgotten completely. He was beautiful in his dejected misery.

Thanking the tinted windows, Niki spread his legs to give room for his cock. He wasn't a sadist — far from it — but he loved a good mind fuck. And punishing someone without laying a hand on them always gave him a rush of relief.

He waited until there were fresh tears on Copley's cheeks and he had stopped greeting people before he finally gave in. Glancing at the clock, he saw that over an hour had gone by as he waited for his boy to settle. Copley's tears were running freely, and he didn't look up as Niki got out of his car and approached him on the sidewalk.

He touched Copley's chin, tilting his face so he could see those tear-streaked cheeks with nothing between them. He was beautiful, his red-rimmed eyes drawing Niki in further until his heart ached in time with his groin.

"Do you know why I left you here crying for the last seventy-two minutes?" asked Niki, lowering his hand to his side before he gave in to his need to soothe Copley's tears.

"N-no." Copley hiccupped, his voice threaded through his sobs. His shoulders shook, trembling from either grief or the chill in the air.

"You nearly broke one of my limits today," said Niki softly, taking a step to the left to shield Copley from the breeze. "I know this is your first submissive relationship, but I need you to know how serious this is. You waiting for me out here was your punishment."

"I'm s-sorry." Another sob escaped Copley's throat and Niki couldn't hold back any longer. He pulled Copley closer, bringing their foreheads together.

"I know. I know you're trying so hard to be good for me. That's why your punishment is over, and you're forgiven." Niki took a deep breath. He'd missed Copley more than he'd thought, right down to the way he smelled of cheap aftershave and second-hand smoke. "Are you going to be good?"

"Yes, Sir."

Niki nearly growled at the way 'Sir' sounded on Copley's tongue. "Good. Now, do you have somewhere safe to stay tonight? I don't want you to sleep on your brother's couch again if you don't feel safe."

Niki wasn't exactly sure what was going on, but it had to be big if Copley looked so upset.

"Yeah. I already talked to Sweetie after I talked to you. I'm going to crash at her place tonight to let Sauble's temper cool before I go home." Copley let out a sigh before sinking further into Niki's embrace.

"Good." Niki pulled back, wiping the tears from Copley's cheeks before he turned away. "Go, Copley. I'll talk to you tomorrow."

Copley blinked, surprise creeping over his face. "Wait. Aren't we going in?" He looked to the closed door of Unkinked as if it were a lifeline.

"Do you deserve me, Copley?" asked Niki, licking his lower lip. If Copley thought that it was only hard on him, he was terribly wrong. Niki's longing was almost visceral.

"No." He looked down at the sidewalk. "But I thought you said you forgave me."

Niki nodded. "I do, but I'm not going to reward you when we just finished a punishment. Get your rest, and I'll talk to you tomorrow. Be good, and you'll get to go inside and I'll take care of you then."

Copley brightened, shoving his hands into his pockets as he let out a soft smile. "Okay."

Fuck, this boy is too sweet for me. Niki wondered if he should send him away now, before they crossed boundaries that were best left erected. How long would it be before their lives could no longer be separated?

Niki slid into his car, waiting to pull away until Copley started toward the bus stop. A few people looked at Copley as he walked down the street, and a man's gaze lingered longer than it should have. It was already past dark, and even the safest parts of the city were no longer completely safe. *And I'm letting him walk right into the middle of it while his cheeks are still stained with tears?*

As he reached the bus stop, Nikita pulled his car over to the curb, lowering the passenger window and calling out to Copley. His sub rushed over to the car, his eyes wide and excited. Niki's cock ached in response, almost Pavlovian in his need.

"Get in the car. I'm driving you," said Niki, flexing his hands on the steering wheel. The leather was smooth in his grip, the scent of it thick with fresh polish.

"I can take the bus," said Copley, leaning against the door and sticking his head through the open window. "I don't want to be any more trouble for you today."

"Just be good and get in." Niki let out an exasperated sigh. *Is there such a thing as too perfect?*

Copley closed his mouth, his protest dying on his lips before he opened the door and dropped into the seat of the car. Before he could reach for his belt, Niki pulled it over him and snapped it into place. Taking a deep breath, he lingered, glancing at Copley's lips. They had only kissed once and that had been a poor substitute for the real thing. The fact burned into him at that moment.

He pulled back before he could break his own rule about keeping relationships to the club, turning into traffic and gripping the wheel hard.

"Her place is on Frank Street," said Copley, pulling out his phone and squinting at the screen. "She sent me a screenshot of what it looks like, so just let me zoom in to see the number."

Niki snickered before leaning over and squeezing Copley's thigh. Copley gasped at the touch, and Niki had to bite back his own groan. It was bad enough that he was already aching, but touching Copley again was somehow better than the first time. He couldn't wait to get them a private room at the club so he could expose and explore every inch before he took those lips properly for the first time.

"I already know where it is, boy." He curled his hand over Copley's kneecap, dragging his nails over the fabric. *What am I doing?*

"Oh, you know Sweetie, too? I've only known her for a few weeks, but she's such a nice lady." His voice trembled as Niki moved his hand along the inseam of his pants, fingering the threaded ridge.

That was the first, and hopefully only, time Niki had heard Sweetie referred to as a '*lady*'. She was all claws and teeth, but her regulars loved her, and she took care of them as long as they didn't try to push the boundaries. On the plus side, Niki and Maxim rarely had to step in to teach someone a lesson on her behalf because she usually did it herself.

"I know Veronica, yeah. Her boss is my boss, remember? She's good at her job, and her place is one of the nicer ones. I wouldn't trust you with anyone else." It wasn't *the* nicest place out there, but Niki's place was out of the question. Even if it hadn't been a limit, he still hadn't figured out what was going on with Maxim.

"Veronica?" asked Copley, his eyes wide.

"Did you think her mother named her Sweetie?" asked Niki, chuckling and bopping Copley on the nose at his adorable nod. "Her mum wasn't a prostitute. She was actually mayor at one point, believe it or not. They're still on good terms, too. Amazing woman, that one."

Maybe Niki was a touch biased. The mayor had helped loosen laws against sex workers during her time and had done Nestor one hell of a favor.

"But do you guys like *work together* work together? You were very...skilled. I don't think I've ever been with someone that made me feel so good before." Copley flushed, his face beaming in the dark car.

Am I supposed to take that as a compliment? On one hand, sex work *was* work, but it wasn't exactly Niki's skill set. Having ten different partners in one night turned him off.

"You asking if I get paid for sexual favors?" asked Niki, forcing a growl in his voice as he sent Copley a playful glare.

"N-no!" he squeaked, leaning toward the far edge of his seat.

"I don't," said Niki. "But maybe I should if you're saying I'm that good. A little extra cash would always come in handy."

"Yeah, it would," Copley said softly, his lips dropping into a frown. He looked to the window where traffic had started to pick up as they moved farther into town.

"I'm just a glorified bodyguard," said Niki, pushing through the awkwardness that suddenly draped the car. "Most days I'm by Nestor's side, but I still run an errand or two now and again."

Despite his efforts, the tension remained, the soft music on the radio doing nothing to help. Copley's gaze was on his knee where Niki's hand was still resting. He squashed the urge to pull away.

"Is that what happened with my brother? An errand?"

Niki scowled before easing over to the shoulder of the road. Sweetie's apartment building was to their right, the red brick and identical balconies ominous in the low light. Some of the streetlights were out, but a few glowed bright in the darkness. A man stood at the front door beneath the main floodlight, smoke puffing from his lips as he took a drag from his cigarette.

The tattoos on the man's neck had Niki on instant alert, and he reached for the gun at his waistband that wasn't there. He never took a weapon into Unkinked or if he knew he was going anywhere close. It wasn't so much that he was worried he would shoot someone but bringing a weapon onto another man's property—a friend's—was practically sacrilege.

After leaning over Copley, he clicked open the glove box, grabbing the handgun that was hiding in a special compartment above the owner's manual. The metal was cool against his palm, the minimal weight of it hiding its strength.

"Stay in the car, and don't come out, no matter what you see. If something happens, call Maxim." He slid Copley his phone before he eased out of the car, slamming the door shut behind him and locking them tight.

Niki glared as he watched the man snub out his cigarette against the brick before reaching beneath his jacket and bringing out a piece of his own. The scar over his eye told Niki exactly who he was. Although he'd never met Dimitri, he was known by reputation alone.

A reputation to shoot first and ask questions later. He was more of a hothead than Maxim, which was saying something. And the dagger tattoo through his throat meant that he was for hire to whoever paid the highest price.

"What the fuck are you doing here, Dimitri?" Niki called out, pausing a few paces away and relaxing his grip on his gun so it hung at his side. He hated the fucking thing, but risking going against Dimitri unarmed was suicide. Maxim would dig up his grave just to slap him silly over it.

Dimitri smirked, tapping the brick with his knuckles before he closed the distance between them with a few quick strides. The tip of his gun rested against the sensitive skin of Niki's belly, pressing through the thin layer over his abs. He reeked of cigarettes, his yellow-stained teeth dark and rotten.

Niki chuckled, slowly moving one hand to Dimitri's neck and bringing them closer, before raising his own weapon to Dimitri's groin. Dimitri had balls, he had to give him that. There weren't many people who played with the Twin Tigers.

"I heard your boss has been scooping up some of our ladies," said Dimitri, digging the gun into his belly until Niki had to fight the wince. He eyed Dimitri's finger that was hovering over the trigger.

"So your boss sends you to rough up Nestor's people?" Niki sneered, resting his finger on the trigger, his hand steady. One flinch and everything would be over. "Looks like you're going soft. No wonder you didn't take it straight to him. Afraid he would eat you up?" He moved his own gun into the paunch of Dimitri's stomach, digging into the layer of fat.

"Just checking up on an old friend of mine," said Dimitri, tugging free and backing away with a glimmering smirk. "Sweetie was always a favorite, you know." His threat hung in the air, and Niki had to bite back the urge to pull the trigger. It was really too bad that he wasn't a murderer. It would make a lot of things easier.

"I'll talk with Nestor, but until then, stay off his fucking territory or you'll wish you were never born."

Dimitri shrugged, tucking his weapon into the front of his pants before he turned away. With any luck, he'd blow his own dick off.

"I'd watch that side piece of yours, Nikita. Wouldn't want him to know that his Daddy is a cold-blooded murderer." Dimitri melted into the shadows, the reek of his body clinging long after he was gone.

Niki's vision blurred red as he marched back to the car, the alarm blaring as he pulled the handle before remembering to unlock it. Clicking it open with a growl, he slipped inside, starting the car and tossing his gun back into its safe spot. Copley was exactly where he'd left him, looking curious but no worse for wear.

"But, that was Sweetie's place," said Copley, looking out of the window as Niki pulled away from the curb. His voice trembled, his face pale as he looked from the glove box to Niki.

"You're staying at my place tonight," said Niki, biting his tongue as his voice came out rough and ragged. *Fuck the rules.* He wasn't leaving Copley out there. "I didn't mean to frighten you, Copley, but it's not safe here. I need to keep an eye on you...for me." He let out a breath, the tension draining from his shoulders with every foot between Copley and the threat.

"I'm not afraid," said Copley, his voice barely above a whisper. "I've never seen a gun before is all. I thought you were going to shoot that guy. Then I would have to call the cops on you with *your* cell phone, and that just seemed wrong on every level." A tiny smile touched his lips. "They'd take you away from me."

The last words were so quiet that Niki wasn't sure if he was meant to have heard. They put a bolt of fear straight into his heart. There was no way he could resist Copley another moment...

"I'd never let that happen. You're mine, boy. Don't ever forget that."

Copley shuddered, leaning against his seat and closing his eyes. "I won't."

Chapter Eleven

Copley

Hollywood and romance novels had apparently ruined him. He'd expected Niki to live on the top floor of a penthouse with a stripper pole in his living room and a champagne fountain, but when they pulled up to a nice-looking townhouse, he did a double take.

Six identical porches looked back at him, with crisp lawn furniture and fall decorations. It was all brick and new looking, with yellowed grass that still had the delicacy of fresh sod. Copley nearly melted as Niki parked in the driveway of the farthest home on the left.

The porch display pulled him in, the ornate pumpkins and fancy gourds piled on a bale of straw, like something you'd find on a postcard. He glanced at Niki, a smile on his lips as he looked at his Dom in a whole new light. Niki stared back at him, his eyes darker than he'd ever seen them.

When he'd seen the flash of the gun, his heart had nearly stopped. He knew Niki worked for the Bratva, but he had trouble aligning that with everything else about the man. Debt collection aside, his Dom seemed like a saint.

"Maxim picked the place out a few years ago when it was just being built," said Niki as he slipped out of the car. Circling around, he held the door open for Copley, taking his hand to help him out. "Took them until this summer to put the sod down, though. Most of it died, but we're hoping it comes back next spring."

"It's beautiful," said Copley, squeezing his hand once before letting it drop away. The inside of the house was unexpected, too, with rich wood furnishings and décor that looked like something out of a magazine. The only thing that took away from it was the stale scent of cigarettes that lingered near the kitchen.

"I have to make a few calls," said Niki as he emptied the ashtray that was on the table before rinsing it out in the sink. "Make yourself at home. There's beer in the fridge if you want." Niki disappeared into the backyard, pulling the glass door shut behind him.

Taking a breath, Copley circled the house once before pushing the bedroom door open and stepping inside. Instead of one bed in the room, there were actually two, both doubles and set only a few feet apart.

One set of identical covers was pulled tight and neatly made with almost military precision while the other was a heaping disarray that didn't fit with the rest of the house. The messy side had a stand stacked with gay porno mags while the neat one had an empty glass and a thick hardcover book.

It was like seeing two sides of the same coin.

"What the hell are you doing?" Niki's angry voice startled him, and he whirled around, clutching the door frame as his heart pounded.

Niki looked pissed, his eyes wild and his hair mussed. The frown on his lips was downright ominous and had Copley gripping the frame until his fingers ached.

"You said I could make myself comfortable?" Copley said quietly. He had just finished fucking up and somehow, he was already doing it again. Maybe he shouldn't have checked out the bedroom. Was that too obvious when Niki had already turned him down?

Niki scowled, pushing past him before pulling his shirt over his head. Copley's mouth dropped open at the sight of more muscles and flesh than he could ever dream of possessing. He'd guessed his Dom was ripped, but seeing it for himself was something else entirely.

"Are you going to join me in the shower?" Niki's voice dropped into an unfamiliar purr, and Copley blinked in surprise. His Dom flicked on the lamp before he reached for his belt buckle.

The 'yes' was on the tip of his tongue, but something caught his eye. The spots on Niki's wrists that were supposed to be marked by dark manacles, were smooth and bare. The tiger on his neck was on the wrong side, too, its casual growl looking so much more menacing.

Copley took a step into the room, his breath catching as the belt fell on the messy bed with a slither of leather. The V going down to his groin was obscene, along with the small tuft of hair peeking over the brim of his pants as they sagged. Copley couldn't look away.

"You aren't Niki," said Copley. His heart thudded in both desire and panic, not really sure what the hell he was seeing.

The man smiled, light touching his eyes for the first time. "No, I'm not. And you shouldn't be here." He stalked forward until Copley was backed against the wall with barely a breath between them. "My brother doesn't bring his toys back here, so you must be lost. Or are you a treat for me?" He leaned in, his breath tickling the side of Copley's neck.

He should have been terrified. He should have screamed for help or pushed his Dom's lookalike away...but he couldn't. Arousal sparked in his gut as he came face to face with everything Niki was and wasn't.

"What's your name?" asked Copley, fisting his hands so he didn't reach out. His palms were sweaty, his face flushed and getting hotter with each breath. The smell of cologne and stale cigarettes was strong, along with something almost coppery.

"Maxim," he said, the first hint of an accent slipping into his voice. "I saw you at the club with my brother." He dragged his lips over the shell of Copley's ear. "I would have pushed you further than him. I would have ripped your pants off, fucked you where everyone could see and made you keep coming until you couldn't move for days. He let you off easy."

Copley shuddered, closing his eyes as Maxim's lips loomed closer to his own. He licked his lips, quivering as Maxim touched his waist and sidled ever closer.

"Would you let me do that, Copley?"

Maxim's lips touched his neck and he shuddered, his entire body flushing. *He knows my name?* Nodding, he swallowed against the need to resist. Niki had brought him home to his brother. Perhaps it had been his plan all along.

"That's right. I know who you are. My brother won't shut up about you...his perfect little sub who doesn't even make his Dom come." He placed a wet kiss on his neck and Copley let out a small whimper of need as his body throbbed. "You'd make me come, baby. I wouldn't be able to stop myself from filling up every one of your pretty holes. You'd choke on me as you swallowed me deep, before I took your ass to breed."

"Fuck," said Copley, gripping the wall as he shuddered. He opened his eyes and Maxim was so close that he nearly saw double.

"Oh, you have a dirty mouth too. That's my favorite."

"Maxim!"

Niki's voice cut between them like a knife, throwing a bucket of water over Copley's quivering form. Turning his head, he spied Niki's narrowed eyes, the frown on his lips and the way his phone looked close to breaking in his grip. *This wasn't his plan.*

"What are you doing?" A moment after the rage disappeared, raw hurt flashed over Niki's face before a mask slammed into place, cutting his emotions off like a fractured tether.

"Introducing myself," said Maxim, pulling away slowly. "You can't say that you haven't thought what it would be like to have him between us, taking him at the same time. It's been a long time since we pushed the beds together to have the same man."

Copley's jaw dropped as Niki rubbed his forehead and let out a sigh. It sounded like a great idea to him, but Niki just looked exasperated. His heart sank as he remembered his punishment. Apparently, he hadn't learned a thing from it.

"He's not here to get fucked. He's here because Dimitri is on a warpath and happens to know who Copley is."

What does that mean? Copley wasn't sure if he was supposed to be scared or not, but his throbbing cock took every ounce of worry away.

Maxim took a step back, all pretense dropping as rage curled about him like a snapping wind. Copley shrank away, afraid that he'd be caught in the sudden hurricane.

"Tell me when and where and I'll take care of the little bastard. He's the one who set up our girl with that john." He cast a gaze at Copley before lowering his voice. "He's looking to move into the territory."

"I know," said Niki, tucking his phone into his pocket. "Copley, this is Maxim, my brother. Maxim, this is my sub, Copley." He grabbed Maxim's shoulder, gripping tight. "Lay a hand on him again and I'll break every one of your fingers. You know I will."

Copley swallowed, caught between the throb of his cock and the utter terror of the situation. At Maxim's dark look, he pulsed harder, dripping inside his boxers. Niki's eyes went wide as he clearly caught sight of the tent in Copley's slacks.

"Unless… Did you like my brother's hands on you?" he asked before Maxim had even left the hall. Maxim paused, smirking over his shoulder.

Copley nodded, his throat bobbing as he tried to swallow. Heat burned through him, flushing every inch of his skin until he was sure he was beaming red. '*Like*' didn't even begin to describe how good it had felt. Maxim had barely touched his waist, but the spot tingled with molten awareness.

"Was he just like me?" asked Niki, moving until he hovered just out of reach. Copley still had to crane his head to look up at him, licking his lips at everything he saw. Maxim was still at the head of the hall, watching them with a curious gaze.

"No. He was everything that you aren't," said Copley softly, unable to look away. Niki's eyes were light brown with a fleck of green near the edge of his iris. He wondered if Maxim's looked the same from so close. He had spent so much time trying to look away, that he hadn't really *looked*.

"Good." Niki cupped his chin, giving him a small smile before he pecked Copley on the cheek. "It's late. Go get ready for bed. You can borrow a pair of my sleep clothes if you'd like. I'd like to see you in my things tonight."

Copley rushed to follow the order, taking a quick shower in the en suite before throwing on the pair of boxers that he'd pulled from the dresser beforehand. He'd chosen from the dresser where the clothes were neatly folded instead of heaped by the bed. They were soft and loose on him, sagging until his crack was exposed.

He paused at the bathroom door, shivering as the dampness dried from his skin. Niki was already in bed, the neat covers rumpled and pooled around his waist as he sat against the headboard, reading his hardcover book. Glasses were perched on the end of his nose, and he pushed them up before he turned the page.

Copley looked to his feet, which were slightly wrinkled from the warm shower. *Am I supposed to just get in bed? Do I sleep on the floor like some subs do?* If his research in the last few days had told him anything, it was that every kinky relationship was vastly different. Niki hadn't exactly set out protocols for him, but their relationship was still fresh.

"I can hear you wondering from over there," said Niki, snapping his book shut and lifting his glasses from his nose. "Come here, boy." He patted the small spot beside him on the double bed, making no effort to move over as Copley approached. "Wait there." Niki stopped him at the edge with a hand on his belly, leaning against the headboard again before spreading his legs under the covers. Copley wasn't sure if he was wearing anything beneath the sheets, but the outline of his cock was tall and glorious.

Niki's gaze swept over him, never pausing as he seemed to take in every detail. Copley flushed at the scrutiny. He wasn't overly self-conscious, but he'd never been examined like a piece of jewelry before. His body was his body, simple enough, but no one had ever looked at it like it was actually a beautiful extension of himself and not just something to find brief pleasure in.

"Very nice. Do you work out?" Niki skimmed his hand over the slight bumps of Copley's abs before scratching his nails against the dusting of hair there. He avoided the edge of the boxers, which were slipping even lower.

"My work has a gym, and sometimes I go there to blow off steam," said Copley, watching Niki's hand as he continued to explore. He shivered at the touch, his skin prickling as he let out a gasp. *God,* he missed being touched, and no one had ever been quite so thorough before.

"This looks like more work than just a little steam. I know men who would kill for a body like yours. You have the perfect tuck above your hips, but your waist isn't too narrow. I know it's nothing to the person you are beneath, but you really are beautiful."

"I-I." Copley snapped his jaw shut, blinking away the tears that suddenly gathered. There was no bigger turn-off than tears that weren't from pleasure. "Thank you."

"You don't have to thank me, boy. No, come back here. I could look at you all night, but I don't want you to get chilled. Come." Niki shuffled down, lifting the edge of the blanket before motioning for Copley to get inside. Copley caught a hint of nakedness before he scrambled into bed, his skin prickling at the sudden warmth.

He shifted around, trying to find a comfortable spot where he wasn't too close to the edge, but also not taking up too much space. Niki chuckled before looping an arm around him and pulling him in tight.

Oh God, he's naked. Copley throbbed, squirming closer to try to brush up against everything that Niki had to offer. A hand on his hip and another chuckle stopped him.

"I told you I won't reward you on the same day as a punishment. Now go to sleep, boy. I'll make you pancakes in the morning."

Tell that to my cock. Copley looked down to the traitorous bastard who was throbbing against Niki's thigh. It wouldn't take much, but the last thing he wanted to do was disappoint his Dom again.

Copley lowered his head to Niki's chest, letting out a sigh as Niki combed through his hair. Relaxing into the embrace, he tried to forget about all the reasons he should have been anywhere else in the world. "Goodnight."

"Goodnight, boy."

Chapter Twelve

Copley

Waking was like one of those illusions that he had been fascinated by when he was a child. There was the never-ending staircase that seemed to go up *and* down, or the two lines that looked to be different lengths but were exactly the same.

He opened his eyes to the sight of Maxim sleeping a few feet away, with the heat of Niki pinned against his back. A hard cock was between his clothed cheeks, heavy and hot against him. All he had to do was reach for it and he could have touched it with his hands for the first time.

He clasped his fingers together instead, determined to be good. It didn't help that his own cock was rock hard, with no sign of flagging like his usual morning wood. *Niki didn't say I couldn't touch myself.*

Instead of slipping his hand under the blanket, he tugged the edge down, exposing himself one inch at a time. It was almost obscene with two men in the room who could wake at any moment and see him. But maybe that was the point.

Taking a breath, he reached for himself, touching the wet spot on his borrowed boxers and gasping at the fire that zinged up his cock. His skin prickled in the cool air, every nerve in his body alight. His heart thudded as his adrenalin surged and he came closer to public indecency than he'd ever been.

He tugged his boxers, wiggling to get them down his legs while trying not to move too much. As he went still, Niki's cock slid between his naked cheeks, the wet head gliding a path straight to his hole.

"Fuck," he whispered against the pillow, drowning his moan in the fluffy cotton as Niki humped in his sleep. Copley's cock throbbed, pre-cum dripping to the bed as he edged closer without even touching himself.

"Are you riled up this morning, boy?" Niki asked, humping once more until his cockhead nearly tried to breach Copley's hole. His voice didn't sound sleepy at all, with only its usual gruffness at the edges.

"How long?" Copley arched while keeping his hands buried in the sheets. He had no shame as he rubbed against Niki's cock, testing the limits of his hole until he felt like he was about to be breached.

"I've been awake the whole time," said Niki with a chuckle. "I was listening to you sleep and waiting until you woke up to give you your reward. You sound wonderful when you moan my name."

Copley's dream came rushing back. Maxim's idea had apparently seeped far into his thoughts, and he'd dreamed about the brothers as he writhed between them. It was no wonder that he was hard enough to pound nails.

"But don't stop on my account. I want to see how you fuck yourself." Niki curled around him, resting his chin on top of Copley's head so he could peer down and catch every moment of action.

Copley's arousal spiked, and he wondered if he was going to have actual heart palpitations if he didn't come soon. Niki wasn't trying to be quiet, and Maxim was still sleeping, his eyes shut and his nose squinted as he let out a soft snore.

"Fuck, that's hot." Copley breathed out before taking himself in hand. Getting himself off had always been more of a science than an art. He knew what felt best, and he usually hammered out a good orgasm in five minutes or less. Stamina didn't mean much to him when he had no one to fuck, and he hadn't done the fucking since his college days.

Gripping his shaft just on the side of too tight, he pulled back the foreskin before he smoothed his pre-cum over the head with his thumb and focused on the little divot. He bucked into his hand as he touched the right spot, his balls going heavy as he got ready to bust. His breathing stuttered, the edge so close as he moved his hand over his shaft fast and hard, so ready to wring himself dry.

"Stop."

Copley's hand stopped of its own accord at Niki's command. He slapped the bed as a fierce ache traveled up his shaft, his balls throbbing as they were denied release. He moaned into his elbow, the sound much too loud in the quiet room. It fucking hurt as much as it felt good, bringing tears to his eyes as his orgasm dwindled away.

"Try with your other hand, and go slower." Niki kissed the top of his head as he asked, his breath hot in Copley's hair.

Sweat dripped down his back as he panted, Niki's cock still poking its way between his cheeks. Niki was barely rocking, showing more control than Copley could ever possess. The head was slick, pre-cum dripping against his entrance until he was wet enough that he wondered if Niki could slide right inside.

"Oh, God." Copley shifted, freeing his left hand from where it had become partially pinned beneath him. His left hand was almost useless, except for tugging his jeans up or doing the occasional button. His letters were beyond recognition if he ever tried to use it for writing.

He fumbled on his shaft, gripping too softly then too hard, consciously trying to go slower and utterly failing. Hissing, he tried to find a rhythm, only to stutter to a stop as his biceps began to ache from the strange angle.

"Try again. You are doing so good for me." Niki kissed the back of his neck, the touch sweet and soft.

The praise was enough to pull Copley out of his self-made hole of doubt. He touched his thumb to the head again, trying to swirl it over the pre-cum, only to slip off the edge and hit the rim of his foreskin. He groaned as the fumbling touch sent a new sensation through him. It was like puberty all over again.

Maxim was still sleeping, the furrow on his forehead creasing as he mumbled something. Copley's cock thrummed harder as he found a new rhythm, unable to tear his gaze away from the beautiful sight before him. His rhythm built, his orgasm rushing ahead even faster than the last one.

"Stop."

Copley clawed the bed in agony as he dragged his hand away, cursing as his cock flexed and slapped his belly. He humped the air, searching for anything as his orgasm drained away for the second time. Niki only shushed him, praising him as he hooked a hand between Copley's thighs and pulled his leg back so it rested on Niki's hip.

The pose left him even more exposed, Niki's cock sliding up the seam of his cheeks with Copley's package and hole on full display. Cool air touched the heated flesh of his entrance and he hissed, trying to squeeze his legs together. Niki's thighs held him open, unyielding and layered with muscle.

"Play with your balls this time. You can use your right hand and slick it up, so it feels better. There's lube right there."

Copley snapped his gaze to the lube bottle that definitely hadn't been there the night before. He would have noticed it and cursed it for rubbing his punishment in his face.

Maxim shifted on the bed, drawing Copley's gaze as he froze, his breath stuttering to a halt. Maxim blinked once, rubbing his eyes before blearily gazing at the sight before him. He let out a sigh before he rolled off the bed, coming within a few centimeters of Copley's package as he passed by them and headed for the bathroom.

"Why did you stop?" asked Niki, petting Copley's ribcage before reaching for his nipple and giving it a gentle tweak.

Oh God. Oh God. He trembled, glaring at the lube bottle that was a similar brand to the one he had at home. Was it mocking him? He wasn't even sure if he *should* continue. They had to be crossing a line.

Fuck it. Niki had given him an order and he was going to follow it, even if it humiliated him.

Reaching for the lube, Copley slathered his right hand as he caught the sound of the toilet flushing from beyond the bedroom. His head swam, his vision going momentarily bright as he brought his hand to his sac, smoothing the lube over his sensitive flesh.

It *did* feel good…way better than it should have for just touching his balls. It amped even higher as Maxim appeared in the doorway, scrubbing a hand through his short hair as he lay back down in his bed.

For a moment, Copley wondered if Maxim would roll away and bury his head beneath his pillow to block out their noises, but he resumed the exact same position as before, his bright gaze locked on Copley.

He has the same green fleck in his eyes. With Maxim's mouth closed, and some of his tattoos hidden beneath his pajamas, he could have been Niki. Only Niki was behind him, his naked skin a blazing heat in the cool room. They stuck together, Niki's breath steaming over his neck with every puff.

Copley was on the edge again in a matter of seconds, and he whimpered as Niki stopped him, touching his elbow when Copley couldn't pull himself away.

"Please." His cock throbbed, his balls aching as if they'd accidentally been kicked. At the rate they were going, they were bound to explode from the sheer backlog. "Please let me come."

Maxim shook his head, a smirk on his lips at the same time Niki rumbled out a *no*. It was mind-boggling, and Copley hovered on the edge for far too long before his orgasm retreated to the safe zone again.

"Now I've seen how you treat your cock and balls, but there's one more place that you have to fuck," said Niki, squeezing Copley's hip. "That tight hole of yours is feeling so left out. Slick your hand up again and show me how you fuck yourself open."

"Fuck, please." Copley trembled, clutching Niki's arm that was across his chest as he stared at the tent in Maxim's pajamas. There was no way it could be real. There was no way that anything was real. He had to still be dreaming, his thoughts like the most depraved nightmare of his life.

"Fuck your little hole, and I'll ask my brother to push the beds together some time," said Niki, his voice a growl. "One day, I want you between us when you come."

The lube bottle nearly slipped out of Copley's hand when he squeezed it too hard, squirting a huge dollop on the bed in his haste. There was no teasing when he arched and reached for his hole from behind, accidentally brushing against Niki's cock. It certainly felt like it matched the picture before him.

Copley lined up two fingers, smearing the barest hint of slickness over his entrance. He'd taken more faster, and there was no way he was taking his time. He had to come in the next thirty seconds or he might combust.

Niki stopped him, tightening his arm across his chest until he could scarcely breathe.

"Where did you learn to treat yourself like that, baby? Take it slow. Give us what we want and make yourself feel good. Don't rush." Niki released him, dragging a hand over Copley's belly.

How can I not rush? His need to come overpowered almost everything at that moment. The only thing that stopped him was the urge to please his Dom. He *wanted* Niki to be proud of him and praise him. He wanted to hear the 'good boy' on his lips again.

Touching one finger to his rim, he lifted his leg so he was splayed wider, giving them the view that they wanted. He'd never been so exposed, with his skin flushed with humiliation and need. He couldn't think of a single thing he would change.

"Fuck, that's good." He hissed as he eased one finger inside, going slow as the strange feeling of fullness washed over him. It had been longer than he cared to admit since he'd fingered himself, and the sensations were almost strange. He could take a bit of pain and didn't mind being split open without much prep, but he'd forgotten how good it was to take it slow and enjoy.

"Can I?" He pushed one finger all the way to its base, closing his eyes at the heat of his own silken walls. It was impossible for him to touch his prostate at that angle, but he still tried, twisting his wrist as he reached for it. "I can't reach. Let me put two inside, please."

Niki chuckled, kissing Copley's shoulder. "Not yet. You have to show me that you deserve it before I give you more."

Copley wiggled his hips, Niki's cock brushing his perineum and slipping in the trail of lube. No matter how he moved, the angle was all wrong, his prostate far out of reach. He needed more, and he needed it *now*.

Rolling onto his back, he pulled one knee to his chest, looping his arm behind it to hold on tight. He reached past his cock, slipping back inside with a single finger. Turning his head into Niki, he ducked beneath his chin as his skin burned. He felt like nothing more than a wanton slut, vying for the attention of two dangerous men. But fuck, it felt good.

"Is your subbie acting shy?" asked Maxim, his cocky voice rolling over Copley and making his breath catch. "You should have seen how he reacted when I told him I would have fucked him in front of the whole crowd at the club."

Niki chuckled, the rumbling of his chest vibrating against Copley's lips where they had somehow found themselves against his flesh. His cock throbbed as he strained, his prostate still out of reach, no matter how hard he tried. How long did he have to torture himself until Niki let him come?

He didn't want to tell Maxim that it wasn't even so much shyness as his reaction to his own humiliation. *I mean, who gets hard from being humiliated?*

But I can't take it. Rolling away, he crawled to the bottom of the bed, putting his head at the edge so his ass was on clear display for both of them. Still on his knees, he spread his legs and folded himself in half, reaching for himself in a way he only ever did when he was alone.

His cock went rigid as he peeked over his shoulders one at a time, seeing both twins locked on his ass as if it were a beacon. Niki had shuffled up against the headboard, leaning with such nonchalance that it calmed him. Maxim was the opposite, the hunger in his gaze like a dangerous spark as he leered.

There! Finally. He gasped, prodding his prostate as he finally reached it, and tapping the swollen gland until his cock wept. His breaths came faster as his sac tensed, his hole clamping around him as he edged closer. He'd never come from his ass alone, but with how frazzled he was, it was becoming a real possibility.

"Such a nice hole, isn't it?" asked Niki, looking to Maxim, who nodded. Copley shuddered, biting his lip as he prodded himself deeper. "You can put another finger in, boy, but you aren't allowed to come. Tell me if you're close. I can help you if you can't stop yourself."

"Oh, God." Copley slid a second finger inside, the stretch nothing compared to the pure pleasure that was starting to radiate through his whole body. It was unlike anything he'd ever felt. "I'm close. Fuck, I'm coming."

Niki was there in an instant, clamping over the base of Copley's cock in a way that stalled his orgasm in its tracks. He writhed, pushing against Niki's hold as his skin throbbed, too tight for his body.

"Thank you, Copley. You are such a good boy for telling me you were close. You listened so well." He stroked Copley slowly from base to tip, his hold so tight that there was no way that Copley would be able to come. "Put in three fingers now, baby. I won't let you come." He moved his hand back to the base, his fingers like the world's biggest cock ring.

If two fingers had been torture, three were punishable by law. Copley groaned, humping against the hand that gave him no relief as he spread his fingers wide, opening himself up for what he hoped would come. Niki's naked cock was in reach, but Copley kept his free hand to himself, yearning to do well enough to gain permission.

"I can't anymore," said Copley, going still as he choked, the pleasure too much for him to stand. His eyes were wet, but it was like nothing he'd felt before.

"I know, baby. Take your fingers out now. I'm going to put my big cock in bare and fuck you until you black out. If you need me to stop, just say your safeword or tap my thigh twice."

Copley went lax, whimpering in disappointment as Niki moved behind him. It wasn't that he didn't want to get fucked into oblivion, but...

"What's wrong, baby?" asked Niki, stroking down his sweaty back before combing through his short hair. His hair felt like it was standing on end, and he was practically soaked from being edged so many times.

"I tried to be good. Was I good? Do I deserve to touch you now?" For some reason his cheeks were wet. He shoved his face against the blankets to try to hide his tears. *Why am I crying?* It didn't make any sense.

"Oh, baby. Turn around."

Copley blinked before he sluggishly went to his hands and knees, turning to Niki, even though he was terrified of what he was going to see. He struggled not to bury himself in Niki's chest again as his gaze was drawn to Maxim and the concerned furrow on his forehead.

"You can touch me, baby, but don't make me come. That's my only limit." Niki smiled, a look that was so much softer than his brother's, but no less sexy. Copley couldn't think of anything in the world that he would rather do than please the man before him. *Or men.*

He took a moment to simply look, tracing the lines of intricate tattoos with his gaze and the dark hair on Niki's chest. His pecs looked firm, and his abs were covered by enough flesh that they were nearly hidden. The strength in his body was more than any man Copley had ever been with, but it was nothing to who his Dom actually was.

Instead of reaching for Niki's nipples or cock, which were the first places his cock was trying to pull him, he laid his head against Niki's sternum. Spreading his hands over the plane of Niki's chest, he closed his eyes, listening to the deep thud of his heart.

He had fallen asleep to the noise the night before, and it had followed him in his dreams. But now it was fast, giving away the emotions that Niki was so obviously desperate to lock away.

"Fuck, baby." Niki pulled him closer, wrapping his arms around him and hugging him tight. "Maxim, get over here." Niki released him, but only long enough to cup Copley's chin and bring him up for a kiss.

It was everything that Copley had imagined, but so much more. Where Niki was always soft-spoken, his kiss was demanding and possessive, stripping Copley of the last bits of himself as Niki slipped his tongue into his mouth. He groaned, sucking Niki even deeper as Maxim pressed against his back, the heat of both of them overwhelming.

"I can't wait any longer, baby," said Niki, his voice straining with need for the first time. "If you touch me now, I'll come."

Copley blinked, smiling as he looked into his Dom's eyes. Usually he avoided making eye contact, but he couldn't help himself now with his gut humming with euphoria. He eyed the green fleck that practically glowed against the rest of his light brown iris. "I can wait, as long as I get to touch you later." He paused, stroking Niki's cheek. "You're beautiful. You both are."

Niki cracked a smile as Maxim chuckled. "And you're in subspace, baby. You like it?"

Copley nodded, giggling as Maxim pressed a kiss along his spine. It tickled, Maxim's hands a touch colder on his skin. "Can I touch Maxim, too? I want to suck his cock."

Oh my God! Where is this coming from? It was as if every filter he'd ever possessed had evaporated.

"Fuck yeah." Maxim breathed out, biting into Copley's shoulder until he hissed. Maxim was so much rougher. His hands were callused where Niki's were softer, stopping before he would ever cause Copley pain. But he liked the pain, too. He liked the way it pushed him beyond even what Niki made him feel.

"Maxim was tested three weeks ago, so you can suck him bare, baby." Niki moved him until Copley was face to cock with Maxim's prize.

"How the fuck do you know I was tested three weeks ago?" asked Maxim, even as he threaded his fingers into Copley's hair and tugged him to his cock.

Niki's answer drifted over him, inconsequential to the prize before him. It looked bigger up close and heavily veined, the head nearly purple and gleaming with pre-cum. The foreskin had slid back, revealing all but the ridge of the glans.

One day, he was going to sit the twins side by side to see if every part of them was truly identical.

Niki prodded at his ass, his fingers slick and cool as he smeared fresh lube over his hole. He slipped his fingers inside one by one, until he was three-wide and scissoring them apart.

"He tight?" asked Maxim, hissing as Copley leaned in to lick the pre-cum from his cock. It was salty and bitter, but lighter than Copley had expected. He smeared it over his lips before sucking Maxim's cockhead into his mouth, keeping his lips pressed in a tight ring.

"So fucking tight, baby. You're unreal." Niki retreated and the sound of the lube cap came a moment before his cock pressed against Copley's entrance.

Copley hummed, flinching as Niki nudged ahead and started to breach his tight ring. It was a close fit, stretching him as if he hadn't prepped himself at all.

Is it even going to work? He whimpered as Niki's cock started to sink inside, pulling away before it could split him apart. His rim ached, even as he longed to be filled again.

"It's too big," said Copley as he popped off Maxim's cock, licking his lips to clean the drool that had gathered there. Maxim chuckled, easing him back onto his cock as if he hadn't said a thing.

"Did you want me to finger you instead? I don't need to be inside you to blow your mind, baby," said Niki, rubbing Copley's lower back. The touch worked wonders, easing the strain from his back and pushing him into subspace again.

It wasn't like he hadn't taken a cock before, but Niki was fucking huge, and he was a bit out of practice. He hadn't touched himself except for brief moments in the shower, too afraid that someone would catch him on the couch or Sauble would walk in.

Or maybe it was that his time with Niki had been all pleasure, the pain so unexpected that it shocked him to his core.

"I-I want you," said Copley, tugging free of Maxim's grip before turning his head to place a kiss in the center of his palm. "Just go slow."

"How about you let me take care of you instead," said Niki. "I'll decide what you need, and if I think you need my cock, then I'll give it to you."

That sounded so much better. The tension drained from Copley's body in an instant, and he fell back onto Maxim's cock, lowering his mouth down the shaft until the head hit the back of his throat. He choked, dragging back as his jaw started to ache.

"You're a good cocksucker," said Maxim, shooting Copley a grin as he looked up. Maxim turned his gaze on Niki. "Do you think he could take it if I fucked his mouth?"

Copley giggled, weaving a bit as he tried to find his balance. The idea sounded hilarious. If Niki didn't fit in his ass, how was Maxim going to even attempt fucking his mouth? He had a good head game, but his gag reflex was alive and well.

Niki moved behind him, three fingers back as if they had never left. Copley gasped as his prostate was hit dead-on, his cock surging and leaking onto the bed. He was close again, his orgasm already starting to simmer. A fourth finger toyed with his hole, and he pushed against it, welcoming it inside.

It was...*wow*. His cock throbbed, seconds from spilling as he tensed. He could feel it building at the base of his cock and in his balls, ready to smash into him and take his breath away.

"Niki!" Copley called out the warning, knowing he'd never be able to stop his orgasm in time. It was too far along, and he had no way of pulling back.

"I know." Niki's prodding sped up, the tension at the base of Copley's spine starting to unwind.

But Copley couldn't do it. He couldn't have his pleasure without giving anything to Niki in return. Maxim was right. He hadn't even made his Dom come.

Pushing Maxim's cock away, he grabbed Niki's wrist, holding him still with every ounce of control he possessed. It wasn't much, and he couldn't stop his hips from jerking as he sought out more pressure, but it was the best he could do. He pulled Niki's hand from him, spinning around and straddling Niki's lap as soon as he was free.

The position felt strange, almost dominant, until Niki brought their lips together and took his will and his passion, all in one kiss. It wasn't hard to find Niki's cock below him. He reached for it, guiding the slick head to his hole.

"I can't come without you inside me. Please don't make me," said Copley as he leaned back, lowering himself down. Niki grabbed his ass, taking some of his weight as the head popped through his tight ring. The pain was over in a fleeting second, but his strength drained as pleasure overwhelmed him. If Niki hadn't held him up, he would have impaled himself to the base.

"Maxim." Copley reached behind him, finding Maxim's hand and tugging him close until his chest was against Copley's back. Maxim was rugged and even more rigid than his brother, his breathing fast as he pressed a kiss to Copley's neck.

Copley let out a breath, sinking all the way down until his ass settled against Niki's groin. He *had* split apart, his ass throbbing and his rim stretched farther than it had ever been. He could feel Niki all the way in his stomach, a steel rod piercing straight through his gut.

Niki flexed his hand on Copley's hips, grinding as Copley tried to adjust. Maxim breathed against him, cursing before he bit down into Copley's shoulder. It stung, but not as badly as the ache in his ass.

"Stretched so fucking wide."

Maxim's voice sent a shiver down Copley's body, and he clenched automatically, a fresh ache zinging through him. Those words were something that should never be uttered outside the deepest darkest bedrooms on the wrong side of town. They made him dizzy and drunk, pushing him so high that he wasn't sure if he was even upright anymore.

Niki's hands grounded him and the gentle touch of his lips against his neck. Copley's cock was so hard that it was painful, the head purple and weeping where it was squashed against Niki's belly. His peak was right there, one nudge the only thing between him and oblivion.

Niki lifted him and Copley turned his head away, seeking Maxim's lips as Niki's gentle thrust grazed over his prostate. The touch ached and he flinched, whimpering as Maxim drank him in. He could scarcely breathe as Niki continued to move, stripping him of the last sane thoughts as his vision started to darken around the edges.

"Breathe, baby."

He sucked in a breath before Maxim took his mouth again, brutalizing him with tongue and teeth as Niki peeled his soul back layer by gentle layer. It was too much, his entire life pinpointing into that single moment.

"I can't," he gasped between kisses as Maxim thrust against his back, spurting with a grunt and a drawn-out moan. "I can't."

"Yes, you can," said Niki, sucking the base of Copley's neck as he changed his angle, his strokes becoming unbearable. "Just be good and let go for me. I've got you."

Something snapped inside him, his orgasm building throughout his entire being until he shook with the force of it. His vision went dark as he clutched Niki's neck, his cock releasing every pent-up drop between their bellies.

"*Niki.*"

Niki never paused, ramming his cock deep until Copley's consciousness blinked out of existence.

Chapter Thirteen

Maxim

His fingers were covered in cum from when he'd snuck his hand around Copley's belly as he'd started to shoot, the stickiness begging him to wipe it away. But he couldn't. He stared at it with his mouth dry and his cock still stiff after his own epic orgasm, wondering what it tasted like and how it would feel if he used it to lube his cock and push himself in Copley's hole next.

He was almost certain he wouldn't fit at the moment. Copley's rim was red and stretched so wide that he looked close to breaking. The echo of his own cock was before him, taking everything that he longed for.

Whatever that had been — sex wasn't the right name for it. He'd never tortured someone at the edge until they cried. He'd never been able to hold himself back like Niki had. And his brother made it look so fucking easy, even if Maxim could see the cracks at the edges in the way he tensed his jaw with every thrust, and the wrinkle around his eyes that was more pronounced than usual.

But it wasn't his brother he was looking at—far from it. It was Copley—the most beautiful man he'd ever met, who responded like a dream wrapped in a secret wish. Maxim wanted to grab him and carry him back to his bed, wrapping him up in the covers before he explained to them both that he was never letting go.

It was fucking terrifying.

Anything more than a one-night stand wasn't worth the effort, and the power exchange he'd just witnessed couldn't have been real. There was nothing—no one—he wanted to do that with, except maybe the man who was passed out against his brother's chest, still impaled deep as cum started to drip from his filled ass.

Maxim pulled away, rubbing his forehead as he stumbled from the bed. He didn't have a huge problem with his brother's nudity because he had been seeing it since he was born. He'd seen his brother fuck before, too, and vice versa, but it had never been anything more than a way to pass the time.

He'd kept his hands to himself like a gentleman and hadn't even compared their dick sizes. Watching them together had been like watching a porno that starred himself.

"You okay?" asked Niki, his voice much too calm for the situation. Cradling Copley against him, he laid back against the pillows, making no move to pull out.

"That was fucking intense." Maxim flopped against the bed. "Sorry if I accidentally touched your dick or something. I'm just not into you like that." He closed his eyes, grabbing his pillow as Niki chuckled.

"Feeling's mutual, Max, but I don't mind sharing. You're the only person I'd trust to share someone like Copley with."

Maxim swallowed. He'd known that, but it still made his chest go tight every time he thought about what his brother had given up for him. *Six years.* Niki had trusted him then, but Maxim had still managed to fuck it up.

"I didn't know it could be like that," said Maxim, turning to look at Copley's face. His eyes were half-open, but his gaze was lost, like a hooker who had indulged on her pimp's hidden stash. "Is he going to be okay?"

"Yeah." Niki placed a kiss on Copley's head, lingering in his hair for a moment before he let out a sigh. "Sex didn't really do it for me either until I became a Dom. Now it's the opposite. I can dominate someone and be more satisfied from that than six hook-ups. I don't even *need* to come. It's different...better."

Maxim nodded, finally understanding what his brother had been talking about for years. "All this time I just thought you were just whacking someone with a belt for kicks. But maybe you do that, too?" His mouth went dry as he thought about slapping a belt — or even better — his hand, across Copley's ass. His pale skin was longing for a bit of red on it.

"Not my style, but neither are home visits," said Niki, furrowing his forehead. "I like to praise my subs and encourage them to do well with rewards, if I can. I only punish them if they cross a line that threatens our dynamic, and even then, I never hurt them. I can't hurt them. It's...not like that for me."

A frown tugged at his lips and Maxim's confusion deepened. "But what if I wanted to spank him? Would

I just...?" He slapped the bed in demonstration, the hollow springs humming from the strike.

"He shouldn't even be *here* to begin with, but we'd have to discuss Copley's limits before you set up a time at the club. If he sets a limit for no impact, then you would have to respect that." Niki scratched down Copley's back before letting out a sigh.

Maxim snorted, rolling his eyes. He didn't respect a single thing or person in his life except for his brother. He didn't even respect Nestor, who could be a manipulative little bastard when he wanted to be and who had convinced Niki to keep his homosexuality quiet in the first place.

"I'm serious." Niki's gaze was steady, and Maxim's smile fell away. "If you didn't respect his limit or he safeworded and you didn't listen? We'd have some big fucking problems, Max."

"You can't be serious." Maxim leaned over the bed, clenching his fist to try to keep his anger in check. "You'd pick him over me? That little snack? You went to jail for me, Nikita, for six fucking years. Don't kid yourself."

Niki let out a long sigh before resting his cheek on the top of Copley's head. Copley roused a bit, mumbling under his breath.

"I love you, Max, and you're my brother, but having a sub is a special relationship that simply can't be replaced. I would protect Copley, for him and for me, and I wouldn't let you hurt him. If you want to force someone, you can do it on your own, and you can enjoy your time in prison after I beat you bloody."

What the fuck am I supposed to say to that? Moments ago, he'd been floating on a high that had felt like it was never going to end, but now he was pretty sure that an alley cat was worth more than him. His brother was everything he had, and without him…

"But I know you're just talking shit," said Niki. "You don't know much about dominance and submission, but you know right and wrong, even if you like to ignore it from time to time. You're freaking out, aren't you? And you're deflecting because nothing makes sense right now."

Maxim threw his arm over his head, blocking out the light from the window. It had to have been past ten in the morning, but neither of them were making any move to get up and make breakfast. "I'm not going to force someone, Nik, but I have no clue what just fucking happened. I mean, I've never even really *liked* sex before, and that was just *wow*. But where do I go from here? I'm a thirty-five-year-old murderer who works as an enforcer for Nestor. I *can't* be unsure. I have to have everything figured out, and the only thing I know for sure is that he's yours."

Niki was silent for a long time, the thermostat clicking as the temperature fell in the room and the baseboard buzzed to life. The smell of burning hair puffed into the room as it heated, one of the side-effects of it being on Maxim's side of the room where things only got dusted on rainy Tuesdays in January.

"I'm scared, too," said Niki softly. "I'm scared that I went too far and that he'll wake up and say he's going to find someone else. I'm scared that he'll figure out that being with me isn't safe, and he'll just go. I'm worried I made a mistake bringing him here, and now we've crossed a line and there's no going back. It makes my chest hurt when I think about it, but I can't stop. I'm not a good person, but I think I could be for him."

"Wow." Maxim took a long look at his brother, surprised he hadn't realized it before. "I know he's something special, but I didn't think I'd be hearing wedding bells already. Can I bring Nestor as my plus one?"

Niki shot him a light glare that pushed a surge of relief through Maxim's body. They'd been through the ringer in the last few days, but they were still brothers and best friends.

Copley blinked awake, a cute groan pushing through his lips as he looked around the room, then down to his ass where he was still leaking. For whatever reason, his confusion calmed what anger was left, soothing Maxim's soul until he felt almost normal—which was weird, for *him.*

"Yep, you got fucked good, boy," said Maxim, moving to sit on the edge of his brother's bed. It dipped under his weight, the frame groaning from the strain. He was honestly surprised that it hadn't collapsed with the three of them on it. They weren't exactly small men, except for Copley, who was a bit more package-sized.

Copley's cheeks tinted pink, but instead of tucking into Niki like he had before, he let out a laugh, scooting away just a tad. "It sounds different when you say it." He smiled, his eyes lighting up until they almost glowed. "When Niki calls me 'boy', it's like he's talking to a kitten, but when you say it, it's like a southern rancher yelling at someone who just lost three cows."

Niki chuckled and Maxim shook his head, failing to hold back his own snicker. "I was going for the grown man with my brother's cock up his ass kind of *boy*, but that will do."

Copley laughed, throwing his head back as his chest shook from the sound. It trailed off into a small *aww* as Niki finally slipped out.

"Did you have fun, baby?" asked Niki, his uncertainty nearly heartbreaking.

The thing that most people didn't know about his brother was that Nikita was, and always would be, a softie. As a kid, he'd cried when he'd found an ant that had been missing a leg, and he'd lovingly stitched a teddy bear back together when it had ripped. He didn't even scold Maxim when he found out that Maxim had been the one to pluck the ant's leg off, and that he had torn the teddy a new armhole because he'd thought that three arms were cooler than two.

It was one of the reasons that Maxim had always worn his heart on his sleeve. He didn't want to hide anything from anybody, especially not his brother. And if no one accepted him exactly the way he was without exceptions, he knew that Niki would always take him back. It was the only certain thing in an uncertain world.

"I loved it," said Copley, leaning in for a quick kiss. "To be honest, my prostate actually hurts a little bit now, so if we could hold off for a bit, that would be great." He winced as he shifted his hips from side to side before reaching between his legs with a furrow on his forehead.

"There's a lot—like a lot a lot." He dug a finger into his hole before bringing it around to stare at it. He gave them both a quick little look before he darted his tongue out and licked the thick cum he'd gathered.

Maxim grabbed at his spent cock, which was showing signs of life, glancing at Niki, who practically glowed. "Keep doing that and you won't be able to walk."

Copley held out his finger toward Maxim, a bit of white still clinging to him. Maxim screwed up his face, not fighting the gag. There was a reason he didn't go down on anyone, but he could eat someone out in a heartbeat. "No thank you. That's fucking gross."

Copley giggled, sucking his finger into his mouth. "I kind of like it. I mean, not because it's cum — let's be honest, that's no milkshake — but because it's Niki's. He left it there to claim me, so it's only polite if I have a taste."

"Reason number two that it's gross," said Maxim, reaching for his boxers and pulling them on. His stomach grumbled, giving him his cue to get his ass out of bed and get moving. "Pancakes okay?"

Copley beamed and nodded while Niki gave him a much more refined nod. "I'll pull out the apple butter, too," said Maxim, reaching for the door frame.

"Max, wait," Niki called from the bed. Reaching for his own boxers, he started to pull them on. "We good?"

Maxim gripped the frame, searching out the sharp edge with his fingernails. *Good* didn't exactly fit. He had feelings for his brother's...submissive, and he had never been able to share anything in his life. He just wasn't sure if he was turning over a new leaf or if things were just getting primed and ready to explode.

"We're good, yeah. Get cleaned up, you two. You're both a fucking mess."

Chapter Fourteen

Nikita

Can we talk?

He stared at the message on his phone that he had missed three hours prior. The three little words terrified him, even if he didn't show a single sign. Copley had sent them, and that alone didn't bode well.

Since their night together, things had *changed*. Copley had come out of his shell, his fear long gone as he spent every opportunity trying to please Niki. His sub was as affectionate as he was beautiful, and every day his heart swelled with love as he fell deeper. He'd never had a sub submit to him so prettily, then look at him like he was the best thing in the world. He almost didn't regret removing some of the boundaries between them, although he'd made it clear that Copley's stay in their home had been a one-time thing.

It had been stiffer with Maxim. Maxim hadn't kissed Copley since they'd sat together on the couch while

Niki had been doing up the breakfast dishes. When Niki had dried his hands, Max had pulled away, disappearing until long after Copley had left.

They hadn't said much since, tiptoeing around it like cowards. It grated on Niki's nerves, even as his sub blew his mind. But he couldn't help but wonder if he was asking too much of Copley to be *their* sub. He'd dropped a few little hints, and Copley had seemed on board, but they had yet to have a real discussion.

Niki wasn't sure how to start. He'd always coveted his subs, holding tight until it was time for them to move on—or until he dismissed them. He'd never considered sharing one, especially not with his brother. It would be two separate relationships, where Copley would coexist with men who were polar opposites. He wasn't sure if Copley would be able to handle something like that.

But maybe Copley already knew his intentions, and he was ready to back out. There were other Doms who would be more than happy to have a versatile sub like Copley, who seemed up for almost anything except for some truly painful adventures.

Taking a deep breath, he mustered up the courage to type a reply.

Yeah.

He glanced around the house, toeing Maxim's shoes into their proper place on the mat before he moved deeper, seeking out his twin like he did every day after work. He had always been afraid that one day he would come home and his twin would have fallen at Nestor's orders.

"Hey," he said, and he spotted Maxim on the couch, seemingly engrossed in the television. Max blinked, sending him a panicked look before he grabbed for the remote. It slipped through his fingers, thudding to the floor as Niki circled around the back of the couch.

"Oh." He blinked at the screen, his mouth watering instantly at the erotic display of a hardcore BDSM scene. The volume was down so low that he could only catch the little yelps as the Dom brought his hand down on one of his sub's asses. "This is a good one."

Maxim spluttered, diving for the remote before shutting the television off. The player was still going, the timer counting as the scene continued, unwatched. "I thought that wasn't your thing," Max whispered, his face a touch pale.

Niki frowned, pulling his jacket from his shoulders as he moved around the couch. "Why does that matter? What does anything *I* like have to do with your preferences? If you want to watch someone get spanked until their ass is red, then by all means. The sub comes from it at the end, if you wanted to know."

"I know." Maxim scowled, reaching for the remote again and attempting to turn the player off. "It doesn't matter." He gave Niki another look. "Really it doesn't. I've never been ashamed of anything in my life, Nik, but I'm just trying to figure this shit out."

Nodding slowly, Niki reached for his phone as it started to ring. It took him a moment to recognize the number when it appeared, and he let out a breath. It wasn't Copley.

"Hello?" He turned away, heading for the back as he answered the call. Sliding the glass door open, he slipped outside, instantly wishing that he hadn't taken his jacket off. The wind had picked up and the temperature was dropping closer to freezing every day. Only a few leaves still clung to the trees, their burnished skin crumpled and mottled.

"Hey, it's Clint. Did you have a minute to talk, Nikita?"

Niki frowned at the tone, his stomach instantly clenching. He had only heard Clint sound so forlorn a few times, and it had never boded well for the person on the other end.

"Yeah sure, whatever you need." He swallowed before sagging onto the metal chair on the back porch. He'd already taken the cushions in for the season and the seat was frigid through his jeans.

"I wanted to do this in person," said Clint before letting out a sigh, "but I know I wouldn't go through with it. I've known you for a long time, Nikita, even before you were on the scene, and before you went to prison."

"Old times, right?" He tried to smile, but he knew it was a pathetic farce, his cheeks strained for nobody to see. He'd known Clint because he'd gotten banged up a few times and Clint had patched him up at the hospital. They'd made fast friends, even if they only saw each other every couple of months.

But as things in his life had turned to chaos, he'd pulled away, only finding Clint again after he'd gotten out of prison, and he'd finally realized what he needed with his life in order to be complete.

"I know I never asked what you went to prison for, and I don't exactly watch the news, so this is my fault too," said Clint, each word another nail in his coffin. "But we are running the background checks. We have to in order to keep everybody safe. I thought maybe robbery or assault, but I didn't expect to find… murder."

Niki let his head fall into his hand. It was all coming apart. He'd known that his past would haunt him for the rest of his life. Even if he someday managed to leave Nestor behind, he would pay for his service forever.

"I should have told you," said Niki, gripping his hair and holding it tight to keep his emotions in check. "I shouldn't have put you in a position like that in the first place, but I was desperate, Clint."

"I know. I know, but that just makes this so much harder."

There was a pause and Niki wondered if the line had gone dead, but the call's timer was still counting.

"You can't come back, Nikita. You may be rehabilitated or a changed man, but I can't have a convicted murderer in my club. I'm sorry."

"Don't be," Niki mumbled, not sure what he was even saying. "I understand. It's probably for the best." *No it isn't. I need the club. I can't just live and not go there anymore.* It was his life, as much as Nestor owned him, but Unkinked was more his life than anything else. No other club or munch was anything like it.

No club meant no kink and no sub to call his own. Bringing Copley home with him had been a mistake because it had almost cost him his brother. Maybe it already had.

Which meant he had nothing left. He didn't even have a cat that would make him feel any better, because he was too afraid that he would get shot and Maxim would forget to feed it.

"I gotta go," he mumbled into the phone, the speaker almost touching his lips.

"I know, but I want you to know something, Nikita. This doesn't mean that you can't call me if you need something. You're still my friend, and I've got your back. As far as I'm concerned, you are one of the best men I know."

"Bye, Clint." He ended the call, blinking back any tears that tried to escape. Selecting Clint's contact info, he deleted the number.

A leaf skittered across the porch, catching the edge of his socked foot. It clung to him, the sharp fibers of its edge barely hanging on until the wind dragged it away, tossing it out onto the lawn.

Goosebumps prickled over his skin, but he could barely feel them. He stared at his arms, dragging his fingertip over the bumps that had risen in the tattoos on his wrists.

When he'd walked into the tattoo shop, determined to get the dark manacles that encircled his wrists, there had been nothing in the world that could have stopped him. His skin had already been inked in so many ways that the new pair shouldn't have meant much more. He remembered the addictive hum of the needle as it had pierced his flesh too fast for him to see, dragging fire everywhere it had touched.

It was the first thing he had actually *felt* after he'd gotten out of prison. When he'd walked his short path to freedom after his greatly reduced sentence, thanks to a team of lawyers and good behavior, he'd met Maxim at the gate, hugging him close as soon as he was within reach.

Maxim had been a shadow of himself at that time, so riddled with guilt that he'd buried himself in rage and anger that still followed him to this day. Maybe he didn't understand that Nikita would do it again in a heartbeat, even if the sentence was life in prison. It wasn't a place that Maxim would survive—not that anyone would be able to catch him unawares because he was too good for that, but he was born to be free. A jail cell would squash his spirit.

The tattoos were a reminder of what was truly important in his life. He'd lost six years, but he'd saved something so much more valuable. People feared him, now more than they ever did, but he would take their disdain if it kept his brother safe.

He refused to regret his actions, even if it cost him what little was left of himself. He could let go of the little slice that Nestor hadn't broken and that prison had left intact. He could live without sex, and he would have to live without dominance, too. *If only I could figure out how.*

But fuck, he loved taking care of Copley, even holding him and whispering into his ear. He loved holding the door open for him and wanted to bring him flowers when they met at the club, just because he could. He wanted to be there and take the burdens off his sub's shoulders, but he also wanted to keep him as far away from Nestor and Dimitri as he could.

His phone chimed once as a text message came through. He knew in his gut who it was, but he couldn't bring himself to read it. Dialing Copley's number instead, he brought the phone to his ear. His knuckles brushed something wet on his face, but he shook it off.

"Hello."

The warmth of Copley's voice sank in deep, his chest aching as he longed to feel him closer. What he wouldn't give to have lived a different life, where he could give Copley what he deserved.

"You wanted to talk," said Niki, his voice low and gravelly. The cold seeped under his shirt, clutching him deep until he wasn't sure if he would ever feel anything again.

"Hey, Niki!" Copley chimed back, so fucking positive even though his life had devolved into a shitstorm too. "Thank you for calling, but I just sent a message that I thought maybe we could meet up? I'm not trying to push any limits this time or take you out for coffee or anything, but I just wanted to say something in person."

He *was* still pushing, and for once, Niki wasn't in the mood. "No. Say what you have to say." His voice was dull, even to his own ears.

"Oh, okay." Copley paused and Niki thought he may have heard a sniff. *Just another thing I've fucked up today.* "It's not about us, well, I guess it kind of is. It's about the money."

Niki blinked, taking a few minutes before he could comprehend what the hell Copley was talking about. Everything had just gotten so side railed since they'd met that he'd forgotten all about the hundred grand owed to Nestor. *Probably not the best thing to forget about.*

"You mean Sauble's debt," he said, biting his lip to keep back the growl. "You shouldn't be worrying about any of that shit, Copley. It has nothing to do with you." And taking worries off Copley's mind was *his* fucking job. *Is there anything else I can fuck up?*

He looked to the sky, a few raindrops falling and painting the porch with a speckle of gray. His laundry was still hanging in the backyard from the morning when he'd hung it out to dry. There was no way he was getting it in time. *Yep, I guess there is.*

"He's my brother. Of course I'm worried about it," said Copley quietly.

And wasn't that a punch to the gut. Niki reeled back in his chair, pulling the phone away from his ear before looking over his shoulder. His brother was standing against the glass door that was cracked a few inches, concern etched on his face.

"What about it?" Niki grumbled, wiping his cheeks until they were clean. There weren't a lot of things that upset Maxim, but he hadn't seen Niki lose it before. *Just be the rock that you're meant to be. Hold him steady.*

"I managed to save a bit. It's not everything, but I couldn't come up with that much in a month and the bank wouldn't give me a loan either, even though I lied about what it was for."

Fuck, could it get any worse? He looked away from Maxim before he lost it. Copley had been running around during their time together and he hadn't said a fucking thing. He'd let his sub be burdened like that and he hadn't even known.

But of course he didn't. The rules had been club only, right? So how the fuck was Copley ever supposed to be able to come to him in the first place?

Useless Dom. He didn't deserve them…not Copley's submission or Clint's proffered hand. He craved it, but he was too fucking weak.

"How much?" He wasn't even sure why he was asking. In a heartbeat he could have Nestor forgive the debt—or pay it off himself.

"Five thousand," said Copley, his voice strained. "I know it's not a lot, but it's all I have. I can give you five thousand a month until the debt's paid off, and you can even tack on interest. Just please don't hurt my brother."

His ears buzzed, his hands flushing hot then cold again as he started to tremble. "What do you mean, 'give me'? Why would you pay *me*?"

The money had nothing to do with him. Even though he was a sometimes enforcer, it was Nestor's fucking money. He didn't want a single bill to pass through his own hands.

"It's... I don't understand. Sauble owes you...or your boss. Whatever... It's the same thing. Will you take the money or not?"

He must have looked close to puking when Maxim stepped through the door, grabbing the phone from his hand and ending the call without a word. Niki fought to drag in each breath as his lungs protested and his head swam. A touch to his shoulder was like a red-hot poker.

Pulling away, he stumbled from the chair, reaching for the glass door and nearly falling through as his knees went weak. He forced a smile on his lips, even as his vision blurred, sending a smirk toward his brother. "You leaving too? I wondered when you would finally give in. I know you can't stand to look at me...your soft big brother who wouldn't hurt a fly but paints his skin like he's some kind of champion."

He choked as his throat went tight, slapping Maxim's hand away as he reached for him.

"What the fuck happened?" asked Maxim, looking to the phone in his hand like he didn't know what it was.

Maxim's panic was quickly setting in, his jaw going tight. Niki knew all the signs because he'd seen it before. Usually, it wasn't his fault though.

"I'll kill the fucker if he hurt you. It was Copley, wasn't it?" Maxim growled, squeezing the phone so tight that Niki worried the screen would crack. "I can do it, Niki. Say the word and I'll take care of it. I'll kill anyone who tries to hurt you."

The chuckle that came from Niki's throat was so thick that it hardly sounded real. That was what had landed them both in this mess, wasn't it? The Twin Tigers, whose reputation preceded them across the fucking country. "I know. I went to jail for it, remember?"

Maxim blanched, his jaw going tight. "That's low, Nikita. You know I didn't mean for that to happen. How many times can I apologize before you actually believe me? It was my fault that Nestor brought us into the fold, and it's my fault that I stabbed that asshole. I'm fucking sorry." His voice grew louder with each word until he was shouting in the back yard, his voice echoing off their neighbor's homes.

"I'm going to go," said Nikita quietly, moving inside and grabbing his coat off the couch where he'd tossed it. The porn was playing on the screen again, but it was bland and tasteless.

"No, we are in the middle of a discussion here. You can't run off to your kink club or your sub right now, asshole." Maxim slammed the glass door, stalking after him.

"The club kicked me out because I'm a murderer, and my sub thinks I'll kill his brother if he doesn't pay his debt. My brother hates me, too, because he thinks I'm a coward. Maybe he's right." Niki reached for the front door, turning the knob under his hand. "Just do me a favor and stay out of jail."

Chapter Fifteen

Copley

Copley stared at the phone in his hand, tears streaming down his face as he tried to figure out what had gone wrong. Was it something he'd said or done? It had taken him nearly a week to muster up the courage to talk to Niki about the debt. The end of the month loomed closer every day, and he'd finally snapped, unable to take it any longer.

Niki was like two beings that he couldn't quite piece together. On one side, he was gentle and generous, dominating him in the most loving way that Copley could imagine. On the other hand, he was a beautiful and mysterious demon who worked for the Bratva, his tattoos telling the story of his crimes.

Copley had looked them up after he'd spent the night with the twins. He knew what the manacles on Niki's wrists and the skull on Maxim's chest meant. But that hadn't stopped him from calling Niki nearly every day since. He'd even jerked off in the bathroom at work with his Dom's voice telling him exactly what to do over the phone. He still had the sore on his tongue where he'd bitten too deep trying to keep quiet as he'd come.

There had been mind games, too, like when he'd been left on the street, but Niki had never sounded so cold, and he'd never hung up on him. That hadn't been his Dom on the phone at all.

He looked up from his pathetic little bed on his brother's couch, which he had reluctantly crawled back to when Sweetie had told him to stay away from her place for his own safety — whatever the hell that meant. He'd tried calling up a few of his friends, but apparently Spencer had finally figured out that Copley wasn't coming back and had steamrolled them with stories of how Copley had seduced him.

That part didn't even hurt that bad, seeing as he *had* dropped to his knees first when they'd both had too much to drink. It didn't mean that he wanted his friends to know about it, though, and apparently hold it against him.

Sauble had made it abundantly clear that he was no longer welcome, either. The apartment had grown cold with only Copley there six days out of seven, Sauble's bed empty most mornings and nights. The fancy shakes in the fridge had expired, so Copley had dumped them, but he kept the rest of the fridge stocked.

It was almost like being a bachelor again, but sleeping on an old couch was starting to take its toll on his neck and back. The night in Niki's bed had been like a dream that had shattered into a nightmare within the last ten minutes.

Looking to his bag that still spent its nights and days on the table, he zipped it shut, tossing the strap over his shoulder as he stood. Buried beneath three layers of socks and tucked in a pouch, was five thousand dollars in cool bills.

He'd never carried that much cash in his life, and even now he felt like there was a target in the middle of his back. He wasn't sure if he was hiding it from the neighbors, his brother or any other random person who decided he looked like an easy meal. Even if they did manage to grab the bag, they probably wouldn't find the money in its hiding spot.

He glanced around, taking one last look at the apartment before he headed to the door. It had grown on him, even the numerous water spots on the ceiling that made spooky shadows during the night. He barely heard the steady music anymore, so accustomed had he become to the constant beat. He still wasn't sure if he would exactly miss it, though.

Grabbing for the doorknob, he stumbled back as it turned under his hand and the door swung wide, narrowly missing his nose. He let out a startled yelp as he tripped, landing on his ass as his bag rolled toward the couch.

"Shit, Copley, are you okay?" Sauble hurried forward after he slammed the door, offering Copley a hand and dragging him to his feet. "Why are you crying?" He looked to the bag that Copley had been holding. "Or are you headed out? You could have said goodbye, you know. I would like to know where my brother ends up so I can send him that Christmas card."

He threw his arm over Copley's shoulder, leading him back to the couch. His arm was heavy, especially under the thick layer of his winter coat. It must have started snowing because there were a few speckles of moisture clinging to the coat, looking much too big for raindrops.

"Did you take Mark up on his offer?" asked Sauble, grabbing the bag and setting it into Copley's lap.

Copley stared at it, touching the zipper that he had just pulled closed. Sauble seemed like his regular self, without any of the cold shoulder that he had been sending Copley's way. He must've been happy to see him go.

"There's five thousand dollars in this bag," said Copley as he stared at the zipper. Grabbing the end of the pull, he dragged it open, watching as the teeth separated and gaped wide.

Sauble sucked in a breath before he leaned away. "What are you doing with that kind of cash? You know how unsafe that is in a place like this? Besides me, any one of the people in this building would take it in a heartbeat."

"It's for you." Copley bit his lip, reaching inside. *What am I doing?* "I worked sixty hours a week this month, so I could make enough to bring this home. I only bought food, some clothes and one set of pajamas. Everything else is in there. Every dime."

Pulling the money free from its hidden compartment, he eased it out of the socks, placing it on the table before him. The brown bills were almost anticlimactic. All his hard work was laying before him, without a single hint of his blood, sweat or tears.

Sauble hissed, moving to the edge of the couch as if the money would bite him if he got any closer. His hand twitched before he closed it into a fist, resting it on his thigh. His face was tight as he stared at it, his tongue coming out to trace his lips.

Five thousand dollars and his brother's gaze was lost, everything else seemingly forgotten in the face of his addiction.

"I'm taking the money to Nikita and Maxim," said Copley, grabbing it and stuffing it back into the socks before hiding it in the compartment. The zipper closed so much easier than it had opened.

Sauble's eyes went wide. "The Twin Tigers? Are you fucking nuts? They'll chew you up and spit you out if you show up with anything less than a hundred grand."

"Funny." Copley shook his head, wiping his cheeks as his tears started to dry and itch. He was so sick of crying.

"This isn't the little league, and it sure as hell isn't funny. I can't believe that you're this naïve." Sauble threw up his hands, standing from the couch. His shoulders were tense, his temper apparently ready to roll.

"No. it's funny because the last time I went to their house, I showed up with nothing, and I still made love to them both." He dropped his head into his hands.

Maybe that was where he had gone wrong. He never should have brought the money up to Niki in the first place. He didn't want his Dom to feel like Copley was somehow involving him in something that wasn't his concern. Their relationship was club only, despite their night together and the calls afterward. Niki had made that very clear.

Maxim was a bit more of a mystery.

"You...y-you *what*?" Sauble went pale as his mouth dropped open. Copley had never seen him so shocked or afraid.

"I'm going to take care of it." Copley took one last look at the lumpy couch as he headed toward the door. "I'll see you for Christmas. Don't forget." He pushed into the hall, heading down it with his head low. The pack smacked against his hip with every step, five thousand dollars so heavy that his shoulder already ached.

It was funny how he had managed to live for a month with the contents of one duffle, when he'd had a walk-in closet with Spencer and still hadn't been able to find anything to wear. Sure, he'd gotten a few looks at work with his steady wardrobe of exactly five outfits that he'd grabbed from Spencer's apartment when he'd snuck there one last time. If he ever did go back for the rest, he doubted anything would be intact with Spencer's rampaging and his girlfriend moving in.

He wasn't sure if he even cared. He was ready to burn what had been left of his life and start fresh. And if that new part would get him a punishment, then he would submit to whatever Niki gave him. He wasn't afraid — even if he should have been.

It took him nearly two hours to get across town to where Niki and Maxim's house was. He'd stopped once when Sweetie had called out to him as he'd approached the bus, plowing on after he'd given her a sad smile and a wave. Hopefully he'd see her again sometime soon.

Dragging himself down the street to the row of identical townhouses, he stared at the arrangement of pumpkins that were looking a little closer to expiring. There was a clump of leaves that had made its way onto the porch and had started a wet pile in the corner that was bound to stain. He gritted his teeth as he stopped at the edge of the steps, staring down at the soggy mess.

The last time he had seen the front of the house, it had been as spotless as the inside, except for Maxim's side of the bedroom. The leaves were so out of place that they left a terrible taste in his mouth.

Tossing his bag on top of the decorative bale of straw, he grabbed the broom, sweeping the porch with even strokes until it was spotless. He looked down at the sidewalk that was spotted gray with melting snowflakes. A few of them lingered on the yellowed grass and on his jacket before they slowly melted. *How long until it stays?* Sweetie had been in her typical getup of a tube top and short skirt. He couldn't imagine being so cold all the time.

"You've been staring at the same thing for ten minutes. Are you coming in?"

Copley turned toward the voice, glancing to their wrists to confirm his suspicion. It was Maxim, sounding quieter than Copley had ever heard. They hadn't had time to speak much since their first meeting, but he hadn't forgotten his Dom's twin.

"I wasn't going to stay," said Copley, looking down at his feet when Maxim's gaze became too hard to hold. "I don't want to bother you, Maxim, but I don't know what's going on."

"That makes two of us." Maxim let out a sigh before reaching for him, taking Copley's hand in a grip so warm that it was nearly molten.

He shuddered from the touch, grasping his bag before letting himself be led inside. A few pieces of straw clung to it, dropping to the spotless floor inside the threshold. He shivered as Maxim closed the door, pinning him to the wall with one hand.

Copley let his eyes fall shut, breathing in deep. With his eyes closed, he could almost tell Maxim apart from

Niki more easily. Maxim had the edge of something wild, and he could almost taste it with him so close — that, and his frame was that much stronger than Niki's, his hand rougher as he touched Copley's neck. The calluses scratched against his skin, and he hummed under his breath.

"Niki left," said Maxim softly, "and I'm not sure if he's coming back."

Copley sucked in a breath, wrapping his arms around Maxim and tugging him close as his stomach sank. He was too damn short sometimes, and his head only came up to Maxim's collar. His skinny arms weren't great for comforting, but he did his best to offer his support when he was ready to break apart himself.

"I'm sorry," said Copley, closing his eyes and leaning into Maxim as he pulled him tighter. "I'm so sorry. It's all my fault. I never should have brought up the money. I just didn't want my brother to get hurt."

"This isn't your fault."

It was the thing he had been waiting to hear for hours as his heart had pounded. His guilt was cut like a marionette on strings, leaving him weak and senseless.

Copley whimpered as Maxim led him to the couch, taking the bag from his hands and tossing it to the floor. Maxim looked to him, hope in his eyes. "I have to admit that I don't know much about the dominance and submission thing, but I know we're both hurting and I'm just going to do what feels right. Will you submit to me, baby? I know I'm not my brother and I'll never be able to treat you the way he does, but I think we both need this right now."

Copley nodded, the ache in his chest easing for the first time in hours. For some reason he'd thought he'd been alone, but he was so wrong. He offered Maxim his hands, not knowing quite why.

Maxim took each one in turn, placing a kiss to the inside of his wrist. "Will you kneel for me?" He leaned back on the couch, spreading his legs to leave Copley room.

Everything was happening so quickly. One moment he was looking for Niki and losing him, and now...

Fuck. Will I? Blow jobs aside, he'd never knelt for someone in his life. If he had to choose one person, it would have been Niki. He barely knew Maxim, but he was right. They both needed this.

He dropped to the hardwood, wincing as his knees struck the surface that was firmer than he'd expected. Shifting closer, he moved between Maxim's spread knees, keeping his gaze low. "Can I have a pillow?"

Maxim reached for him, combing through his hair. The touch was like wildfire cooled by a summer's downpour, and every muscle in his body went lax. He leaned against the couch, lowering his head to Maxim's knee.

"No," said Maxim, tugging his roots softly before scraping his nails over his scalp. "Not unless you have an injury that I don't know about. You can stand to kneel on the floor for me for a bit."

Copley nodded, his eyes half-lidded. The ache wasn't even as bad as he'd thought, and with Maxim's hand in his hair, it hardly mattered.

"Did you do something like this with Nikita?" He tugged again, and Copley moaned, letting his eyes fall all the way shut. *Fuck* it felt good to simply give in, to let go and be taken care of. The money didn't matter, and it wasn't his burden to bear with Maxim looking after him.

He shook his head, unable to bring himself to speak. Niki had made him feel good in other ways, and maybe they would have done this if their relationship hadn't been confined to the club.

"Tell me what you need. I can't be Niki. I could never replace him." Maxim let out a sigh, dragging Copley that much closer. "He thinks I hate him. Maybe he's right. Maybe I'll never forgive him for taking the fall for me. He could have gone to prison for life, but he took that risk, and he still ended up behind bars for all those years."

"What happened?" Copley didn't know why he was asking the question when he already knew the answer. "I know someone died…" He swallowed, shifting a touch as his knees started to ache again. He needed to shut up and let go, not ask questions.

"Someone came after one of our girls. I took care of it like I always do, but I messed up. I stabbed the fucker—which he deserved—but I got sloppy, and someone saw me. With only an eyewitness, the cops showed up at the door. I answered it because I knew there was no use running. But when they went to arrest me, Nikita confessed."

Copley's heart pounded even as he sank deeper.

"I can still remember the look on his face telling me to keep quiet. I was so fucking stunned I couldn't say a word until they had him packed away in the cruiser already. Fuck, if I could go back, everything would be different." His voice cracked, and he dug his nails into Copley's scalp.

"Would you stop yourself from killing the guy?" asked Copley, barely able to keep his eyes open. His head was telling him to run far and run fast, but he couldn't move an inch.

"No, he deserved what he got. Some people think they can beat on a hooker and almost kill them, just because their body is for sale. Pieces of shit like that don't get to live. I would have changed everything else, though. Niki never would have made it to the back of that car. I would have turned myself in before I even came home."

His grip was tight but not painful as he touched the back of Copley's neck, moving him until Copley's head was in the middle of his lap. He was soft beneath the layer of fabric, but the position had so much more heat than when Copley had been resting on his knee.

"You don't hate him. You hate what happened but not *him*," said Copley, placing his hand on Maxim's thigh to balance himself. "I hate what my brother does, but I don't hate *him*. I couldn't."

"Niki said you left him." Maxim touched his chin, lifting him until their gazes met. "But you're here."

Looking at Maxim was like looking into the sun. His eyes watered until his cheeks were wet, his promise not to cry broken like the rest of him.

"I offered him five thousand dollars to leave my brother alone." He licked his lips as Maxim's eyes went dark. He looked terrifying in every way that Niki was serene patience, but Copley couldn't help but fall under.

"I said I don't know much about dominance, but I do know one thing." He pinched Copley's chin until the touch burned. "Nikita would have done anything to protect you, because his bond was deeper with you than any sub he's ever had. I know he had rules, but he wouldn't care about the money, and he wouldn't let you get hurt."

"I don't care about *me*. It's my brother who's going to get himself killed." Copley's voice rose, and he tried to tug away, but Maxim's grip only went tighter.

"Stand up. *Now*." Maxim's voice dropped into a growl, and he stood from the couch, dragging Copley to his feet when he didn't follow right away. Gripping the back of his neck like a collar, he pulled Copley from the living room to the bedroom, tossing him down on the messy bed without hesitation.

"Now I know why Niki left," Maxim hissed, pinning Copley to the bed with one hand as he loomed over him. "There's only two people in the world that he cares about, and neither of us give a shit about ourselves."

Copley trembled, gripping the sheets when Maxim didn't let up. His world was crashing down. It was *his* fault that Niki had left them, and he had no way of getting him back.

A month's worth of panic and stress came rushing forth at the same time, battering at his mind until he wanted to scream. His breaths came fast, his mouth half-smothered in the sheets as Maxim refused to let up. Tears choked him, soaking into fabric as sweat prickled along his hairline.

"I'm sorry." He could scarcely get the words out through his chattering teeth, everything coming to its breaking point.

Twenty-nine years old and he had planned to stay in a motel until he found a place to stay. His brother had a gambling addiction that he could do nothing about and had stolen his ring, which he had bought for a man who had only been looking for a fun time. His life was a clusterfuck of positive thinking, and it was all crashing down.

"You aren't sorry now, but you will be," said Maxim, finally easing his grip. "I'm going to punish you so we can move on from this, and you are going to take every bit of it because you know you deserve it. Nikita gave you a safeword. What was it?"

"'Red'," said Copley, biting his lower lip to keep from sobbing. "'Yellow' to slow down."

Maxim chuckled, the sound making the hair rise on the back of Copley's neck. "You don't get to slow down. You're either green or red, so what is it? Will you let me beat you so you can forgive yourself?"

How could a man he barely knew seem to *know* him better than every other person, save one? He had been holding every moment of the last month over himself, beating himself down constantly as he tried and failed to make amends.

He would never make amends with Spencer because their love was a one-sided carnival game that had been rigged from the beginning. He couldn't control Sauble, either, and five thousand dollars was nothing to a man like Nestor. All his hard work and there was nothing to show for it except sleepless nights and the five pounds that he would probably never gain back.

"You're doing it right now," said Maxim, grabbing the waistband of Copley's pants and tugging them past his ass. The button on the slacks popped free in distress, flying somewhere in the tangled sheets. "Don't fucking think of yourself like that with me standing right fucking here."

The first slap to Copley's ass made him yelp more in surprise than pain. It was a dull thud that would probably bruise later, then a prickle of skin that had his hair standing on end. The pain didn't start until a moment later when he lifted himself to his hands and knees.

The next slap landed in the same spot, and the tingle rushed through him faster, burning bright until his nerves weren't sure what to do. He could hardly breathe through the ache in his chest, his thoughts rushing faster as he spiraled. "I can't."

"You don't have to."

His thoughts came to a grinding halt. *I don't have to?* A resounding slap battered his ass, then another before he could recover. Tears streamed down his cheeks unchecked as the pain and humiliation set in, and he started to sob. He grabbed for a pillow, clutching it close as he tilted his ass into the hits. He deserved every single one of them.

"Do you know why Niki and I care for you so much?" asked Maxim, his voice so much softer than it had been before. He smoothed his hand over Copley's flushed skin before spanking him twice more. "Answer me."

"I don't know." He yelped as Maxim slapped him between his cheeks, one finger landing across his hole in a burst of pain. His hole ached, and he clenched it tight.

"Because we want to look after you. We want to be there for you every day and take your hurt and worry away. We want to own you and please you and watch you crawl to us."

It doesn't make sense. Copley shook his head, fighting for breath. "He said only the club, though. He only wants me there but nowhere else. Our night together here was a mistake. He doesn't want me."

He caught Maxim's intake of breath and his skin prickled. Hadn't he known?

"Then he was wrong, and we'll make sure he knows it," said Maxim, pulling another metaphorical rug out from under Copley and wrapping him in a bubble of warmth instead. "He was so fucking wrong, baby. He was wrong about everything, just like we were, and when we find him, we're going to make sure he knows it."

Heaving in a few breaths, Copley let himself go, sobbing into the bed as Maxim smacked him over and over, moving to a fresh area as soon as his skin started to go numb, only to move back to the spot when fire erupted. He was wrung out and stretched so thin that nothing in his life mattered except for Maxim's hands on him, punishing him until he was forgiven.

Finally, when he knew he couldn't take another strike, Maxim stopped, leaning over and pressing a kiss to Copley's neck. Maxim's breath came fast, his teeth scraping over the knobs of his spine.

"You're forgiven, baby."

Copley's limbs went slack, and suddenly he wasn't on the bed anymore, but cradled in Maxim's arms. Every movement was whispered agony, but the sensation was so distant that it was barely a hum against his thoughts. Maxim touched him slowly and gently for so long that the minutes blurred, and his tears dried to itchy streaks.

When he came to, he felt as if he'd woken from a sleep that had lasted a week. He was lighter than he'd ever been, almost enough to flow away on a snow-filled breeze. Maxim was the only thing making sure he didn't float off.

"You feel better?" asked Maxim, his voice quiet and calm.

Copley nodded, leaning into Maxim's chest and listening to the beat of his heart. Something throbbed against his ass, but Copley made no move to touch it and neither did Maxim.

"Did I hurt you?" He sounded a touch worried, and Copley had the sudden urge to laugh. His ass throbbed from where his waist band would sit to the tops of his thighs.

"No. You made me whole." He kissed the side of Maxim's neck, licking his pulse that had started to pick up. "Thank you."

"You won't thank me when you wake up tomorrow and you can't sit. But I'll take it for now." Maxim smirked, his eyes bright as he patted Copley's ass.

"Ow...fuck." Copley groaned, flinching away from the touch. "You're right. I take it all back." He squirmed under the touch, noticing for the first time that his own cock was aching and hard. He wasn't even sure when it had happened.

"Punishment's over. You ready for your reward for being such a good boy?"

Copley's breath caught as warmth filled him. He'd never thought that being called a good boy would be one of his buttons, but apparently it nailed it head-on. He nodded, not sure if he wanted to snuggle into Maxim tighter or reach for his cock. It was still as hard as an anvil beneath him.

"You think you deserve a reward?" asked Maxim, playing with the hem of his shirt. Even with the smile, his voice was serious. The tiger on his neck was menacing, ready to snap its quarry in two with a single bite. Copley stared at it, his mouth dry.

"I do," said Copley after a moment. If he had his way, he would get a month's worth of rewards and epic sex. "I'm a good boy." It should have felt juvenile, but Maxim beamed at him, patting him on the head as he nodded.

"Don't I know it. Now be a champ and suck me off." Maxim lifted him, setting him gently on the bed before reaching for his own pants and popping the button. His cock lunged free as soon as he pulled the zipper down, no underwear caught in the way of freedom. "Fuck, that's better. I'm not sure how Niki can stand it for that long."

Copley tilted his head, looking closely at the cock before him. It wasn't identical after all. "I think Niki's a bit smaller than you, so maybe it doesn't hurt so much in confined spaces?"

Maxim threw his head back as he laughed, the sound filling the room with warmth until it was nearly bursting. The laugh turned into a choke as Copley reached for him with his mouth, pushing the foreskin back with his lips before sucking him deep. He wasn't about to ignore an order.

He was heavy and salty, stretching Copley's mouth wide until his jaw ached. He would have had to have been a sword swallower to take it any deeper in his throat, so he wrapped his hand around the base, stroking the bit he couldn't fit. Drool slicked the way as he stroked in time with his sucks.

"Put your hands behind your back, baby. I want to see you choke yourself." Maxim swept Copley's hair away from his face, looking into his tearing eyes.

Copley blinked before sitting back on his heels. His heels pressed against his sore ass, and he lurched forward again, almost headbutting Maxim's cock in the process. Biting his lip, he spread his legs wider, trying to balance as he put his hands behind his back. His muscles trembled from the effort, and he could barely balance on the squishy bed. He hadn't had a chance to make it to the gym all month, and it was already starting to show.

"Too hard for you?" asked Maxim, making no move to help. Releasing the buttons on his shirt, Maxim shifted a few pillows behind him, leaning against them with a sigh.

Copley shook his head, reaching for Maxim's cock with his lips. He overshot, nudging Maxim's abs before he finally managed to capture it, circling the head with his tongue.

It was like rubbing his belly and patting his head at the same time. The moment he tried to focus on Maxim, he would lose his balance and sink a touch too far, choking himself in the process. When he reeled back, his eyes watering, he touched his aching ass to his heels and lurched forward again.

"I can help you, but you have to ask nicely." Maxim spread his legs wider, stroking his cock once as Copley leaned back for a breather, sacrificing the bruises on his ass to let his gag reflex calm.

Shaking his head, Copley narrowed his eyes before leaning in again, determined to be good. At the last moment, Maxim tilted his cock toward his belly, avoiding Copley's incoming lips. Copley's nose squashed into his abs as he missed his target and sucked in a few deep breaths.

"Come and get it, baby. It's like you aren't even trying." Maxim moved his cock out of reach again as Copley tried to get it from the side, losing his balance and nearly tumbling off the bed before he braced himself with his hand.

"No hands. Are you deaf, too?" Maxim smirked, drawing his tongue over his lips.

Bastard.

Copley flushed, struggling to get his hands behind his back and clasping his wrists tight. When he leaned in, Maxim thwarted him, pointing his cock down until it was tucked under Copley's chin. Maxim clicked his tongue, shaking his head with mock disapproval.

I'm done playing fair. Copley lunged, sinking his teeth into the soft skin over Maxim's abs before biting down hard. He held on, even as Maxim spluttered and tried to pull away.

Leaning back, Copley licked his lips, giving Maxim the most innocent look he could muster. "Sorry. I missed."

"My baby's got teeth." Maxim smirked, touching the red outline that was quickly blooming on his belly. "But that really didn't hurt. You're gonna have to try harder than that."

Copley flopped his mouth open, and he stared. *Wasn't expecting that.* He wasn't really sure what he had been expecting other than maybe a few more swats on his sore ass. Whatever the reason, he wanted to push and find out.

Trembling from the effort, he sucked Maxim's cock into his mouth, choking on it as he lost his balance. Instead of pulling back, he scraped his teeth over the sensitive underside.

Maxim had a hand in his hair and was pulling him off before he could react, squeezing his hand tight enough that a few strands pulled free from Copley's scalp. His eyes were dark pools and almost feral as he glared at Copley.

"Something like that could get you in a lot of trouble, boy. Care to try it again?" asked Maxim, dropping his hand back to his side. He grasped his cock, wincing a little as he brushed the underside.

Guilt flooded Copley as he looked at the tiny red mark that his teeth had left behind. He'd only meant to tease, not to injure. It had to hurt terribly, especially for someone like Maxim to wince. He looked like he could break his arm in a fight and still keep on punching.

"Hey." Maxim gripped his chin, tilting his face up. "What just happened? Where did you go?"

"I'm sorry," said Copley softly. "I didn't mean to hurt you." Every time things were finally going right, he managed to fuck them up. Maybe he wasn't the right kind of person to be a sub.

Maxim snorted before squeezing his chin tighter. "It's going to take a lot more than that to actually hurt me. Just saying, though, nipping a delicate place like that is a great way to earn a punishment, and I'll be giving your ass a rest for that."

I'm more curious now. Should I? He just wanted to let go of everything and let Maxim take over.

Copley leaned in, taking Maxim gently in his mouth. Building a rhythm, he waited until the taste grew thick in his mouth and Maxim's cock throbbed before he dragged his teeth along the underside, nipping at the crown before he pulled back.

His head was somewhere else as he smiled goofily, sitting back on his heels, despite the sting. If anything, the sting made it feel that much better, his head swimming with the possibilities. *Will he backhand me until my cheek is stinging and red?* He'd caught sight of that kind of scene at the club, and the sub had looked so blissed out that it had to feel good.

"Fucking hell, boy." Maxim put a hand over his cock as if he were trying to protect it. His grin turned positively evil. "I've always wanted to do this. Tap my thigh twice if it's too much."

Grabbing Copley by the back of his neck, he pushed his cock through his open mouth until it hit the back of his throat. Copley gagged, his eyes watering, but Maxim didn't let up. He didn't stop until he pushed past the resistance, settling deep in Copley's throat.

He gagged, pushing against Maxim's belly to try to get relief. His head was swimming, his lungs already burning for air as he fought to keep his stomach calm. He was just so fucking big, stretching his throat to its maximum and beyond.

"Bite me and I'll take your ass the same way," said Maxim, giving Copley a moment to breathe before he dragged him all the way back down, going a touch deeper until Copley was sure that his throat would be raw for days.

He scrambled to get free, but Maxim's grip was so strong that he had no chance. Two taps, and he could have breathed again, but he couldn't bring himself to do it.

There was something about the struggle and giving it his all, but still being unable to get away, that had him rock hard. For a second, he considered biting down, but that was one threat that he didn't want Maxim to follow through with. His ass would never be the same if he was taken without prep by a man like Maxim, who probably didn't have the word 'gentle' in his vocabulary.

"You're so close, baby. Just a little bit more."

One breath and Copley was being plunged down again, so far that his eyes rolled back, and the struggles left his body in an instant. It felt like Maxim was in his goddamn stomach by the time his nose touched his scratchy curls, his cock throbbing so hard that it felt like its own heartbeat in his throat.

"So fucking good. Drink it down." Maxim barely twitched as he came, but Copley felt the pulse in his throat, choking as he was pulled back, molten cum flooding his mouth.

He tried to swallow, but he couldn't keep up with the flow that flooded his mouth as his lungs screamed for air. Shuddering, it spilled from his mouth as he let out a silent yell, his body snapping tight as his orgasm rushed through him. He hadn't even known it was close until it slammed into him, the taste and Maxim's touch too much for him to stand.

When he came to, he was back in Maxim's arms, his lips and chin clean and a few crumpled tissues on the bed beside him. He blinked, barely able to move as he sank into the embrace, wishing he would never have to leave.

Chapter Sixteen

Nikita

He wasn't sure if it was still considered stalking if he had Copley's best interests at heart. Perhaps that was what stalkers told themselves before they snuck into someone's bedroom.

Either way, he hadn't been watching Copley's apartment *that* long. He'd parked his ass on the curb a few hours before on the off chance he'd catch his sub coming home. It had been a physical blow when he'd realized that he hadn't even known where Copley worked.

He'd been so focused on keeping their lives separate that he'd forgotten what he had promised himself on the first day on the outside. Hiding from Nestor shouldn't have been his first priority, but somewhere along the line, he had convinced himself that his boss was more important than his life.

Fuck, he'd been a terrible Dom. Copley never should have had to go through any of those things, let alone be terrified about a debt that didn't belong to him.

Three days in a shitty motel had cleared up a few things for him. He couldn't remember the last time he'd slept on his own, and he was positive that he never wanted to do it again.

His guilt solidified until he wished he could take back every word that he'd said. It only grew worse when his fear of facing Copley and Maxim had overshadowed the grief, pure madness eventually driving him from the motel. He hadn't been able to take another second of the sounds of his neighbors fucking through the walls while missing the comforting snoring.

He'd walked from the motel all the way back across town to Copley's apartment, scraping the thin layer of snow off the curb before he'd sat down. That had been three hours before, when there had been still a hint of innocence to the night.

He'd never been afraid of the dark, not even when he had been a child. If he could have lived in the darkness and wrapped it around himself like a blanket, he gladly would have done so. People didn't judge him when they were blind to his appearance. They didn't fear him.

Even under the shadows between two streetlamps across from one of the shiftiest apartments in the neighborhood, he still got a few looks. The dealer who had scrounged up the courage to approach him had quickly scurried off when Nikita had looked up, the lights of a passing car illuminating his face.

Everyone feared him, whether it was because of his brother or not. The only two who didn't, he'd driven away after he'd lost his control. He hadn't thought he could live without Unkinked, but he'd realized he couldn't live without those two instead.

He let out a sigh, leaning back to try to get blood into the frozen parts of his ass. The hookers just down the road were fucking champs compared to him, walking the streets every night without complaint.

The bus pulled up to the stop — probably the last one of the evening — and he leaned forward, biting his tongue as he searched for Copley in the crowd. Even if he couldn't scrounge the courage to stand up and talk to him, he had to see him again. One time in his bed, and Copley had already become a permanent fixture.

The bus's doors closed with a hiss of air, and it pulled back onto the road, a cloud of diesel following it along with a few leaves that were somehow still dry enough to skitter around. One person broke away from the group, heading toward the apartment with a wave of his hand.

The son of the neighborhood. The last person he wanted to see turned down the path to the apartment before disappearing through the doors. Sauble probably didn't have a chance against him in a fight, but he didn't want to risk starting something that he wasn't prepared to finish.

Where the fuck is Copley? His thin veneer of patience, which had been slowly stretching for days, finally snapped. He couldn't wait another moment to see his sub. He had to find him *now.*

He stumbled from the curb, heading toward the prostitutes who were standing in little groups around the bus stop. It seemed like a strange place, but it was the best lit area in the neighborhood, and everyone knew where it was. Nestor had a deal with the cops, so as long as his girls didn't show too much skin, the cops would steer clear of the area.

Skin prickling, he pulled his jacket tighter as he crossed the road, his legs tingling as they slowly came back to life. He still couldn't feel his ass, though, which was a strange sensation while wearing jeans.

There were four girls on the corner, all of them Nestor's. The scent of perfume and cheap sex was almost overpowering.

"What's up, boss?"

He turned to Sweetie. Her legs were probably numb, too, but she made it look easy. Her smooth flesh was exposed from ankle to nearly her hip, the tiniest hint of a bruise just above her left knee. Her lipstick was smeared, her hair a bit mussed, but that was nothing new. Her night had already begun.

"Have you seen Copley?" asked Niki, shoving his hands into his pockets and hunching his shoulders. A few of the girls backed away from him — most of them newer faces who hadn't learned who the real bad guys were. Sweetie had been around long enough that she knew who to fuck and who to fuck *with*.

Sweetie frowned before she touched one finger to her lower lip, the tip coming away painted red. "Thought he was staying with you, boss. Haven't seen him in...three days, I guess...maybe four." She tilted her head to the side, biting at her lip. "Something going on with you two?"

Can you ask any louder? Most of the group weren't looking at him, but he knew he had every one of their ears. Any other time he would have made a sarcastic rebuff or sent out a warning growl to someone who dared ask him something so fucking personal.

Time to leave that life behind me.

"He's my sub and my lover. Do you know where he might be?" He chomped down on his tongue, hating that he had to ask that question.

Sweetie let out a low whistle, her eyes going wide. "I wondered if that was you and him the other night, but I thought I was hallucinating." Her face suddenly grew worried. "Some guys are trying to stir up shit in town. You really don't know where he is?"

Niki shook his head sharply before glancing back at the apartment. Sweetie kept talking, the worry growing thick in her voice, but he turned away, storming up to the decrepit building where Copley and he had met for the first time.

When he'd snuck in on that first day, he had been expecting to throw a few punches at a punk or maybe get his ass handed to him when his permanent marker did nothing. Copley had taken his breath from the beginning, perfect in every fucking way. Niki was ready to go through hell and back again to salvage what they had left, then he would crawl to his brother and beg his forgiveness.

He didn't bother knocking on the door. He had discovered that even with the lock on the door, it didn't actually work. Pushing it wide, he stormed through the entrance, spotting Sauble in the tiny kitchen with a jug of milk halfway to his mouth.

Sauble spluttered, milk running down his chin as he dropped the jug, his eyes going wide. He was in a tank and shorts, still covered in sweat, presumably from the gym. He shouldn't have looked so relaxed with his brother missing.

"I'm not here to fight," said Niki, holding up his hands as Sauble scrambled in the cupboard for something. Niki knew there had been no guns in the apartment last time, but that might have changed since. "I'm just trying to find Copley."

"He's supposed to be with you," said Sauble, giving up his search and grabbing a long butcher knife from the counter that was probably more useful for carving a pumpkin than anything else.

"Fuck." Niki turned away, slamming the door behind him as he rushed back out of the building. His heart pounded as he reached for his phone and keys automatically, knowing that he wouldn't find them. By the time he hit the street, he was running full tilt, barreling toward Sweetie, who stepped back from a john's car as he approached.

"Give me your fucking phone." He grabbed it from her hands before she even released it, her nails cutting against his palm. A few prostitutes shifted away, terrified of the beast that he'd unleashed.

He dialed Maxim's number by memory, not even amused when it popped up as *Double Dickhead* in Sweetie's contacts. Most days, he would have agreed with her anyway.

Three rings later and he smashed his fist into the glass shelter at the bus stop. One person screamed as the glass cracked under his fist, blood blooming as it cut him to the bone. He was so numb that he barely felt it. "Pick the fuck up, Max. Don't fucking ignore me."

"What?" Maxim yelled into his ear as the line connected.

Niki let out a breath, leaning into the rigid corner of the little hut. He touched his face, leaving a wet smear behind that quickly cooled. "I can't find him."

His words came out choked and he realized that it wasn't just blood on his cheeks. Someone touched his back and he flinched away, only to realize it was Sweetie offering him her thin scarf.

"Nikita? Where have you been? Whose phone is this? It says '*That one chick*'."

Fuck, it's good to hear his voice. He held out his hand for Sweetie, who wrapped his knuckles tight with almost surgical precision. "Sorry."

"Wow, never thought I'd hear my big bro apologize. Your sabbatical must've really changed your ways. Which ditch am I picking you up in?"

Maybe I didn't miss him that much. Niki couldn't help but smile through his tears before his gut plummeted a second time. "I can't find Copley. I checked his apartment, but his brother thought he was with me."

"Eh, close enough. He's home, which is exactly where he should be."

For a moment, Niki wondered if Copley had gone back to his ex, but as much as his sub tortured himself, Niki had to believe he would never go that far. "He's with you?"

Maxim let out a sleepy sigh. "Domestic bliss, baby. He makes the best fucking pancakes, too, and his foot rubs are second to none."

Niki went numb, his tongue freezing against the roof of his mouth. At first he thought it was jealousy, but a moment later he realized it was grief. He'd never get their time apart back, but he'd have to get stabbed for him to miss it again. "I'm coming home."

"He'll be waiting."

Chapter Seventeen

Copley

So warm. He snuggled deeper into Maxim's chest, taking a breath to draw him in closer. *Why am I awake?* He'd never been so warm in his life, so cared for — and it still wasn't enough.

Spencer had been enough for years, with only brief touches between sex that was the definition of routine. *I'm sorry.* He couldn't say it aloud to Max. He couldn't bring himself to tell his lover that he needed more.

Sorry, you aren't good enough. I need your brother, too. Yeah, that would go over well. One of the few things he'd learned about Maxim over the last few days was that he was as wild as he was unforgiving. It also took a team of insults working together to actually mean anything, but if one struck true, it hurt for a long time. Copley never wanted to be the cause of that hurt or be the one to dim the fire in Max's eyes.

Shit. He squeezed Maxim tight, grumbling when he tried to roll away. Was it so bad that he just wanted to be praised and taken care of? Max teased him, punished him and made him feel loved, but it was so different from everything that Niki had given him.

Every evening he'd rushed back to Max after work, hoping that he would find Niki seated on the couch. He tried not to let Max see his disappointment, but from the tense lines around his eyes, there were few things that he overlooked.

"You awake, baby?" asked Max without a hint of sleep in his voice.

Copley grunted, holding onto his sleepiness with everything he had. It slipped away, leaving him lonely in a bed that he shared with another man. He bit his lip, trying to keep his feelings at bay.

"Sorry if I was too loud. I didn't mean to wake you," said Maxim, skimming his hand down Copley's back before cupping his ass. "Now that you are awake, I'm going to go out for a while. Nestor has a few things he needs me to take care of."

Copley peeked over Max's shoulder, squinting at the red lights on the clock. Max had gone to *work* every day that they'd stayed together, but always during daylight hours. Copley dreaded what he would get up to at night. "It's one in the morning. What the hell does he need you to do right now?"

He hadn't meant to whine, but oh well.

"Baby going to miss me?" Max taunted, squeezing his ass that was still sore from a spanking earlier in the evening. Copley had found ways to earn one every night since the first, loving and hating every minute of it.

"I'm not sure that I want to know, but I'm a bit worried," said Copley, clinging tight. "The city isn't safe after dark…even the good parts." The good parts were where the easiest prey were—or so Max had told him.

"Baby, I'm the reason that the city isn't safe. The boogeyman doesn't have shit on me." He slapped Copley's ass, pushing a grunt through his lips. Copley's gut burned on the edge of arousal that always seemed to simmer within him since meeting the twins.

"I'm *so* scared." Copley chuckled, biting Max's nipple through his shirt. "Can't you feel me trembling?" He pitched his voice higher, trying to keep from laughing. "Oh, Maxy, please don't hurt me. I'm innocent."

Max snorted, giving him another slap. "You *are* innocent. You are so fucking sweet that I'm gonna get fucking cavities. You're getting the bill for it, too. Nestor doesn't cover shit like that."

"My hero." Copley clung tighter as Max tried to sit up before slipping his hand between Max's legs and brushing against his quickly growing erection. He cupped it, smoothing over the warm flesh as it rapidly went hard. His mouth watered as he thought about getting his lips around it—choking on it again. "You still have to go?"

Max paused, grabbing Copley's hand and moving it away from his lap. Copley bit his lip, sitting back and blinking at Max in the darkness. His insides trembled, his breaths coming fast.

"I think there's something that you just aren't getting," said Maxim, shuffling in the darkness until his heat pulled away from the bed. "I own you. Every part of you. That perfect cock is mine, and those red lips and everything else, too. I decide when you sleep, when you eat and when you fuck. You gotta get that through that pretty little head of yours."

Copley burned. His skin flushed with humiliation and desire so fierce that it nearly blinded him. The thought of being owned, so completely and thoroughly, had him rock hard and weeping.

"Do you know what part of me you own?" asked Maxim, moving close so his breath tickled the shell of Copley's ear.

Shaking his head, he wet his lips, tilting his head for a kiss that he hoped Max would give him. He needed something—anything—if he wasn't going to explode.

"Not a fucking thing." Maxim's voice was a growl in the darkness as he wrapped a hand lightly around Copley's throat. "Get it now, baby?" He squeezed until the blood rushed to Copley's head, and he wondered if he would pass out if Max didn't let go.

I'm going to come. He shook, touching Max's grip on his throat and squeezing it tighter. Closing his eyes, he leaned into it, not even sure why he would ever resist. Max *owned* him.

"I'm yours." He managed to get the words out—barely—licking his lips as Max's grip eased just enough for him to catch his breath. His cock throbbed with each inhale, surging as Max clamped down again.

"You are ours to do with what we please."

Ours? He couldn't think, reaching for his cock and gripping it tight. He wasn't sure if his vision was going dark or if it was just the dimness of the room looming closer. He caught a flash of Max's teeth, his lips stretched into a wicked grin.

"Don't fucking touch yourself," Max growled, dragging Copley to his feet. "You still don't get it."

His knees trembled as Max suddenly let him go and he gasped in a few haggard breaths. Standing between the beds in a dark room with the whisper of cool air against his naked skin, he clutched his hands together so he didn't reach for himself. His cock throbbed harder as his skin flushed with humiliation as Max moved around him and seemingly ignored him. There was the rustle of cloth and a belt buckle, which made Copley that much harder.

The lamp flicked on, casting shadows in every corner. He didn't speak. He didn't dare say a fucking thing as Maxim prowled around the room in the low light, looking more threatening with each layer he donned. A hoodie completed his ensemble, the thickest clothing that Copley had ever seen him wear, even with snow starting to fall outside.

"I—"

"Don't say a fucking word." Max approached him, landing a slap on his ass before he stalked away.

Max not touching him was even more intense than when he did, his eyes raking over Copley and leaving him bare. He'd never been so exposed before anyone. But Max flayed him open as if he had night vision that could see every imperfection and flaw.

"Something's missing." Max tapped his chin, pausing as he looked down Copley's front and eyeing his cock like it was a piece of modern art. "Got it." He turned from the room, returning a moment later with a ribbon in his fingers. "I was going to use this for wrapping Christmas presents, but this will be way better."

Grabbing Copley's cock, which hadn't flagged in the least, he wrapped the ribbon around it tight enough that blood pounded beneath his skin. Max finished it off with a little bow, smirking as he stepped back.

"Maybe I should get the scissors and curl the ribbon a bit." He touched the base of Copley's bound cock, flicking the straight edge of the ribbon. His eyes were dark, an obvious tent in his own ragged jeans.

Imagining scissors so close to something so precious and vulnerable should have been terrifying, but the ribbon's steady grip was the only thing keeping him from coming. *There has to be something wrong with me.* Max cackled, tugging the ribbon until Copley hissed. *But at least it's wrong with both of us.*

"I think I like it just like that," said Max, patting the head of his cock in the same way he would pat a dog. "Now you lie in Niki's bed and go to sleep. You aren't allowed to touch yourself or take that ribbon off unless it really starts to hurt." He leaned in close, placing a single kiss on Copley's cheek. "Make me proud."

Copley stood for a long time in the center of the room...long after Maxim turned away, shutting the lamp off but leaving the bedroom door open and the little light on above the stove that made it easier to move around the house in the dark. He heard the front door open and shut, but not the little click of the lock that usually followed

Looking to Niki's bed, Copley pulled the perfect sheets back, trying his best not to disturb them as he carefully slid between them. They were cold, sucking the heat from his skin and lying against his cock like an ice pack. Everything pulled tight around him, the edges still tucked how Niki had left them days before and the water glass on his bedside getting shallower every evening.

He rolled against the pillow, breathing deep as his cock throbbed between his legs. It hurt, but not enough to remove the ribbon to get relief—just enough to keep him on edge and keep sleep pressed to the far corners of his thoughts.

Max is gone. How will he know if I touch myself? He bit his lip, pondering his options. The answer was simple. Max seemed to know everything—what he had for lunch, how his day at work went and even a few details that set Copley a bit on edge…like how he liked the taste of buttermilk.

Turning over again, he stared at the outline of the light fixture against the ceiling. The ceiling was made up of soft-looking white tiles that didn't have a single hint of a stain on them. It was such a contrast to his usual view that it almost made him miss the lumpy couch of his brother's apartment.

He'd brought up the money exactly one time with Maxim before he'd clamped his mouth shut. Maxim had given him a dangerous look before he'd said he would take care of it. Copley wanted to press to make sure that his brother was safe, but his jaw had stopped working completely.

He drifted, his cock throbbing as sleep started to overcome him. Just when he thought he would truly drift off, the front door clicked open. He came awake all at once, gripping the pillow beneath him to keep from reaching for his cock. There were low voices in the front hall that were too soft for him to hear, but one of them sounded like Maxim.

His head pounded, but he couldn't move, waiting with his eyes closed as the light in the kitchen shut off and two sets of footsteps came closer. He wanted to hide under the covers and throw them back at the same time, his chest aching as he pretended to be asleep.

"Looks like he fell asleep. I've kept him busy for us the last few days," said Maxim, his bed squeaking as he presumably sat down. The frame was identical to Niki's but for some reason, it always squeaked.

Copley drew in a slow breath, his ears almost pricking like an animal's as he tried to figure out who the second person was. His heart was giving him the same answer over and over.

"Even more beautiful than I remember."

It *was* Niki, his voice just a touch deeper and slower and sinking in a second before something touched Copley's face. He opened his eyes, reaching for Niki before he even saw him. Wrapping his arms around him, he dragged him into the bed, Niki's coat freezing against his warm skin.

Niki landed on him with an *oomph*, driving the air from Copley's body with his weight. He clung tight regardless, refusing to let his Dom go. He was trembling already, tears on his cheeks as he reached for Niki's face. Niki was coarser than he remembered, with dark shadows under his eyes that looked even worse in the dim light.

"Fuck, I missed you," said Niki, rolling them over so Copley was on top. The sheets tangled around his hips, pulling free until he was stripped naked and straddling Niki.

"I tied up his cock real pretty for you. You're welcome," said Maxim as he lay back in his own bed before rolling over and facing the wall. He tossed his arm over his head. "Just don't keep me up all night. I've got shit to take care of tomorrow."

Niki shook his head, his lips pressed in a line as he sat up, dragging Copley along with him and setting him in his lap.

Copley flushed, dropping his gaze to his half-hard cock that was still surrounded by the ribbon. It was looser now, giving him room to grow. Niki followed his gaze, tugging the ribbon free and carefully unwinding it from his cock.

"I'm not going to fuck you, Copley," said Niki, cupping his chin in his hands so their eyes met. "It's not because you don't deserve it, baby. You deserve the world, and it took me three days too long to figure that out."

Niki pulled his coat from his shoulders, covering Copley with it. It enveloped him like the warmest hug, soaking him in Niki's scent that he had longed for for days. Tears soaked his cheeks as he shook hard enough that his teeth chattered.

"Help me get undressed, then I'm going to hold you all night. I don't want to forget what that feels like ever again." He wiped Copley's cheeks, leaning in for a kiss that was so gentle it was barely there at all. Copley sank into it, giving himself up with a single touch. "I don't deserve you," Niki whispered, kissing Copley's cheeks. "How could I ever leave you?"

Copley took a breath, his hand steadier than it had ever been around the twins. He dried his eyes, placing his palm on Niki's chest just above his heart. "Don't say that." He dug his nails in when Niki tried to speak.

"Be good, baby," said Niki, grasping his wrists and pulling them away. His eyes were bloodshot, and there was a smear of something dark on his cheek. One of his hands was wrapped with something that left a damp impression on Copley's skin. "I want to hold you, not fight with you. Just be good."

Copley's stomach sank and he looked away. *I thought I was being good.* He wasn't sure what he had expected when Niki returned, but this wasn't it. He'd waited so patiently for his Dom's homecoming, only to be pushed away.

Grabbing the ribbon back from where it had been discarded, he pulled himself free from Niki's grip, stumbling the two steps over to Maxim's bed. Maxim grunted as he poked him in the shoulder, Niki's gaze burning into his naked back.

"Wha?" Max asked, turning to look at him with sleep already in his eyes.

"I'm sleeping with you," said Copley, his voice just above a whisper. Niki let out a pained sigh behind him, and it almost broke Copley's heart. He couldn't do it. He couldn't not be good for a man that he missed so much it ached.

"The fuck you are," said Maxim, turning to face him before rubbing the back of his hand over his eyes. "I had to drive all the way across town to pick Niki's sorry ass up. The least you could give me in return is a proper night's rest without having to fuck you to sleep for once."

The rejection burned, and Copley clutched the ribbon tighter in his fist. Would it be the same if he tied it back where it belonged? *No.* He knew that Max was miserable when he didn't sleep and waking him up was like poking a hibernating bear, but it still fucking hurt.

Niki's gaze burned fiercer as Copley took another step back, caught between rejection and his Dom who couldn't see how hard he was trying. Sleeping with either of them felt wrong.

Without another word, he stormed out of the bedroom, slamming the door as hard as he could. The sound shook the silence of the house, cracking in the night like sudden thunder. Freezing air shivered against his skin as he walked to the living room, sliding the window shut that Max always insisted they leave open, despite the heater just below it.

It was a frigid, with snowflakes drifting past the lamplight. Chilled air creeped through the closed glass, every hair on end as he shivered.

Grabbing the blanket out of the basket beside the couch, he snuggled into it, doing a double take when a beer can rolled out of it and disappeared under the couch. The blanket only went to mid-calf when he pulled it up to his shoulders, but it was the largest blanket in the basket.

It was scratchy and only kept the edge of the chill from his skin, despite the weight of it. Maxim had called it a decorative piece of shit, but Copley had liked the look of it nestled in its place. At the moment, he had to agree with Max.

He snuggled into the couch, curling into a ball as the sound of raised voices reached him. The twins were fighting, but this time it was because of *him*. The walls must've been thin because he could hear almost everything that they were saying, even as he tried to ignore it. Every word stung like a fresh wound.

"What the fuck is wrong with you? I gift-wrapped him for you. Literally gift-wrapped."

"I don't deserve him — not after I pushed him out of my life and walked out on you. I'm supposed to have control of myself all the time, but I fucked up."

"Control con-schmol. You still haven't figured your shit out. You're afraid, aren't you? You fucking asshole. You're fucking terrified that he's going to walk out on you or that somebody is going to steal him away."

"*You* seem pretty comfortable with him."

Copley shuddered at Niki's rebuff. He *was* comfortable with Maxim. Max had been his steady support and pseudo-Dom, which was something that he wasn't even aware that he needed until he'd met Niki.

"Well, joke's on you, Nik. The whole time you were gone, he was wishing I was you. Do you know what that's like? I finally...*finally* find someone who turns me on and makes me want something more than just a quick fuck, and he's in love with my brother. I'm just the stand-in who looks and sounds like you but has never been able to live up to you."

Okay...that was enough. None of that was true, and he certainly didn't know if he *loved* Niki or not. Copley threw the blanket back, storming over to the bedroom door before throwing it open. It bounced off the wall, probably putting a hole in the drywall. He couldn't bring himself to care.

The ribbon was still in his hand, the red sheen cloudy from being clutched so tightly. The twins were both in their respective beds, with Max's sheets torn down and almost on the floor while Niki's were picture perfect again.

Copley pointed at Maxim, putting every bit of anger and despair into his voice. "You are so wrong." His voice rang off the walls, and the twins went silent. "I want you just as much as I want Niki, and you fucking know it. You think I would let you own me if I didn't cherish you, too? Unbelievable."

"And you need to shut up." He rounded on Niki, ignoring Max's dropped jaw. "You are so ashamed of yourself that I don't know if I can trust you. I can't give in to a man who thinks he doesn't deserve this—deserve me—and who doesn't realize how much I've missed you. I want you to show me the world, but I won't sit back and let you bury me afterward. I may not be the perfect sub, but I'm worth more than that."

Niki stared, opening and closing his mouth a few times. Copley held out his hand to stop him from speaking. "Don't say anything, because you are just going to regret it in the morning."

He looked between them, his heart full and broken at the same time. He wasn't sure when he had finally figured out that he deserved them, but he latched onto the feeling. He refused to be disrespected ever again.

"I'm going to sleep on the couch." He took a step back, his courage starting to fail. "And I'm turning the thermostat up. It's way too cold."

"Copley," said Maxim, his voice gravelly and low, "get into bed. I don't care who you sleep with, but you aren't sleeping on the couch. No boy of mine sleeps on the couch."

Copley sucked in a breath, even as he took another step back. The air was suddenly charged and intense, two powerful men looking at him with dark thoughts in their eyes. He glanced at Niki, his jaw set tight, his arms crossed and looking every inch the Dom that Copley knew him to be.

Shaking his head, he took another step away, swallowing as the shadows deepened in the room. It was full night outside and the lamp across the street flickered out, plunging the house into darkness.

"You have three seconds. Don't ask me what happens after that."

Was that Niki's voice or Maxim's? Maybe Niki would leave him in the corner for hours, staring at the same spot and punishing him without lifting a hand. If it were Max, he would be in for a short span of pain followed by toe-curling pleasure.

"No," he said softly, his voice barely above a whisper. He cleared his throat, squaring his shoulders and closing his eyes. "No. I'm sleeping on the couch. I'm not sleeping with you until you both figure your shit out — and that's final."

He heard a low chuckle dipped in a threat that made his cock throb and his skin prickle. He didn't dare take another step. His heart was in his throat, his stomach clenched so tight that he could hardly breathe, but he was so hard that it hurt.

Something touched his cheek, but it was gone again before he could flinch. Another breath and he was enveloped by someone so much stronger and taller than him. He reached for them, tracing the outline of rigid strength and total control. The laugh to his right was the only thing that told him it was Niki.

"When I told you to be good, I meant it," said Niki, kissing the top of his head. "My brother may like a bratty sub, but that won't fly with me, and you know it." He dragged his hand slowly down Copley's side, pausing at the dip in his waist.

"Get in the bed, Copley, or you'll be begging to sleep somewhere as comfortable as the floor. I could make up a spot for you there and let you earn your way back into our beds. There would be so many nights with you sleeping alone, cold without the arms of one of your Doms around you. You'd be colder still, knowing it was your own fault." Niki trailed a hand up his chest, clutching Copley's chin and turning his face to the side. "I will never abandon you again, and you need to trust me on that. Regardless, you will *never* speak to me like that. I will dismiss you, even if it would hurt me more than it would hurt you."

His heart pounded, his head swimming. "D-Dismiss?" He had no idea what that word meant, but it didn't bode well. It settled into his gut like a boulder, weighing him down until he felt like he wouldn't be able to lift his feet from the floor. Max shifted on his bed, his outline just barely visible as Copley's eyes adjusted.

"When a naughty sub doesn't listen to his Dom, he's punished." Niki prowled around him like a predator, his voice coming from every angle. "You've been punished before. Tell me, how did it feel?"

Copley trembled, remembering his despair on the street. He'd gotten there early, so desperate to see Niki again that he'd been willing to wait for days for the opportunity. After a few minutes, he had started shifting, little twitches from side to side as he looked up and down the street, wondering what kind of car Niki owned.

But as the cold had settled in, he had stopped moving and stopped smiling at the couples that had gone into Unkinked. Soon, he hadn't been able to feel his hands, even after he'd stuffed them in his pockets. His watch had clicked away on his wrist, but the numbers had been meaningless.

An hour after their meeting time, he had given up hope. He'd slumped, unable to swallow with how tight his throat had been, hating Niki, even as he craved to see him again.

He'd started to wonder if he should leave...but he hadn't. He'd waited on the off-chance that Niki would remember him and show up. He would have waited longer still, feeling more worthless with every passing second.

"I hated it," he said, gnawing the inside of his cheek. "But I needed it, too. I didn't understand your limits, but you showed me the consequences of ignoring them and not asking questions. You showed me what would have happened if I broke the rules."

The light outside the window flickered on, sending a surprising amount of light into the room. Niki nodded, his jaw clenched tight. "Would you break the rules again?"

Copley chewed his lip, gasping as he accidentally bit too deep. He touched his fingertip to it, glaring at the dark spot. "Yes. It was worth it, even on the off chance that I could see you outside the club. What we had wasn't sustainable." He snapped his jaw shut, wondering if he'd pressed too far.

"How would you do it?" asked Niki, his hands resting by his sides. His face was an unreadable mask.

"I would… I would call you and ask if I could see you again…ask you out for coffee, dinner — anything, really. I would text you to see how your day went, so I could know if you were happy or not. I would take any punishment you had, just so I could see you again."

Niki nodded, but he didn't smile. "And what did you say to me just now? Did you ask me nicely? Did you say please? Or did you tell your Dom what to do while yelling like a toddler who just had his favorite toy taken away?" His voice dropped to the tone that always gave Copley shivers. "You told me to shut up, then disrespected me." He touched Copley's chin, pinching tight enough that it started to ache. "If you speak to me that way again, you will no longer be welcome here as my sub or my lover. If you disrespect me, you can find another man to toy with. Do you understand?"

Copley nodded, swallowing even though his mouth was bone-dry. "I'm sorry."

"No, you aren't, but you will be," said Niki, releasing Copley before turning and grabbing a pillow from the bed. He tossed it on the ground in the small space between the beds where it settled with a flat thump. Maxim looked on silently, his expression unreadable.

"Max doesn't want his boy to sleep on the couch, so the floor will have to do. You can ask for our punishment and our forgiveness in the morning." Niki pulled his sheets back, slipping into his own bed.

Can I ask for a blanket? Copley crinkled his toes in the carpet. It did feel soft against his callused feet, but he doubted it would be the same against his skin. Carpets were scratchy as fuck, and this one was none-too-plush.

"May I have a blanket please?" he asked softly, wrapping his arms around himself. He was trembling, and although it was only partly from the cold, he could feel it sinking into him.

"No," said Niki steadily. Max stayed silent, his gaze unblinking.

Dropping to his knees, Copley lowered himself to the ground, curling into the pillow and wrapping his arms around it like a stuffed animal.

How can I explain? Other than his time on his brother's couch, he hadn't slept alone in years. Not having someone beside him — someone he could reach out and touch when his nightmares surfaced, was more terrifying than the dreams themselves.

Niki couldn't know that, though. He had probably slept alone for most of his life with his brother across the room. Max wouldn't understand it, either, especially since he didn't like the sleeping part of sleeping together.

He clutched the pillow tighter, willing the chill away, even as it sank its tendrils deeper. It probably wasn't even that cold, but it felt like there was ice against his skin, with enough to freeze him solid as he curled into a ball. Even the pillow went cool as it grew damp with his tears.

Was Niki watching? Or even Max? Or had they both gone to sleep already? The same sinking feeling touched him that he'd felt on the street, only this time his savior was lying next to him, snoring softly as the night stretched on.

"Yellow."

There was a touch on his shoulder and a hand in his hair less than a second later. He let out a breath, leaning into it. It must've been Niki's, coming from his side. *He's not asleep.* He hadn't left Copley there to shiver alone.

"I don't want to see you suffer, Copley. It fucking kills me. What can I do to make it better?"

Even hearing Niki's voice made him feel better. But he was still *Copley* and not *baby*. He didn't want to sleep on the floor that night or any other night. He just wanted to be close to his Doms. He could worry about a punishment later, but he *needed* to be close to them.

"I can't sleep alone." He clutched the pillow tighter, dragging it with him as he scooted closer. The carpet scraped against his skin, rubbing him in all the wrong ways. He wished it was worse…enough for a punishment. "I'm sorry for what I said, Niki, but please don't make me sleep alone. It's different on the couch. I can do that so much easier because it's like my body knows there's no room for another person. But not the floor. *Please.*" The last word was a sob, but he muffled it with the pillow, not wanting Niki to know how fucking pathetic he was.

"Are you afraid of the dark?" asked Niki, his voice even. It didn't sound like he was teasing, but Copley couldn't be sure. *I'm not a kid, and I'm not weak.*

"It's not that." He looked around at the long shadows that stretched beneath the beds. They were like horror movie corpses reaching for him. "I don't like being alone. I can't stand it. I could have stayed in a motel or got my own apartment instead of crashing close by, but I needed someone close."

"We are close...me and Max. We would never let anything happen to you."

And *fuck*, he knew that, too. His frustration built, his stomach going tight.

"It's not the same. You're up there and I'm down here, and you're both upset at me because of what I said—and I don't know how to make it better. Can't you just punish me now and get it over with? I don't want you to look at me, knowing I did something wrong when I can't do anything to fix it."

"That's life, baby," said Max, his voice just a tad higher than Niki's exhausted timbre. "But for the record, I'm not pissed off—surprised that you were so rude but not pissed. You've always been so sweet, and I'm surprised you even had it in you."

"But Niki's upset," said Copley, wanting to clutch the hand in his hair and wrap his body around it. "I haven't seen you for days, and I should have been so happy, but I got angry with you instead. I should have forgiven you, but I just made you want to leave again. Maybe I should just go." He said it, but it was the last thing he wanted to do. It would kill him to leave them.

"I'm not upset, Copley," said Niki, patting him on top of his head before withdrawing his hand. "I'm exhausted beyond belief, hungry and so happy to be home that I could scream, but I'm not upset."

"I don't understand." Copley reached for him, but only found air between him and the edge of the mattress. "I thought you were going to dismiss me or kick me out or whatever you call it. If you're going to do that, just do it and put me out of my misery."

He wasn't sure why he was digging the hole deeper and deeper, but he couldn't let it go. He shivered on the floor, the pillow no solace as the silence stretched. He could have gotten up and left, but he just wanted to be *good*.

"I don't want to be bad," he said.

"Good," said Niki, the sheets rustling as he moved around. "Then sleep on the floor tonight for me. I need my space right now and so do you. We'll talk more in the morning."

Something loosened in Copley's chest, and he dropped his hand back to the floor. He had thought that the floor itself was the punishment, but if he was doing it *for* Niki and not because he was angry, it made it so much easier. Scratchy carpet and perpetual chill aside, it wasn't the worst he could endure. He couldn't think of many things that he *wouldn't* do for Niki.

"Sound good, baby?"

Copley shuddered at the pet name, letting it wash over him to take the last of his doubt away. "Yes, Sir."

He wasn't sure why he said it, but it felt so right that it slipped right off his tongue. They weren't in a scene, even if it felt like they could have been.

"Good boy."

Chapter Eighteen

Maxim

Niki's punishments were the most boring activities he had ever heard of in his life. He had been half-hoping to tie Copley up and spank him with his hand or a spoon or *something* until he called red, before fucking him until he begged to come. *That* sounded fun — not what Niki had him doing.

Max sighed, leaning against the couch and lifting his feet as Copley went by with the vacuum for the second time. The stress lines around his eyes from this morning had relaxed, though, each task seeming to ease him a little bit more as Maxim descended further into boredom.

Copley wasn't even naked. Vacuuming wasn't tolerable on the best of days, which was why he always left it for Niki. It might have been exciting with Copley naked, with the carpet burn on his skin glowing. But nope…clothes.

Max sent a glance to his brother as Copley whirred away to the other room, switching on the beater bar as he transitioned to the carpet.

"I don't get how this is a punishment," said Max, taking another sip of his coffee. It slid down his throat like liquid gold and was the only thing keeping him awake. He hadn't slept a wink with Copley on the floor.

"Do *you* like vacuuming?" asked Niki, looking over his newspaper. Why he didn't just read it on his tablet had never made sense to Max. Something about *smelling the words* or however Niki had put it.

"I *don't* vacuum." He kicked his feet up on the coffee table before setting his drink down next to him. It was almost empty, and he would have to get up for another refill soon if he didn't want to crash halfway through the day.

"Then it's a punishment. I'm a pleasure Dom, Max. Pain doesn't turn me on, and I don't like dishing it out to my sub." Niki went back to his paper like it was the most natural conversation in the world.

They hadn't really discussed things, but Max wasn't sure if they actually needed to. He could almost see the contentment coming off Niki in waves as he took a sip of his own coffee.

"So you're a softie. At least you admit it." Max snorted.

"You've seen me with him. Did it look soft?"

"No, I guess not." He shifted on the couch, wincing when something dug into his back. Reaching between the cushions, he dragged out a can of beer. His *missing* beer. *Bastard.*

What Max had seen had been an eye-opener. He'd never thought of torturing someone with their orgasm before and Copley hadn't looked like it was all fun and games, either. "What am I, then? I spanked his ass every day since you've been gone. I thought it was a punishment at first, but he kept pushing for it."

"You're a sadist and a brat," said Nikita, raising one brow as he lowered his paper again. "And he's a brat for you because that's your dynamic. It's good that he's flexible, because a lot of subs wouldn't be able to handle two Doms who are so different. You don't have to look for labels, though. Just do what feels right, with consent, and the rest will fill itself in. And use your imagination. He likes getting spanked, but how about a belt?"

Whistling, Max crossed his arms. "I thought you were a pleasure Dom, but now you want me to beat him with a belt?"

"I said I didn't like to dish it out myself, but that doesn't mean I don't like to watch sometimes."

Max looked over the back of the couch to where Copley was just coming out of their bedroom. Copley sent him a little smile that melted something in his chest that had never really been touched before.

"He's good, though," said Max, once Copley had headed out of the room again. Niki hummed in agreement. "Would you really dismiss him?" Max had had the sense to look a few terms up when he'd been stewing over his boredom. Subs that broke the rules repeatedly or didn't respect their Dom could be sent away with all ties cut off. The idea of that left a sour taste in his mouth.

"I don't think we'll ever have to have that discussion," said Niki with such calm collection that Max did a double take. "Like you said, he's a good boy, but he's new, and just like you, and he needs reminders from time to time."

"Plus, this gets you out of vacuuming for one day," said Max, looking from his coffee and back to the beer. His stash had mysteriously disappeared, and he'd been fresh out of brew for a few days, but it was only eleven o'clock in the morning—and warm beer was shit.

"Yep." Niki gave him a wicked smile that had Max laughing.

"You're worse than I am. I just fuck with people, but I usually leave their heads out of it."

"What's life without a bit of a mind fuck?" Nikita grinned, looking like he'd gotten a full night's rest, even though Max knew that he had laid awake too, even as Copley slept between them.

"I didn't think you did all this just to fuck with his head." Max motioned from the empty garbage bins to the dishes that Copley had washed and dried before carefully putting them away. Max had even helped once to put things back in the top cupboard when Copley hadn't been able to reach.

"This is so he can feel like he had a punishment. With everything he's doing, he's getting more and more relaxed. He's forgiving himself and letting his mind empty so he can please me. Serving us is a privilege, and he sees it that way, too. That's why he's perfect," said Niki, looking at Copley out of the corner of his eye as he pulled the plug on the vacuum and started to wrap it up.

Oh. Max hadn't thought of it that way.

"Come here, Copley," said Niki, pointing to the floor next to the couch. There was a pillow waiting there that he must've grabbed at some point. It looked way more comfortable than their decorative ones that lined every fucking couch for some reason.

Definitely soft. That didn't mean Max was going to say it out loud to Niki. In a fair fight, he was evenly matched with his brother, although they rarely wrestled anymore.

Copley knelt without protest, his gaze fixed on the floor in a way that made Maxim's cock go instantly stiff. *I should have gone to the club so much sooner.* It was strange that he would be welcome where his brother, a long-standing member who deserved it a hell of a lot more than he did, was barred for the rest of his life. He tried not to let that sit too deep in his gut.

"How are you feeling?" asked Niki, immediately threading his hand through Copley's hair. Copley leaned into the touch as if he were starved. Maybe he was. He had been so close to a leech with Niki gone that Max had almost been a touch claustrophobic. *But I still missed him last night.*

"Good," said Copley, bobbing his head as he closed his eyes. "A little bit tired and hungry, but good — relaxed. Not how I expected to feel during a punishment."

It was the same way he had responded to the spankings, now that Max thought about it. At first he would yelp and wiggle, but as soon as he settled down and let Max turn his ass pink, he seemed to relax, so much so that his gaze had looked distant.

He was bright-eyed now, but he seemed to be slipping — his smile just a bit loopy. Max wasn't sure what to make of it.

"The house looks perfect. You did well, Copley."

Copley let out a sigh, sagging his shoulders the tiniest bit. It was like a beacon to Max. He looked to Niki and saw the same expression that he felt on his own face.

"Tell me what's wrong." Niki lifted Copley's chin, even as his eyes stayed shut. There were tears on his lashes, brimming but not ready to fall yet.

"You haven't called me 'baby' once since last night. Am I still being punished? Did I not do good enough?" Copley asked softly, one tear escaping down his cheek and leaving a line of glistening moisture. Max's chest twisted. He didn't want *that* kind of tears.

"You remember what I told you about the bed, right?" asked Niki. "It's something that you need to earn, just like being called 'baby'. You're doing very well for me today, and you are being so good. I'm sure it won't take long."

Copley let out a small huff, but his lip stopped trembling. When he blinked his eyes open, they were focused, a new goal obviously in mind. He turned to Max, licking his lower lip. "You haven't said anything about *your* punishment, Maxim. Are you going to spank me?"

He seemed to perk up at the idea, which made Max purse his lips. Nikita was right. As much as that pained him, spanking wasn't a punishment if Copley liked it so much. He didn't want to hurt his boy, though, and a belt seemed a little harsh, even for him.

Maybe that's because I've strangled people with belts before? The last thing he needed were flashbacks.

Besides, when he spanked Copley and fucked him, it always morphed into some of the most intense sex of his life. He didn't want to relate anything negative to that and risk turning Copley off.

"No sex," he blurted out after the two gave him expectant looks. *Real imaginative, dumbass.* "I mean, Copley, no sex until either Niki or I say so. We can come all we want, but your cock and ass are off-limits until you earn privileges back."

Niki's grin was downright feral while Copley looked like he'd swallowed a bug. *That's more like it.* His one-track mind had finally done something right.

"This is going to be so much fun." Max snickered as Copley shot him a glare. Thinking about getting himself off—loudly—with Copley listening in from the scratchy floor had him hard already. He was good at edging himself, and he could last all night if he needed to.

"You're mean." Copley pouted, shifting on the pillow. His tears were dried, though, and there was a small smile on his lips. *Thank fuck.*

"Tell me something I don't know." Max picked himself off the couch, running his hand through his hair to brush it. "Anyway, I'm out. Nestor has some shit he needs me to do. I'll be back late tonight. He wanted to speak with you, too, Nikita, when you got back. Let me know if you want me to come with."

Niki shook his head, his expression immediately serious.

He could guess what was in his brother's thoughts. Having Copley with them, when Nestor barely tolerated their sexuality, was pushing a line that best stayed unpushed.

The thing was, Max had been trampling those lines since he'd been born, and he wasn't about to stop anytime soon. If Niki only knew his reputation on the street of being a badass motherfucker with a heart... There wasn't a single soul who didn't fear him and who wouldn't stand on his side.

"Call me if you need me," he said, smiling at Copley, who had rushed to pick up his coffee cup and take it to the sink. He could get used to being treated like a prince, just as long as he used every opportunity to show Copley the same thing. "That's one point in your favor, baby."

The grin that Copley gave him warmed him all the way to his toes.

Forgoing a coat, as he always did, he pushed the front door open, shuddering as a few snowflakes swirled his way. The pumpkins on the porch were looking sadder by the day but had lasted longer than the carved lanterns at their neighbor's.

Still, he didn't wear a coat...ever. They were too bulky, and they slowed him down if he ever had to defend himself. The last thing he needed was a puffer jacket getting him shot. He'd never live down Niki's glare.

He jumped in the car, then backed out of the driveway, keeping an eye out for the neighbor's kid. She was only three and always pointed to his tattoos, asking about his drawings when they were on display. It cracked him up something fierce, but her mother never seemed overly impressed.

Drumming his hand on the steering wheel, he headed to a part of town that he never thought he would willingly go back to. He cranked the music, trying to get lost in the beat as his stomach clenched.

It's just a club. Nothing to be afraid of. It wasn't the club so much that he was afraid of...it was what his brother would do to him if he found out. His shit for Nestor could wait.

He pulled up to the curb a short time later, shutting his car off and spying a couple that was moving down the sidewalk toward the unmarked door. As easy as it would be to slip in with them, he didn't actually want to cause any trouble. It was just shortly after noon, so he didn't think there would be many people there, but still. *Don't make a scene.*

He leaned against the wall next to the door instead, wishing he had a pack of smokes so he could at least pass the time with something. Crossing his arms, he suppressed his shivers, trying to look like he was just a bouncer who was supposed to be there. From the strange looks he got from a few people, he didn't succeed.

"What are you doing here?"

Max looked up, following the sound to find the little spitfire bartender who had called him out. He looked over his shoulder, a touch worried that Derreck would be at his back. That was a man he had no desire to piss off. No one would ever find his body.

"Clint said he talked to you."

It took Max a moment to realize that Maddy must've been confusing him with his brother. He pulled his hood down, pointing to the tiger tattoo on his neck that was different than his brother's. He should've just worn a T-shirt.

"Oh." Maddy's snarl fell but he took a step back. Probably a safe bet.

"Can you get me in here?" asked Max, resisting the urge to flirt. "I need to talk to Clint." He held his hands out when Maddy glared at him. "I'm not going to cause any trouble. If I was, I would've just broken in the back. You know that lock is loose, right? If you wiggle the handle, it pops right open."

Maddy gave him a strange look before he nodded, tapping a card next to the door. It unlocked with a beep and a clunk, and he pulled it wide. Pausing in the doorway, he pointed at Maxim's chest. "If you do cause trouble, I'm gonna mace you, just so you know."

Max nodded, holding back his laugh as Maddy patted his pocket where he presumably kept his pepper spray. Max couldn't remember the last time someone so cute had threatened him, but honestly, it was adorable. If Maddy ever wanted to give up working at the bar, Max would be on board to have him as a sidekick. *Derreck would kill me, though.*

Clint wasn't hard to find. He was standing behind the bar as they entered but marched toward them as soon as he caught sight of them. Grabbing Maxim's arm, he dragged him off to the side, his grip like fucking iron.

Max pulled his arm away, letting out a low snarl before he turned on Clint with a low voice. "I don't know if my brother is into all of that touchy-feely shit, but don't fucking touch me."

Clint's eyes went wide, and he dropped his hand, looking pained. "Sorry... I shouldn't have touched you, but what the fuck are you doing here? I told you to call me if you needed something. You can't come back here."

Max rubbed the back of his neck, letting out a sigh. *It's going to be a long day.* He tapped his tattoo, but Clint just looked baffled. "I'm Maxim, Nikita's brother. We met before."

It took Clint a second before he blinked and nodded, a flush rising to his cheeks. "Yeah, sorry, man, I keep forgetting Nikita has an identical twin. Is he holding up okay? I still feel terrible about the situation, but with his record, I could lose my license."

"Yeah." Max let out a breath. He was shit dealing with delicate situations. Give him someone to interrogate and he could pull out every finger and toenail, but hugs practically gave him hives. "Nikita told me he knew you before the club and before prison. He used to talk about you when he came back from being patched up — the cute little nurse with arms like a god."

Clint chuckled, rubbing the back of his neck. "Yeah, that was me, I guess. I used to be in better shape, but not much time to bench press behind the bar." He flexed his biceps, which were still rather impressive, if Max had anything to say about it.

"He's a good guy, my brother. He's been doing his best to get out of the game, too. Now that he has a nice sub to settle down with, that might just happen. Me on the other hand?" Maxim shrugged. "I live for that shit."

"Okay," said Clint, looking a tad confused. "So you came here to plead your brother's case?"

"Nope." Max shook his head slowly. There were more people than he expected inside, the booths almost full and two people at the bar. The lights were dim, soft music filtering through the speakers. "I'm here to tell you that he's innocent."

"Look… I know this is hard on him and probably you, too, but he went to court, so there had to be proof —"

"I killed the fucker, not him. That proof enough for you?" Max kept his voice low, even though he wanted to scream. "He turned himself in when the cops came to pick me up, and of course they believed the eyewitness who said that they saw *him*. Funny thing is, he's never killed anyone in his life. He doesn't have the heart for it."

"But you do," said Clint, his voice grim. "Don't take this the wrong way, but I'm going to have to ask you to leave. I don't want things to get out of hand." He looked back to the bar, probably giving some signal to Maddy who had moved to take over drink orders.

"Shit, well, I had to try." Max shrugged, holding out his hand. Clint looked shocked but accepted it regardless. "Just do me a favor and think about it, will ya? I've already fucked up my brother's life too much, and I don't want to take this away from him, too. Thanks for your time."

He kept his rage tightly wrapped until he was out of the door then slammed his fist into the brick and watched the blood bloom on his knuckles, painting the brick and dripping down his wrist. He'd need bandages that would match his brother's.

After pulling his phone from his pocket, he dialed Nikita, putting the phone to his ear. His brother answered on the second ring.

"You talk to Nestor yet?"

Nikita grunted in reply, which was his usual no response.

"Then give our baby a kiss and get your ass over to Highbury. We've got a debt to collect."

Chapter Nineteen

Nikita

Pulling in front of Copley's apartment that he'd shared with his brother, Nikita put the car into park, letting it idle as he stared out of the window. It was slightly cooler than the last time he'd scoped the place out, but somehow it was a hundred times worse.

Money was the bane of his existence. Surprisingly enough, Maxim was the one who paid the bills, even if he left it to the last minute, then grumbled when it didn't go through on time. He would vacuum every day for the rest of his life if it kept him away from the Mastercard statements.

He scowled at Maxim as he knocked on the window, his hood pulled up against the wind. His face was already flushed, and he looked ready to go as he bounced from foot to foot. Something shimmered on his knuckles, catching the light.

Niki looked away, flicking on the radio and popping the locks. He shook his head as Max knocked again, sending Niki a pointed thumb over his shoulder toward the building. Niki stayed rooted to his chair, flicking on the seat warmers since the furnace didn't seem to be doing much to help the guilt that was freezing him from the inside.

Maxim circled the car, yanking the passenger door open and sliding inside. Slamming the door behind him, he turned the radio and heat all the way down, plunging the car into silence. Niki shivered in the cold.

"You want me to go solo? I'm sure the kid can't hit that hard, even from what I've heard about him," said Max, peering back toward the building. One of the other tenants emerged, their hair astray and a beer bottle clutched in their hand. They tossed the bottle toward the street, wobbling once before they keeled over. The bottle shattered as it struck the sidewalk, glass spewing out into the street.

"He can't come back here," said Niki, staring at the drunk as they rolled over, their arms and legs flailing as they fought something Niki couldn't see. They must've been fucked on something more than just booze.

"No shit, brother," said Maxim. "He's like a beacon in this place. I can't believe he wasn't mugged or propositioned on a daily basis. I mean, I can see three whores and one drug dealer from here, not to mention whatever the fuck is going on over there." He pointed to the drunk who had started puking on the sidewalk.

"The only reason he was safe was because of his brother," said Niki, closing his eyes before rubbing his temples. The heated seats weren't helping. If anything, they were making his nausea worse.

"I told you I can go solo," said Maxim, crossing his arms and giving Niki a flash of his brass knuckles. They were silver, each knuckle carved with Cyrillic lettering.

"I don't want you to go at all....either of us. I can't do that to Copley." His stomach flopped again, and he brought his hand to his mouth, biting his knuckles.

Maxim gave him a long look. "You really like this guy, don't you?" It wasn't a question worth answering. "Then we have to take care of his brother, so Nestor doesn't come down on both of them. You know how he is and what he can do."

Niki nodded. He'd been there. Sometimes he wished he'd known that before he'd wrapped himself tight in the Bratva lifestyle.

"Then what the fuck are we waiting for? We can have a pity party later, and I'll even buy the drinks. Let's go."

"Can't," said Niki, burying his hand in his hair. "I can't go in there then go back home to Copley and pretend like everything is fine. I can't be that monster anymore." That was what everyone had always called Niki—one of the Twin Tigers, more a monster than a man.

"I hate to break it to you, but you've never been a monster, Nik. That's more my style." Maxim gave him a soft smile before patting him on the knee. "I'll take care of it, and you buy the beer." He reached for the door.

"Don't." Niki grabbed his arm, pulling him back into his seat. "We have that money saved up..." He trailed off, leaving the rest unsaid. They had a cushion for rainy days and retirement which Max had painstakingly set aside with each job.

"Fuck no." Max reared back as if he'd been slapped. "We've been saving that up since we graduated. I'm not giving it to some bum with a gambling problem."

"Then give it to Copley." He looked out to the street at the drunk who was probably going to freeze to death if somebody didn't drag their ass back inside. "Give Nestor the money and call the debt paid. It will mean Copley's safe, and we'll ask him to stay with us to keep him out of this place." He looked back to his brother. "We need to do this."

Maxim was silent for a few minutes, scratching at a hole that was starting in his jeans. The blue fabric was frayed and scraped raw in places and couldn't have done much to keep the cold at bay.

"Fine. But I have conditions." Max finally broke the silence, pushing out of the car door before Niki could say anything.

Niki clambered after him, tugging his coat tight as the wind swept through him. The guilt had started to recede, but it hadn't been replaced by warmth yet. When their retirement finally came, he was going to convince Max to settle down south where he'd never have to face snow again.

Max lifted the drunk before Niki could reach him, dragging him into the building before tossing him into the hall. The front door didn't shut, but it was warmer in the building at least. He wouldn't wish the place on his worst enemies.

Something flashed at the edge of his vision and Niki scrambled to duck a second before Sauble's fist slammed into the side of Maxim's face. Maxim stumbled back, cursing as he grabbed his cheek and crumpled against the crumbling wall.

Heart pounding, Niki lunged as Sauble pulled his arm back for a second blow. He'd underestimated someone before, and it had almost cost him his life. He struck Sauble hard enough to throw them both off-balance, sending them into the opposite wall. The drywall buckled, leaving a dent that crumbled as they twisted.

Grunting, Niki wrapped his arm around Sauble's neck, jerking to the side and cutting off his air. Sauble dug at his arm, choking and gasping as Niki used every bit of strength to lift him off the ground. There was only a couple of inches of height difference between them, but he was determined to use every one.

Maxim wiped the blood from his lip, spitting on the carpet before securing his brass knuckles from where they had slipped. His eyes were glowing, his hood down and the tiger on his neck ready for the kill.

"Don't." Niki jerked Sauble to the side, loosening his grip when his face started to turn purple.

"Get the fuck off me, you bastard," Sauble hissed between choking breaths, twisting as he tried to break Niki's grip. He kicked out, nicking Maxim's shin before he could sidestep the blow. Maxim let out a snort, his nostrils wide as he eyed up his prey. Niki had seen that look enough times to know that someone was about to end up dead.

"Calm down or I'll break your fucking neck," said Niki, his voice barely above a growl. It was the same voice that kept terrified subs away from him but had caught Copley and reeled him in.

Sauble went still, his chest heaving as he fought to catch his breath. He was ready, with every muscle tense under Niki's arm. "I saw you bastards out there. I knew you were coming to get me to prove a point or whatever. I don't have your fucking money, and you'll never get it."

Maxim laughed, blood dripping down his chin. The drunk at the end of the hall stirred, gagging and rolling once before falling back into a stupor.

"Maybe we were just checking in. Your brother is worried about you," said Niki, keeping his voice deceptively soft. He could see Sauble's confusion and feel it as he went slack.

"Leave my brother out of this. He's got nothing to do with it." Sauble grabbed at Niki's arm with frantic movements. He was no match as Niki clamped down a second time, cutting off his struggling breaths.

"Nestor doesn't see it that way. You don't give him his money, and he will take out your family first. He likes to teach people a lesson before he kills them," said Maxim, leaning against the opposite wall.

Niki's stomach sank as he met Maxim's gaze over Sauble's shoulder. It hurt how true that was. Maxim had been protecting him from it his entire life, taking care of the dirty work so Niki could keep his hands clean.

Niki released him, pushing Sauble into the opposite wall. His head cracked against the busted drywall, but Sauble never even went to his knees. He was persistent. Niki would give him that.

"You guys would know." Sauble's voice was strained as he touched his neck. "Fucking murderers. Copley's in way over his head if he thinks he has you two tamed."

Niki cracked his knuckles, holding Max back with a single arm across his chest. "We're only here because of him."

Somehow Sauble managed to gather up the strength to lunge, diving straight at Max. Maxim closed the distance first, pushing Niki's arm aside and slamming his fist into Sauble's face once. Blood burst over Sauble's eye as the skin split from the force of the brass knuckles. Sauble dropped to his knees, cradling the side of his face.

"What did you do to him?" asked Sauble, the edge of a sob in his voice as blood poured through his fingers.

"Nothing he didn't want," said Maxim, a smirk taking over his features as he knelt next to his downed prey. He looked away from Niki's glare. "He's at our place, which is a hell of a lot safer than here." He motioned to the drunk, who had an impressive pool of vomit next to him.

"This is how I see it." Maxim turned, pacing toward the drunk before flipping them onto their front just in case they vomited again. "*We* take care of your debt, and *you* let us take care of Copley. He stays with us as long as he wants, and you get clean." He leveled Sauble with a heavy look. "Gambling is just like any drug. You're always seeking another hit, even though you'll never feel as high as that first time. Disappoint Copley, and you'll have the two of us to worry about. Got it?"

Sauble nodded slowly, rubbing his neck as the redness of his face started to fade. His eyes were pinched, the bleeding starting to slow. His shirt was ruined, though, along with most of the carpet.

"If you hurt Copley, you'll have the entire neighborhood to worry about," said Sauble, clearing his throat as he looked to the drunk. "But for now, help me get this guy to his couch. If you want to talk about falling off the wagon, here's your guy."

Sauble stooped down and Niki followed, grabbing the drunk by the opposite arm so they could half-drag him along the hall to his apartment. They tossed him onto the couch as Maxim paced the apartment, grabbing a five-dollar bill from the table.

"Service fee," said Max, tucking the bill in his pocket. Niki rolled his eyes before swallowing his protest. He would never understand some of the things his brother did.

"You know he's on welfare, right?" asked Sauble, shooting Maxim a glare. "That five bucks could mean the difference between him eating and not."

"Or drinking and not." Maxim shrugged, crossing his arms. His brass knuckles had disappeared, but his hand was still tinted with blood. "I'm doing the guy a favor."

"You want to take that chance?" Sauble squared his shoulders, sending a bloody glare at Max.

Niki rubbed the base of his nose, trying to suppress his growing migraine. Some of it eased as Maxim tossed the bill back on the table with a grumble before he stormed out of the apartment. Niki tagged behind him, hanging back at the door.

"Take care of my brother," said Sauble, his face drawn as he looked at the filth strewn about on the floor. There were full garbage bags, flies circling their openings, along with enough empty bottles to fund a liquor store. The fridge door hung open in the kitchen, a green goo slicking across the filthy laminate.

Niki shook his head before touching the tattoo on his neck. He remembered getting it and what it had meant to him at that time. But his past was far behind him, along with every ounce of aggression he'd ever had in his bones.

"Copley is something special," said Niki as he turned away. "I'll treasure him for as long as I can."

Chapter Twenty

Copley

The floor was spotless and scrubbed, the dampness of the carpet cleaner just starting to fade. The last round of water had come out nearly clear, as opposed to the black sludge from the first. Cleaning had never really been his thing, but cleaning *for* someone had a whole different meaning to it.

He'd pushed past his exhaustion from so little sleep the night before, scrubbing everything in sight in the hope that Niki would reward him in the end. *You're forgiven.* That was all he needed to hear, over and over until he could believe it. Cleaning kept his mind utterly empty as he pulled the dishes from the cupboard, scrubbing them spotless before putting everything back.

It was something that he had never considered doing for Spencer, but for Niki it felt *good*. He wished Max was there to dirty it up, just so he could clean it again…maybe on his knees and naked so Max would have something to watch.

Tossing a pillow to the ground, he let out a sigh as he sat on the couch. Luckily, he had the day off, because there was no way he was in any shape for anything that related to numbers. He also needed a nap, but at the same time, he wanted to surprise Niki and Max when they got home.

He twined the ribbon between his fingers, eyeing the crinkles and little tears that had started to form. Unwound, it was long enough to wrap around his wrist, but he had no way of tying it. He wished it was longer — long enough to wrap around his throat.

His phone chimed and he scrambled to grab it, smiling as soon as he read Niki's text.

Be home soon.

He tossed the phone back onto the couch, stripping off his shirt before he lost his courage. His palms were slick as he fumbled with the button on his jeans, yanking them down along with his boxers. Tossing both in the laundry, he scrambled back into the living room, arranging the pillow before kneeling on it.

The clock ticked beside him, each second stretching out. *I should have picked some music.* He shifted on the pillow, glancing at the radio. He didn't dare move. He had no idea how long *soon* was, and he didn't want to be caught in the middle of the room and not on his pillow.

Do I have to pee? Every sensation in his body was heightened as he closed his eyes and took a deep breath. His belly tensed with anticipation and worry as he gnawed his lip almost to the point of drawing blood. *No. Maybe I should go anyway?*

Glancing at the clock, he let out a huff. It had only been three minutes since Niki's text. *Wait... Should I have made dinner?* It was getting close to the time he would usually eat, but he hadn't been prepared. He wasn't even sure what his Dom's favorite food was.

A scratching click that didn't quite sound like a key caught his attention. *That was fast. Thank God.* He held his breath as the front door opened with a creak before someone's shoes squeaked on the front tile. A few shuffled steps and he closed his eyes, clasping his knees and holding tight.

I can't do this. He bit his lip, forcing himself to stay put. His hands were shaking, his heart beating fast as something thumped and the footsteps came closer, joined by a second set that were nearly identical.

He fought to keep his breathing steady, face flaming and cock hard as he waited. One pair of socked feet headed for the kitchen, the light turning on and off once, while the other pair headed to the bathroom. Copley watched them, the tightness in his chest slowly easing with each passing moment.

Being called out or praised for his position was probably the last thing he wanted at the moment. *Probably*—because he had no fucking clue. He loved the way his heart raced, but if either of the twins spoke up and asked him where his clothes were, he was going to die.

Someone settled next to him, the couch letting out a soft groan at their weight. He shot a quick glance up, letting out another breath when he saw Niki. A moment later there was the pop of a bottle cap and a hand in his hair. Niki's fingers sank straight to the roots, draining the last of his worries away. He tensed only for a moment when Max joined him, close enough on the couch that Copley could have reached out and touched his toes.

"You want some frozen peas or something?" asked Niki, his voice a soft rumble as he reached for the remote and flicked on the television.

Copley glanced up in confusion, spying the purple and red bruise blooming on Max's face. He gasped, even as Max sent him a wink.

"Nah. It's already starting to feel better." He was so full of shit. Maxim's left eye was swollen almost completely shut, red flesh already turning blue and purple around the edges. The eye itself was bloodshot, matching the ragged corner of his lip.

"Uh-huh." Niki nodded, taking a swig of his beer and letting out a sigh. "Looks great."

Reaching out, Copley touched Maxim's knee, asking without words if he was okay. He hadn't checked the freezer, but there had to be ice packs or something that would make him feel better and at least help with the swelling. Niki didn't seem concerned, though. In fact, he looked completely relaxed, flipping to a sports channel with his bandaged hand before he took another swig of his beer.

Crap. Hockey. Copley could only take a few minutes of hockey before he zoned out, and those were the games he'd watched *live*. The twins seemed to jump right in, pointing at the television and cursing the ref when the whistle blew.

Wrapping his arms around Max's leg, he shifted closer, leaning his head onto it and letting his eyes close as Niki continued his head massage. His nudity melted away, until he was nearly asleep between them, drifting within a peace that he had only felt a few times in his life. Thoughts of his punishments drifted away along with the looming curse of his brother's debt.

He didn't even have to hear them thank him for all his hard work. He knew that they saw it, just from the tone of their voices, and the little way Niki smiled as he caught sight of something that Copley had done. That was more than enough.

"You want Chinese?"

Copley let the question wash over him, an answer so far beyond reach that he could never respond. His stomach grumbled, aching from his missed dinner. He couldn't even fathom what time it was, but from how stiff he was, it had to have been late. The hockey game had changed to another team with different colored shirts and a ref that seemed to blow the whistle every few seconds. The players looked the same beneath their helmets.

"Copley?" Max touched his shoulder, but Copley only grunted, kissing Max's knee before snuggling closer. Wherever he was drifting, he wanted it to last forever.

"He's in subspace," said Niki, his hand going still for a moment. "He probably won't be able to answer you. Get something easy to eat and you can hand feed him if you like. I've already asked him about allergies, and he doesn't have any."

"I don't want to leave him like this," said Max, touching Copley's chin. Copley blinked, smiling before wrapping his arms around Max's thigh. The change of angle made his back scream before it settled beneath a wave of something that flowed like molasses beneath his skin.

"Call the order in, and I'll take care of it when they get here." Niki shifted in his seat, and when Copley turned his head, he saw that his pants were tented. Max's were, too, only it was harder to tell as he had adjusted himself already.

His hand twitched with the desire to reach for one of both of them and take care of them in the way he longed to, until he remembered Max's punishment. 'No sex' was going to be harder than he thought, especially with his own cock somehow rock hard and aching.

It was more restful than dreaming, but when the couch shifted and something warm touched his lips, he jolted in surprise. His heart was slow as he blinked his eyes open, staring at Maxim.

"Shhh, baby, just a bit of food. Eat for me. That's it."

He slowly closed his lips over Max's fingers, snatching his teeth along the morsel while being careful not to scrape too hard. He had no desire to tease or play when everything felt so fucking good. Even the chicken ball in his mouth tasted better than anything he'd ever eaten. Returning to Max's fingers, he licked them clean, getting every last drop of sauce.

"You like that, baby?" asked Max, holding out a second piece before he had swallowed the first.

"Go slow," said Niki, grabbing a plate of his own and balancing it in his lap. "If he gets deep enough, you'll have to remind him to chew and swallow and even breathe sometimes."

Copley smiled, stroking Niki's leg before he drew his hand back, unsure if it was okay. Did he even deserve to or was he still being punished?

"You can touch me, Copley, but remember Max's rule."

Copley. So he still wasn't completely forgiven, but it was a start. Somehow, it didn't even squash his buzz. If anything, he sank deeper as he slid his hand under Niki's pant leg to touch his calf. Coarse hair tickled his fingertips, too sparse for him to get a good grip.

"Open, baby."

At Max's words, he realized that there was something new pressed to his lips and he had no idea how long it had been there. It took a huge effort to open his mouth for it, and even more to slowly chew. He hummed at the taste of beef and ginger mingled with the saltiness of soy sauce and probably enough MSG to kill a cow.

Giggling, he swallowed it down, licking his lips to find more of the taste. Max was back with more as soon as the bite was gone, but this time Copley sucked his fingers into his mouth as well, swirling his tongue around them.

Max chuckled, pulling his hand back. "Nice try, but I'm not in any shape for that right now, no matter how good you were today."

Copley glanced up, frowning at the swelling that had spread over Max's eye. From the puffiness alone, it looked like something was broken, and his lip looked to be bleeding again. Some of the fog drifted away to worry and he reached to touch the split seam.

"What happened?" He touched Max's lip, prodding gently and blinking when his fingertip came away red. Somehow, he'd imagined the twins to be invincible, and seeing the blood was almost unreal.

"You should see the other guy," said Max with a smirk that split his lip wide open. Niki turned a glare on him, but Max seemed unaffected. "Your brother has a mean left hook on him. I should have known. He looks like he spends most of his week in the gym."

Cold air stroked his skin as Copley flinched, blinking rapidly as the fog faded fast. His heart picked up, his stomach twisting as the ginger became overwhelming. "M-my brother?"

The debt. Is it the end of the month? He had to get to a calendar. He had to know. He scrambled to try to get his feet under him but his legs had gone completely numb.

"Copley, it's okay. Just relax." Niki touched his chin, giving him a soft smile. "We went to let your brother know that his debt is taken care of, but he didn't like the idea of you staying here with us. We had a…difference of opinion."

"That's one way of putting it," said Max, stroking Copley's lip with a sigh. "He's a nice guy, but a bit of a dick. He didn't like the idea of getting any favors from a couple of Russian *pricks* like us." He smiled, but it didn't reach his eyes.

Copley grabbed Max's hand, ignoring the sauce that slicked his fingers. "You are not a *prick*." He hissed out the word, hating how it tasted in his mouth. There were a few words in the world that he hated to use, and that was one of them.

"But I am Russian," said Max with a chuckle. "Just because I was born here and I've lost most of my accent doesn't mean I can hide my roots."

Copley shook his head as panic started to fade. *How do I put this?* "Your accent is one of the sexiest things I've ever heard. When you get upset or angry, it gets thick, and well, *fuck*." He shuddered. "Especially if Nikita growls at me. Our first scene at the club? The sound of your voice will be with me forever."

Niki dragged him from the floor, pulling their lips together briefly before placing his hands on Copley's hips. Copley let out a sigh, sinking into the warmth and bliss as he curled under Niki's chin. He fit perfectly.

"How are you feeling about today...about our dynamic?" Niki kissed his cheek and Copley nuzzled into his neck. There was a bit of growth there that scraped against his skin, pushing him under the veil again. "Did you like the chores, or did you want to explore something else instead?"

Copley leaned back with a frown, digging his fingers into Niki's shoulders. "I don't know. I didn't hate it, and it was actually pretty calming, but it made me really tired. I wouldn't want to do it every day."

"Good. Can I touch you?" Niki reached up, but let Copley close the distance until his cheek rested against his palm. "Tell me what you liked about it."

"It was relaxing. It gave me time to think about things, but at the same time, there was no rush to get anything done. I just wanted to make you happy."

Niki's grin was infectious. "You made me a very happy man and happy Dom today. I don't think this place has ever looked so clean. But my thoughts were a reward system based on chores. Let's say you did the dishes or went out of your way to tidy something, you could earn points toward certain things that you like. What do you think?"

Copley chewed his lip. "What kind of things? Like, I don't want an allowance or anything like that. It just doesn't feel right."

"Back rubs, foot rubs, a night where you pick the television channels, or, if you are really good, an all-access pass to touch whatever you want."

Copley glanced to Maxim, watching him roll his eyes before he smiled. "I would like that, but I honestly thought my stay here was temporary. I've already made a few calls, and I have a showing tomorrow at a place close to my work. It's in my price range."

Copley swallowed at the twin glares shot his way. He hadn't *wanted* to look for other places, but it felt wrong staying in a house where he'd just shown up. They'd never talked about him leaving, but they'd never talked about him staying, either.

"You're staying," said Max, his voice the low growl that Copley craved. "I don't care if it's too fast or whatever, but I don't want you away from us."

"What he means to say," said Niki, shooting his brother a glare, "is that we would like you to live with us. You could be our sub full-time, or we could discuss setting certain times aside for play and others where we go vanilla for a bit. I've always dreamed of having a full-time relationship, but I need to know if you're ready for it or not. If it's too much or too soon, we can always wait."

Copley stared at the rise of Niki's collar. It looked like it had been broken before and was just a touch out of shape, but it was almost impossible to tell beneath the inked skin that peeked above his shirt. *Do I have to decide?*

"Whatever works for you guys." His tongue was leaden as he spoke, uncertainty building in his gut. He loved submitting *now*, but he couldn't be sure about his future. The only thing that was certain was that he wanted them, even if that meant going out of his comfort zone.

That wasn't a new concept for him. Everything had been out of his comfort zone with Spencer at first, until he'd given in and expanded his horizons, sometimes drunkenly. A few times he'd decided never to try things again, but Spencer had slowly worn him down. Most days he'd just wanted to snuggle after sex, whereas Spencer had wanted a second or third round right away. Spencer had never understood how sore Copley would be.

"That's not how this works, Copley," said Niki, touching his chin in the comforting way that he always seemed to do when Copley was uncertain. "This is a relationship, one that is built on more trust than most. I may be your Dom, but you have the final say in what we do and when we stop. You are our first and second priority, and if you're uncomfortable, it's your responsibility to let us know. We need to be able to trust that you'll tell us."

He swallowed as that sank in, almost feeling worse for it. His brother yelling at him hadn't made him feel as guilty as Niki managed to.

"I want to stay," he whispered, peeking at Max out of the corner of his eye. He was easier to make eye contact with than Niki. "But I don't want to sleep alone again. I'd rather have my own apartment than sleep on your floor again."

"Thank you for telling me," said Niki, stroking his back. "You're a good boy — *our* good boy. Max has his punishment for you, and if you do well, then you can sleep in his bed tonight, okay? Remember that you can always safeword if you need to."

Another punishment? He'd honestly forgotten that things weren't over with yet. But he had disrespected them both, and even though Niki had seemed to forgive him, Max was always a bit more of a mystery.

"I can do no sex. That's fine. I just want to sleep with you—*sleep*, sleep. I'll keep my hands to myself." He looked down at the ribbon that was still clasped in his fingertips. It was almost broken beyond repair. "Can I have a new ribbon that I can tie on my wrist? I kept wishing it was there today, but I couldn't tie it myself and now it's all frayed."

"You want my collar, baby?" asked Max, shooting him a smirk. "I'll make you a deal. If you can make it through my punishment, then I'll let you come *and* I'll get you a bracelet that will be a lot nicer than a cheap ribbon."

Copley flushed at the idea, imagining wearing something that Max or Niki bought him. It was a different feeling than the bland taste of an allowance as a reward. "I want to wear something that shows everyone that I belong to both of you. How many times do I have to clean the house to earn that?"

Niki chuckled, kissing Copley's forehead. "They already know you belong to us, and if anybody doubts it, it's their funeral."

Chapter Twenty-One

Copley

He had underestimated Maxim…again. When Niki had rolled into bed, grabbing earplugs as he went, Copley had actually been brimming with excitement, and on edge with anticipation with every smirk Maxim sent his way. But he'd forgotten a key point.

Maxim was *evil*.

He wasn't just the 'trip you when you're down' kind of evil, but the 'convince you to trip yourself' kind.

Max had tucked Copley into his bed, pulling the sheets around him tight before grabbing the lube, condoms and a few toys. He'd set them on the bed stand before slipping in next to Copley, settling beneath the warm sheets with a sigh. Even the sight of the lube had Copley's cock hard, his strange calm from before all but gone.

If lube and toys were a punishment, then he was down for it.

Niki snored softly as he turned away from the lamplight, his arm coming up to cover his eyes. He'd fallen almost straight to sleep as Maxim prepared the stage, giving Copley a quick kiss before he'd retreated to his bed alone.

The bed was small, leaving maybe two inches between himself and Maxim. It felt like fifty and none at the same time. It was hot beneath the covers, warmer than he'd felt all day and all the night before. Every time Maxim shifted, it moved them closer for just a moment before they drifted apart, lighting up his nerves from the almost-touch.

It was killing him, and they hadn't even begun.

"No touching, baby. Did you want me to tie your hands, or can you do it?" Max reached for a belt that he'd left on the side stand. "Nikita gave me this beauty. You can wear it as a belt, but it converts easily to restrain someone. This is going to come in so handy."

Copley gulped, eyeing up the belt. It was thinner than usual and looked like it had two buckles instead of one. It didn't look like it would hurt, but he also wasn't sure if he wanted to find out.

"I don't know," said Copley. "Can I try just hanging onto a pillow instead? That should keep me from reaching out."

Max shook his head as he pulled the blankets back. Copley was still naked, where Max was fully clothed and in his hoodie. The bulky thing gave nothing away, but at least it wasn't the blood-soaked one Copley had found in the laundry. Max's swelling had started to look a bit better after he'd taken some medication, but it would leave one hell of a bruise.

"I need your hands free, and I need to be able to see every inch of you. Restraints or no restraints, baby? You need to make the choice."

I hate making choices. Copley pouted, staring at the scratchy carpet. He wanted Max and Niki to make the choice for him. Was that so terrible?

"I don't want to." He scowled, even as Maxim gave him a long look.

"You know what I want?" asked Max, a hint of frustration in his voice. "I want us both to have fun. I'm not a fucking mind reader, and I don't have Niki's experience. I won't know if you're uncomfortable unless you tell me, and I don't know the things you like. Answer the question or sleep on the floor. It's as easy as that."

"I'm sorry." He took a shuddering breath. One day, he was going to go a whole hour without fucking up. *One day.*

"Don't be sorry. I'm not upset. I just need you to see this from my angle." Max set the belt back on the stand, pulling at the edge of his shirt and tugging it over his head.

"No restraints. I want to be able to move, even if I can't touch." Copley stared at the tattoos stretched before him. He'd never taken the time to simply look. Max paused as he noticed his gaze, giving him all the time he needed. He even turned a bit so Copley could see the edge of the tattooed knife sneaking around his ribcage.

"Good. No more talking unless it's your safeword. If I need you to answer, I'll say 'yellow'." Max grabbed his pants, pulling them free with a tug before sending them flying into the pile beside the bed. It was the one place that Copley hadn't tidied. The mess seemed almost ritualistic.

Max was already on his way to hard, quickly firming up as Copley stared. Uncut and glorious, his cock was just another thing that Copley wished he had more time to simply stare at.

Taking himself in hand, Max stroked from base to tip twice before he grabbed the lube, pouring it over his cock until he glistened, and his hand made slick noises. He leaned back against the pillows, spreading his legs wide to the room. "Get down to the end of the bed and keep your eyes open. I want you to watch."

Copley scrambled to the edge on his hands and knees without looking away. He didn't want to miss a single moan or gasp that was filling the air as Max slowly worked himself over.

Watching someone jerk themselves had never been Copley's favorite thing in the world. A dick was just a dick, even when it glistened. At least, that was what he had thought. Obviously, he had been looking at the wrong dicks.

He licked his lips, tracing over every vein and ridge. He longed to feel Max inside him again, splitting him wide and making him take it. Or he could take it in his throat — so far that he choked and cried, begging for air while he jammed it ever deeper.

His cock throbbed, his balls aching from the strain of holding himself back. His hands wandered at their own will, one on his belly and one reaching for his nipple.

"Did I say you could touch yourself?" Max's growl cut through him and he froze in place, moments away from touching his nipple. "That's one strike already and we're just beginning. Did you want your punishment now or did you want to wait for the end?"

"Now." He just wanted to be touched, loved and held until all his worries were gone. He wanted to earn that privilege and be the best sub he could be.

"That's two strikes. Did I say you could talk?" The smirk that stretched over Maxim's lips was criminal. "Turn around, little brat, and spread your cheeks. I'll give you something to talk about."

You fucking tricked me. Copley glowered over his shoulder as he turned, grabbing his ass and spreading wide. The exposure didn't even bother him, even as Max moved close enough to touch. A breath graced his lower back and he arched, seeking the feeling.

"Another thing this belt is good for is putting naughty brats in their places."

A smack directly over his hole had Copley crying out and nearly jumping off the bed. It hadn't been hard at all, but he hadn't been expecting it in such a tender and intimate place. Shooting off the bed, he rounded on Max, glaring at the belt still dangling in his grasp.

"You hit my asshole! What the hell?" Copley huffed, grabbing his ass and hissing at the sting. That was going to smart for a long time in such a sensitive place, but Max looked elated. *Sadistic bastard.*

"Oh, three strikes so soon. I thought you were going to be my good boy. I thought you wanted to sleep all snuggled up with your Dom." He wiggled the belt and it practically gleamed in the light. "Get back on the bed, I'll give you two more hits and we can move on and forget that you don't know how to listen."

Humiliation burned through him as Copley climbed back on the bed, willingly presenting his ass for two more strikes. By the first he was aching, and the second made his balls draw up as his body clenched. He grimaced at the sting, reaching around to touch his hole to see if it was swollen.

"Four? What the fuck, baby? You must really feel like a dummy today. Pull yourself wide for me and I'll give you one more taste because you seem to like it so much."

There were tears in his eyes as the belt swung true again, even though the strike was gentler than any of the previous ones. The touch burned through him, making his cock throb and his head swim as he started to feel that familiar drift forming between his body and thoughts. The ragged edge of the humiliation crept away as he realized he was doing it for Maxim.

No one else would ever see him this way. Niki would never ask, and there wasn't another Dom out there that he would willingly kneel for.

"Turn around. Let's get to some good stuff here." Maxim sat back against the headboard as Copley turned around, resting with his ass above his heels. His hole throbbed in time with his heart.

Re-coating his hand with lube, Max reached for his cock, working himself over until pre-cum was dripping from the head. He was so much harder than he'd been the few minutes before, engorged from Copley's punishment. The thought had Copley flushing as he curled his toes.

"It's been a long time since I've fucked myself good," said Max, hovering his hand over the few toys he'd chosen. "What do you think? Plug or dildo?"

Copley bit his tongue. *Not falling for that again.* Max's chuckle made his hair stand on end and a few drops of pre-cum ooze from the slit of his cock. He kept his hands fisted at his sides, his nails biting into his palms.

His chest heaved as the air filled with the scent of sex and Maxim.

"Dildo it is." He grabbed the transparent purple toy that was lined with a few realistic-looking veins. It wasn't as huge as some that Copley had seen in adult stores before, but it wasn't exactly small, either.

"I picked this one because it reminded me of your little cock. Too bad I couldn't just find out with the real thing. I bet you'd feel huge inside, baby, and so hot. You'd fuck me real deep and good until I'd forget my own name." Maxim eyed up the purple cock before bringing it to his lips and wrapping his tongue around it.

Now that's just cruel. Copley's cock throbbed, slapping against his belly as he hitched his hips. He hadn't even considered topping Maxim, but if it was an option, he was on board. It had been way too long since he'd plunged into someone's ass.

Spreading his legs wider, Maxim shuffled down, cupping his sac and bringing it to the side so Copley got his first look at his furled hole. It looked tight and so fucking good that his mouth watered.

"Can I taste you?" The words slipped out of his mouth against his will, and he immediately flushed. *Maybe I should ask him for some duct tape so I can shut the fuck up.*

"Baby. That's five. You like when I spank your hole? I can do it more, just say the word."

The dildo looked huge next to his small hole, his cheeks glistening as the lube spread around his crack. Max rubbed it back and forth over his entrance, letting out little moans with every pass. It took everything Copley had to keep still—half of him battling to reach for Max and the other half keeping his hands off his own body.

"I wouldn't just shove it in, Sir. I'd take my time to lick you open and stretch you out with my fingers before I'd take you. I'd never hurt you." Max would be so hot around him, and Copley was sure that he'd taste like sweet darkness, just the way he'd imagined.

"Off the bed, Copley. *Now.*" Max dropped the dildo, wiping his slick hands on the covers. "Put your head on that pillow on the floor and go the fuck to sleep. You're done for tonight. If you aren't going to listen, then you get time out."

Ice plunged into his belly where warmth had been seconds before. He opened and closed his mouth, gripping at the bedsheets as if they would disappear out from under him. *No. Not the floor.*

"I'll be good." He knew when he said it that it was already too late. How many chances had Max given him? Six? Seven? And he hadn't listened to a single one.

Heart sinking, he crept from the bed, dropping to his knees on the scratchy carpet. His pillow was still there and just as uninviting as it had been the night before. He sank down onto it anyway, a numbness settling over him as the warmth slowly dissipated.

"Do you know what you did wrong?" asked Max, swinging his feet over the edge before looking at him. Even though his face was blank, he was more intimidating than ever. "We've passed yellow and went straight to red. The scene is over, Copley, so you can speak."

"I didn't listen. Even when you punished me, I still didn't listen. I'm sorry." He played with the fibers of the carpet, unable to meet Max's gaze.

"Once or twice, I can understand," said Max, letting out a sigh. "But that many times? Was it the scene itself, or did I do something wrong? Talk to me." He ran his hand through his hair and it stuck straight up, thick lube clinging to the strands.

"I-I don't know. I guess I should have asked you to restrain me. I just couldn't keep my mouth shut, and I couldn't stop touching. I didn't mean to be bad." His stomach was tied in knots, his limbs stiff and his hole aching. He was sure that Max hadn't hit him that hard, but somehow it still stung.

"You had a hard day," said Max, "and so did I. Maybe I made a mistake trying to do this tonight after everything. Did you need anything before you sleep? Cream for your ass or a blanket or anything? Are you feeling level?"

Copley had to wonder how much Niki had coached Max before the event and how much trouble Max had gone through to set something up for him. *And I ruined it.*

"I'm upset right now. You went through all that work for me, and I couldn't even listen. I don't know why I just can't listen." Copley slapped the ground, taking his frustration out on the floor. He wasn't dropping, but he was pissed off — more at himself than anything else.

"We'll work on it, but for now, go to sleep, baby. If you need me during the night and I don't answer you when you call verbally, just shake me awake. Anything you need and I'll get it for you." Max flicked the light off, plunging the room into darkness.

Copley let out a breath, settling down on the pillow. It was probably strange that it was a touch more comforting than the night before when he'd been terrified that the twins were going to kick him to the curb.

"Are you going to find a different sub if I keep messing up?" he asked softly, before scratching at the back of his hand. The carpet was terribly itchy, tickling over his skin until it felt like it was crawling.

"You're stuck with us now, baby. I figure that we both have lots to learn, and it's going to take us some time to figure each other out. I'll try my best if you do, too. I know Niki feels the same way." Max let out a sigh before shifting on the bed. "Night, baby."

"Night."

Closing his eyes, he clutched the pillow, waiting for sleep to slowly take him. He was just on the edge of a dream when he heard the click of the bottle cap followed by Max's grunts and the slick sound of flesh sliding on flesh.

"Is it good?" he asked softly, keeping his eyes closed and picturing what he couldn't see. His cock throbbed, leaking onto the carpet as Max's breathing grew harsh and he finally let go with a gasp and a soft growl.

Next time I'll do better. Next time, he would be so good that his Doms couldn't help but fuck him.

Chapter Twenty-Two

Nikita

Niki leaned back in his chair, the wood creaking under his weight. Nestor stared back steadily, a frown on his lips as Niki laid everything out.

"I'll be your bodyguard, but I can't do any more *extra* assignments." Niki looked at the table, moving his palms over the wooden surface. It was polished and smooth, despite the deaths that had been planned over it. "I don't want to risk going back to jail—not now."

No matter what had happened in the past and the person he'd been, that was one thing that he refused to go through again. He'd been so lucky to get off with a measly six years while some of the men beside him had been in for life.

"Now that you've found yourself some fresh ass," Nestor supplied, the look of disgust lingering on his face. "Everybody's talking about it on the street. It's quite the topic of discussion, you know."

Cold settled into Niki's belly, but he pushed the urge to deny the whole thing away. He would *never* deny his sub, not to his homophobic boss or anyone else. If he did that, he didn't deserve Copley.

"He's my submissive and my lover. I'm not sure why that's your concern." He tried to keep his voice even as the rage boiled beneath his skin. Nestor's disgust turned into a sneer.

"When I took you and your brother into my ranks, I knew of your...proclivities, but I made it clear I didn't want to hear about them. I promised I wouldn't say anything against it as long as it was kept private. But now, I'm hearing from a whore that you like men? And not even one of *my* whores? That's something I can't tolerate."

His skin prickled, and he felt the heat of the gazes of every other man in the room. Nestor had called him along with his five other personal guards, but Niki was the only one seated at the desk.

"Whether you tolerate it or not, it's going to happen. I'm not going to hide who I am anymore." He crossed his arms, trying to keep the rest of his posture relaxed. He knew who would move first. Damon would go for his gun, probably aiming for his knee or his balls so the rest would have a turn at beating him.

"I can't believe this behavior. Your brother—"

"Would kill every single one of you if you so much as laid a hand on me or my lover." He hadn't wanted to bring it up or make that threat, because once it was out, there was no going back. Nestor wasn't stupid, but he was proud—proud of his self-made invincible status.

"We could easily eliminate Maxim, just as we could easily eliminate you. You forget how many friends I have in this world. You wouldn't be able to lift a finger before you'd die."

The click of a gun's safety sounded behind him, and every hair raised on the back of his neck. His palms were slippery as sweat dripped down his back, terror ricocheting through him. He kept his face calm and placid.

"So that's it then? All the years protecting you and your business, and it means nothing because you don't agree with my orientation? That's a pretty shitty thing to get killed over," Niki drawled, tapping his fingers impatiently on the desk. Nestor's gaze was drawn to him, and his eyebrow twitched with irritation.

"People have died for less."

"I know. I was there. I was there for almost every deal and every bit of your dirty work before it landed me in jail. Since then, I've protected your ass and saved you on countless occasions. If you had such a problem with me fucking men, then why surround *yourself* with them?" he motioned to the men behind him who had started to shift uncomfortably. Niki had trained every single one of them and knew where each of their weaknesses lay, but he was treading dangerous territory

"These men would put their lives on the line for you — and so would I." He never raised his voice, even when he wanted to scream at the top of his lungs and pummel Nestor to pieces. As far as gang leaders went, Nestor wasn't half bad — and even had his generous moments.

"Get rid of the boy toy, and we will forget this ever happened. I don't ever want to hear about any of it again," said Nestor, giving him a glare of utter finality.

That was no choice. There would be nothing left but empty walls and the sound of his brother's snores.

"No."

Nestor looked like Nikita had slapped him, his face going pale as he glowered. He looked to Damon, giving him a subtle nod. "Then you give me no choice."

Niki's mouth went dry, his stomach twisting as steel touched the back of his head. He wished he could have sent Copley and Max one last goodbye. Max would never forgive him for this. How long would it take him to find out and stain his hands with the men they'd fought so hard to keep in power?

"Hey, boss?" asked Damon, shifting his gun against the back of Niki's skull. It dragged against the bone, leaving a trail of aches and terror. "I feel like this might be the best time to mention that I sucked my boyfriend's cock last night."

Nestor spluttered as a smile lit Niki's face, the weight of death lifting from his shoulders in an instant. He looked to Damon, who gave him a wink before holstering his weapon and stepping back. *How can I ever thank you?*

Damon had been one of the first students that he'd trained, the blood and sweat between them the strongest loyalty. He'd been fresh off the streets with an anger that rivaled Maxim's and a chip on his shoulder that could swallow parliament.

"Fucking disgusting," Nestor spluttered, moving to his feet as his face flushed crimson. "Bunch of freaks, the both of you. Shoot them."

The others looked to each other, none reaching for their weapons as they stared at Nestor. Niki could see their struggle on their faces. What was worth more?

Years of loyalty to their Bratva brothers or to the man they'd been taught to fear and respect.

"Mutinous bastards, all of you!" Nestor screeched, grabbing a gun from the top drawer of his desk before fumbling to point it Niki's way. "I'll kill every one of you." He spat on the desk, gripping the gun tight as he raised it."

Niki was beside him in a second. He grabbed the gun from Nestor's loose grip, flicking the safety on and unloading it in seconds. Bullets trickled to the floor, tinkling as they bounced and rolled away.

"A few tips, boss," said Niki, handing the empty gun back. He slid behind Nestor, moving to correct his stance as he held the weapon. "You'll never hit anyone with a grip like that. You have to load it, too — safety on and cock it, and that will put the bullet in the chamber so when you squeeze the trigger, you'll actually shoot."

He grabbed Nestor's other hand, placing it on the gun. "And two hands, especially if you're shaky. You'll punch yourself in the face with the kickback and maybe knock yourself out with one. This baby is a mule. I know because your father taught me how to shoot with it."

Nestor had gone pale again, his mouth hanging open as he stared at the weapon.

"He was okay with Maxim and me, by the way. Not sure if he ever told you that. Forty years with your mother, and they only slept together to conceive you. Do you want to know who he was fucking in his spare time?" He patted Nestor's shoulder as he moved back.

Nestor *was* a good boss, but he was also a punk-ass kid who rarely remembered that he was fresh out of his teens. His father's death had rushed him to power, leaving the shell of a man where a teenager had been.

"What's it going to be, boss?" Niki crossed his arms, moving to stand with *his* men. He knew he was pushing it and he was probably one step away from being knifed in his sleep. Nestor was right…people had been killed for less.

"You…you." Nestor held out a shaky finger.

"I'm your friend and protector, first and foremost, and I'd take a bullet for you. I won't be the one shooting anymore, though, and neither will Maxim. We're staying out of prison for the rest of our lives, and we're going to live as we see fit."

Nestor slammed his fist on the desk, a pen rolling to the edge before tipping over and falling next to the bullets. "Get out. Niki, you stay, but the rest of you, get *out.*"

After a moment of hesitation, they filed out, Damon giving Niki one last look over his shoulder before he shut the door with a click.

Niki took a deep breath, his heart pounding and every muscle in his body tense. Nestor took a step, somehow intimidating, even though he was four inches shorter and almost fifteen years shy.

"You know who I am and who my family is," said Nestor, pointing to the center of his chest. "I could destroy you and rip your life and family apart with one order. I could kill every man you've ever trained and still have a hundred more at my side. You fucking betrayed me."

Niki swallowed, refusing to give ground.

"If I've betrayed you by falling in love with someone, then yes, I have. I would do the same thing a hundred times if given the chance." Copley had only been in their home for a few days, but he couldn't imagine it without him. But he *did* know what he would do if someone hurt him.

Nestor spat, a bit of spittle touching Niki's shoe as he swore. Niki blinked at it, more amused than he had words for. He'd seen Nestor enraged before, but he'd never seen him fully lose his temper like a toddler.

"I guess I'll go then," said Niki. *Have I done the right thing?* The Bratva had been part of his life since before he was old enough to smoke. "Will I be looking over my shoulder?"

"Nikita." Nestor let out a long sigh before he collapsed in his chair. There were black lines under his eyes and his styled hair had gone flat. He had aged since he'd taken over his father's duties. Three years in the chair and he'd aged thirty. "You're like a brother to me," said Nestor, shaking his head. "When I was a teenager, I idolized you. I wanted to *be* you, but I still can't condone this. I can't understand it. A woman is your other half—the only thing that could ever complete you. What does a man have on that?"

"He's everything," said Niki simply. "If Max and I were one half, then he is the balance. I'm not giving him up—not for anything."

"If it's sex, then I can get you a whore." Nestor waved his hand. "You can have your pick."

Niki took a breath through his nose before letting it out slowly. "Have you ever had someone who you could tell anything? That you could give yourself to completely and trust that they would do the same? That's what he is for me. I have him completely, and he has me. He *knows* me like no one I've ever met, and he challenges me in ways that just make me love him more."

The first hint of a smile touched Nestor's lips as he leaned back, looking at the ceiling. "One of my infamous Twin Tigers is a fucking romantic. No one would believe me."

"Maxim has his moments, too, but you know him," said Niki, his chest ready to burst with joy. He'd expected more of a fight, but perhaps there was more to Nestor than even he was aware of.

"He'd rather fight than fuck most days. I won't keep him out of that lifestyle because he was born for it. If he kills someone again by accident, that's on him." Nestor gave him a wistful look before he turned serious again. "You ever disrespect me or my family again and I'll slit your fucking throat. Got it?"

Niki nodded, his tongue stuck to the roof of his mouth. Things could have gone so much worse. By any rights, he should be on the floor now, broken and bleeding.

"Good. Then I'll see you on Monday."

Niki left the room in a haze, not really breathing until he stepped outside and hit fresh air. The fountain in the middle of the massive complex had been emptied of water as soon as the weather had started to cool. A few leaves stuck to the inner lining, black and broken like the souls of the Bratva—or maybe there was hope after all.

Other than a few sparse trees, there wasn't much for decoration. Trees were a great place for people to hide before they put a bullet in your brain—a message that Niki had finally gotten across with Nestor after a near miss. Maxim had taken care of the assassin, and Niki had chopped down every fucking tree with his goddamn hands and an ax he'd found in a shed out back. After he'd wiped the dried blood off the ax, it had worked great.

Maxim was leaning against his car at the gate, smoking a cigarette with his left hand. His right was settled on his waistband in a way that probably looked casual to anyone who happened to see him. He could have a hand on his gun in under a second, taking aim in half that. Where Niki had come weaponless, Maxim had armed himself to the teeth, glinting silver in at least four places that Niki could spy.

"How'd it go?" asked Max, snubbing out his smoke before tossing it to the ground. His lips were pressed together, his jaw clenched with strain.

"You shouldn't smoke that shit." He shoved past his brother, circling around to the driver's side. "You shouldn't have come, either. I told you I had this. And were you smoking in my car? It fucking reeks in here." He hissed as he touched the steering wheel, his hands coming away scented of sour cigarettes.

Maxim shrugged, smirking as he shoved his hands into his hoodie pocket. "It was chilly, and I was bored. Found some cool shit in your car, though." He plucked a baggie of weed out of his pocket, dangling it next to the window. His eye and cheek were a deep black, and his lip had turned purple, too, the split so large that it looked as if it would never heal.

"You can have it. I got that off a guy on Elm Street. Wouldn't want my worst enemy to smoke that shit." He scowled at the weed. He'd tried it, and what should have been a relaxing afternoon had turned into a headache and a hangover worse than any of his life.

"You think so highly of me," said Max, slipping into the passenger seat and putting the weed back in the glove box where he'd found it. He smiled as he leaned against the seat. "Our boy was vacuuming when I left. Got home from work and gave me a kiss right away before he grabbed that fucking thing. He's worse than you are."

Niki smirked, guiding the car out onto the street.

"Did you hear the scene last night?" Max asked quietly, looking out of the window as a flashy Corvette whipped by. "It didn't go really well." He looked worried, chewing his bruised lip with a crease between his brows.

"I heard a bit. Even with the earplugs, you guys aren't exactly quiet. It happens, though. Copley is going to push boundaries, and I don't think you're ever going to get him to shut up unless you gag him. His self-control is basically nil, and he has no self-preservation, either. You're doing good, though. Checking in with him is the best thing to do, and never go back on your word."

Max nodded, looking away as they passed by a nearby bush. It was already getting dark, and Niki kept an eye out for deer and other critters. They always jumped out at the strangest times.

"You okay with it like this? Sharing him, I mean?" Max rifled around in the center console, coming up with a piece of gum that he unwrapped and tossed into his mouth. "It's not weird for me, but just thought I would check in."

"Nah, not weird for me." *It's the first time in my life that I'm not a possessive bastard.* If it had been anyone but Max asking him to share, they'd already be broken and bleeding. "You should know that I love him—Copley, I mean."

Maxim's eyes went wide, his mouth falling open and giving Niki a shot of his partially chewed gum. "Fuck off, no."

Niki nodded, tightening his grip on the wheel. "It's hard to find someone who will take a second look at men like us and not be terrified for their lives or just disgusted. Fuck, the first time I saw him..." He hummed in the back of his throat. "I knew I wanted him to be mine forever. Never thought I'd get to share him with my best friend, but here we are."

Max spluttered, a bit of spit sticking to the inside of the windshield. Niki grimaced. *That's going to be shit to get out.* Cleaning the inside of a car window just made it worse, nine times out of ten.

"You are such a fucking softie." Maxim snickered, smothering his laugh under his hand as Niki glowered.

"I can still kick your ass."

"I'd like to see it, softie. You wouldn't hurt a fly, and especially not little ol' me." Max leaned away, avoiding the slap that Niki sent his way.

He reefed the e-brake, and the car slid to a halt. Niki crossed his arms, glowering at his brother. "Say it again. I dare you. Whoever wins the fight gets dibs on our sub for the next two weeks, and last time I checked, I'm still stronger than you."

"Yeah, but I have more to fight for," said Max, getting out of the car as Niki did the same. "I'm way hornier than you. You've been doing this stuff for years, but I just started. I have so much catching up to do. Besides, you couldn't wrestle a limp noodle, softie."

"You're on." Niki lunged, grabbing his brother around the neck and grappling him into a headlock before running his knuckles over Max's scalp. Max shouted at the assault, sinking his teeth into Niki's arm.

Niki released him with a grunt, tossing Max toward the grassy ditch. Max was only on the ground for a moment before he sprang to his feet, a smirk on his lips despite the fresh blood pouring from the split.

"You're going down, big bro."

Chapter Twenty-Three

Copley

Copley sank into the couch, stroking the fabric as he rested his cheek next to his hand. Work had been busy, especially since he'd taken a few days off so he could give himself some time—that, and cleaning, which should have been an Olympic sport. Maxim had watched him for a minute with a smirk and a shake of his head that made Copley want to smack him.

The cleaning was for him and Nikita, *not* for Maxim.

He actually had no idea what he could do for Maxim at the moment. He hadn't done anything about Copley's nakedness the day before, and he hadn't made a single move that morning when Copley had been strolling about in a borrowed robe. His gaze had remained stoic and calm as he'd stared at Copley above his coffee mug.

He *had* given Copley a quick kiss after Copley had returned home from work, grabbing the vacuum to clean up the crumbs that surrounded Max like landmines.

The kiss had left Copley woozy. He needed the touch of lips and warm skin so badly that it was a visceral ache. He'd wanted to smack Maxim just so he could earn a spanking or *something* to get more—more kisses, more sweet touches or hard ones.

He'd hardly been able to focus at work with his cock half-hard and his mind trying to figure out something to do. Sleeping on the floor for another night was not an option. His back and side ached from the unforgiving surface, and his neck had a permanent-feeling crick. One night hadn't been so bad, but the second had pushed beyond his ability. More would probably cripple him for life.

Maybe if he had been twenty.

The idea of having one Dom had blown his mind—in a good way. But...but, maybe two was too much for him. He could barely figure himself out most days. How could he expect them to know what he needed if *he* didn't know?

The idea of getting spanked again had him flushing hot, but he didn't think he could handle another punishment—another failure.

Tears gathered in his eyes as he shoved his face into the couch. He had found two of the most amazing men in the world, only to discover that he wasn't good enough for them. Maybe it would be better if he just slipped away while they were gone. He'd leave a note for them so they didn't worry...if they worried.

Don't think of them like that. Of course they would worry. They were good men, even if they *weren't*. But he'd fucked up enough that he wasn't worth their worry.

Reaching for his phone, he dialed Sauble's number, biting his lip as he brought it to his ear. *Why did I come back here?* He should have just gone to Sauble's right after work. He didn't have many things with him. His bag had been unpacked on the first night into one of Nikita's drawers, but it wouldn't take much to pack it right back up again.

"He lives!" Sauble laughter greeted him as the line connected.

Copley grunted, faceplanting into the couch as his face flushed. His brother was never going to let him live this down.

"Shut up, Sauble."

"I thought you were tied up in some sort of kinky basement," said Sauble, something honking in the background as he chuckled. "My little bro." He clicked his tongue. "Go big or go home, am I right? Not that I really want to know dick size. You sure know how to pick them, though."

"I thought you punched Maxim in the face. Why are you okay with this?" Copley perked up, shuffling so he was sitting on the couch. He'd expected Sauble to yell at him at the very least. They hadn't exactly left on the best of terms.

"You can take care of yourself," said Sauble without missing a beat. "You're the most responsible person I know, and you never do anything you don't want to. You can't listen worth shit, so even if I told you to run, I know you wouldn't. And as for that bastard, he deserved it."

Letting out a sigh, Copley shook his head, a smile on his lips. "Did he emasculate you, Sauble?" he teased. "He's a big boy, and he doesn't even work out that much. And speaking of cock, he has a huge cock." He snickered as Sauble gagged on the other end.

"You okay, though?" asked Sauble, suddenly sobering.

Copley bit his lip, dragging his finger along the couch. *No.*

"Copley?" Sauble's voice dropped. "I'll fucking kill them. I don't care who they are. They hurt you?"

"No, no," said Copley, rushing to get the words out. "I just... Do you ever feel like you're just not enough?" He plunged his hand into his hair, blinking back tears. "They are so good to me, but I just...I feel like *nothing* next to them. I could never take care of them the way they do me. I could never repay them for their kindness, and fuck, I can't even seem to listen to them."

"Reality check," said Sauble, the humor back in his voice. "You don't listen to *anyone*. Why do you think you got fired from your last five jobs before this one? And as for being enough for them? Buddy, I hate to be the one to tell you this, but they'll never live up to you. They could love you every day for the rest of your life, and they still wouldn't deserve you."

"L-love? Did they punch you back? Because you're sounding a bit like you have a concussion." Copley took in a breath, touching his chest in the place that ached every time he was away from the twins. "What would you know about relationships, anyway? You can't keep a woman to save your life."

Sauble chuckled. "Maybe I don't keep a lady because I don't want to."

"What is that supposed to mean?"

"Nothing," said Sauble, and Copley could almost see the shrug. "As for the love thing, you'd have to be pretty fucking dense not to see it, no offense. One of them was storming around the neighborhood looking for you, then they both show up to tell me that my debt is suddenly 'forgiven' and you're staying with them now. Sounds a lot like love to me."

Yeah, it does. I didn't even realize.

"Or maybe it's me they love," said Sauble, letting out a wistful sigh. "Everyone seems to think they are into some pretty fucked up stuff, so maybe our fight was just foreplay or something."

It was Copley's turn to gag. He loved his brother, but no. He didn't even want to think about his brother foreplaying with anything or anyone.

"Gross."

"Fair play, Copley. You started it with the whole 'dick size' thing. I'll have you know —"

"Yeah, I'm gonna hang up. You and your micro-dick can fuck off." Copley laughed, falling back against the couch as Sauble cursed.

"I do *not* have a micro-dick," Sauble pouted.

"Like you said, the neighborhood talks. Word on the street is that those poor girls of yours can't feel a thing." Copley squealed with laughter, unable to keep a straight face as Sauble kept cursing.

"You bastards deserve each other," said Sauble, with no heat in his voice at all. "I'm gonna go. Be safe and give those assholes a punch from me." He ended the call with a click.

Copley rolled off the couch, wandering toward the back door with a smile on his face. Through the glass, he could see a small drift of snow that was starting to gather against the fence, with a few sticks of grass poking through the thinner bits. The neighbor was out at their barbeque, tongs in hand as the thing smoked way more than it should have.

The door clicked behind him followed by the rustle of cloth and a few murmuring voices. *I deserve this.* He nodded to himself, leaning his forehead against the glass. *I deserve them.*

He wasn't going to go to his knees or strip naked in front of them so easily. *I'm worth it.* He was going to make them work for it—work for him—until they earned the submission that he was so willing to give.

His life over the last month had been a clusterfuck, starting with Spencer and ending with him clinging on too tightly to the first man who'd walked by. He'd been nothing for so long that he'd forgotten that he was something.

And they had to come to terms with the fact that he just wasn't going to listen, no matter how much they asked him to. They would have to *make* him. He wasn't going to be anyone less than himself.

"Hi, guys!" he called out to them as they shuffled into the living room. They smelled like snow and fresh air with a hint of danger that had thrilled him since the beginning. His mouth watered and his knees went wobbly as he forced himself to stay standing, pressing his cheek to the cool glass.

"You okay, baby?" asked Maxim, coming up behind him and touching his shoulder. The heat of his palm sank into him, the calluses catching the fabric of Copley's shirt.

He nodded, blinking as a snowflake settled on the glass. It melted after a few moments. How could anyone ever confuse the two? Sure, they looked nearly identical except for the tattoos, but their voices were different. Maybe not *different* so much as they used them differently, one low and steady and the other all over the fucking place.

"I feel like I've been trying to be something I'm not," said Copley, biting his cheek as Max went tense. "That sounded bad. Sorry." He turned to him, lifting his gaze. "I feel like I've been so terrified that you two won't want me anymore that I've lost a bit of myself, trying to be someone that you'll keep around."

Nikita was standing behind Max, his arms crossed and his face unreadable. He nodded slowly, scratching his neck where he'd missed a bit of scruff while shaving. "I know."

He knows? Copley wanted to cry and deny it all at once. *No, wait! I was only kidding. I'll be perfect for you, just let me try harder.* His exhaustion sank deeper until it took everything in him to keep his eyes open.

Nikita leaned on the wall next to him, looking out into the storm as the wind howled through the buildings. There were tiny droplets on his hair and eyelashes — little snowflakes that had melted as soon as he'd stepped inside. He would be beautiful in the snow with it clinging to every part of him. Copley's mouth went dry.

"That first day we met, it was like everything I've ever looked for was before me, in the most beautiful package I've ever seen." Niki turned a glare on Max as he snickered. "I am not making a dick joke when I say *package.*"

He looked back to Copley, reaching for his hand and entwining their fingers. Copley held on tight, sinking into the feeling of Nikita against him, holding him, even if it was only his hand.

"But I gave you too much at once," said Niki, tucking Copley's hair behind his ear, even though it was too short to stay put. "I treated you like an experienced sub while keeping you at arm's length, so

I didn't get too close. Then you and Max were together, too, with a completely different dynamic than ours. I felt like I was scrambling to hold on to you and to me, but still terrified to get too close because I didn't want to get hurt or put you in danger. Worst mistake of my life."

Niki shook his head, and Copley's heart pounded. Max shifted at his side, grasping his other hand as Niki continued.

"I pushed you to be something that you're not—and punished you when you lashed out. It took a gun to my head to figure out that what I was doing had given our relationship a time limit—a short one. I'm so sorry, Copley." His face was grim, his lips tight.

"All I've ever wanted is a sub who I can really call my own. I've had a few snippets here and there with others, but nothing that even came close to how I feel with you. I've never felt more powerful and more in control than when you are in my arms, whimpering and pleading with me and begging for more."

Copley swallowed, his throat clicking. He couldn't look away.

"Would you give me one more chance?" asked Nikita. "Let me prove that I can be the best Dom for you."

"What about Maxim?" Copley's voice was strangled as he asked, and he was unable to look away from Niki, even as Max hugged him closer. Copley melted against him, soaking up his warmth.

"I'm not a romantic because, fuck no," said Max, his voice just above a growl as he nuzzled Copley's neck. Copley tilted to the side to give him better access. "I'm not sure what kind of Dom I'll end up being, either. I'll fuck up and disappoint you, and I'll probably be too rough or too soft at the wrong times. But fuck, I want to be with you. Will you stay? Will you be my man?"

Copley bit his tongue with how fast he threw his arms around Maxim's shoulders. Sauble had been right. The neighborhood did talk...a lot. Maxim had a reputation that was just above a man-whore, tossing out one-night-stands moments after he'd finished. He'd never had the same man twice, and he certainly never asked for any commitment.

Standing on his tiptoes, Copley grasped Maxim by his cheeks, bringing him in and placing a chaste kiss on his lips. When he stepped back, he immediately turned for Niki, throwing his arms around his neck and pulling him close.

"Is a threesome out of the question?" he asked, chuckling as Niki smiled into his neck.

Max huffed behind him before crossing his arms. "I'd rather not touch my brother's dick if that's possible. But I can see the appeal of a subby sandwich."

Niki let out a laugh that shook his entire frame, holding Copley so tight that he had to struggle to breathe.

"I should warn you guys, though," said Copley, biting his lip. "I won't *try* to be a brat, but I have an issue listening and following directions sometimes."

"No shit," said Maxim with a smirk before pulling his hoodie over his head and tossing it toward the couch. "And I have a confession, too." He leveled them with a serious look. "I'm going to love *making* you listen. This hand hasn't tingled from a spanking in days." He held up his hand, cracking a smile.

Copley shuddered, flushing and clenching his ass cheeks. He'd been missing the same thing. That semi-permanent sting in his ass meant so much to him.

"You wanna get spanked, baby?" asked Niki, kissing his cheek. "You want your Doms to take care of you until you can't even think? There'll be nothing left in your balls after I finish with you, and Maxim will leave his marks on every part of you."

Copley nodded, biting his lip as his cock went completely rigid. He humped against Niki's hip, reaching for the button on his jeans.

"Ah, baby, not so fast." Niki grabbed his hips, forcing him back. A slap rang out a moment before Copley felt the sting against his ass. He yelped, trying to jump closer to Niki, but Niki held on, keeping him still.

"What's your color?" asked Niki, giving him another peck.

"Green." His voice was distant to his own ears. He was already slipping away, going deeper as Maxim slapped him for a second time. Niki forced him to keep still, taking his choice out of the equation. He relaxed into the touch, giving himself over to his Doms.

"That's better. Now get naked and get on the bed. I want to see the mark that Max left on your ass."

Copley scrambled toward the bedroom, nearly tripping over his own pants in his haste to remove them. Tossing them to the side of the room, he stripped his socks and his shirt in one go. He ground to a halt a moment later. *Niki's or Maxim's?*

When they had played together the last time, it had been on Niki's bed, but he didn't want Maxim to think he was leaving him out, either. They were both equal in his mind.

"If you're good, I'll tell Max to push the beds together."

He wasn't exactly the strongest guy around, but the beds were on the small side. He moved to Max's bed, pushing on the bottom corner as hard as he could. It caught in the carpet, edging slowly toward Niki's. The frame was solid and a fuckton heavier than it looked.

He was panting heavily, straining to get it the last few inches when he felt eyes on him. Looking over his shoulder, his stomach sank as he saw Niki. The smile on his lips didn't ease Copley's sudden tension.

"Get naked and get on the bed."

He'd fucked that up in two seconds flat. *It's supposed to be different.*

"Good idea. Need help, baby?"

Copley swallowed the lump in his throat and nodded, standing back as Niki shoved the beds together in a way that made it look effortless. His muscles bulged beneath his skin, flexing as he squared up the corners. Copley's mouth went dry.

Kneeling on the bed almost automatically, he couldn't take his eyes off Niki, tracing his tattoos with his gaze and wishing he could feel them under his hands.

"Can I touch you?" asked Copley, rising onto his knees. He tangled his hands in the sheets so he didn't reach out by accident.

Niki paused before giving him a long look. "Do you deserve to touch me? Have you earned it?"

His automatic response was no. How could he ever hope to achieve the right to openly touch someone so beautiful and strong? But he was worth it, right? Worth more than second guesses and unsure thoughts.

"Yes? I mean, yes." His fingers tingled as he imagined touching Niki and raking his nails over that firm flesh. There were so many places he longed to feel that weren't just his cock and pecs.

"And why is that?" Niki asked softly as he moved around to the edge of his bed, his knees touching the side. He was so tall and big that the room seemed too small for him. Copley's heart pounded with the familiar rush of adrenalin.

"I-I…" Copley snapped his mouth shut. Maybe he had been wrong all along.

"I'll help you out with this one because I know it's hard," said Niki, reaching for him and grasping his hand. He entwined their fingers together, smoothing the ridges on the back of his hand.

"You're beautiful," said Niki softly, pulling Copley closer to the edge until their chests were nearly touching. "You're strong, powerful, devoted, loyal and you make me feel like a good man."

Copley flushed, ducking his head as Niki kept touching him, that soft caress on the back of his hand almost too much to stand.

"I want to hear you say it. Tell me why you deserve to touch me." Niki dropped his hand to his side.

"I-I'm beautiful." He bit his tongue, and his flush deepened until it felt like he'd spent too long in the sun.

"What else, baby?" Niki touched his shoulder next, squeezing gently before trailing his fingertips down Copley's arm. Shuddering, Copley closed his eyes.

"I'm powerful and strong. Am I really? Is that how you see me?" He opened his eyes, peering at Niki, who smiled back. "I'm loyal and I make you feel like a good man. I can't take credit for that one. You *are* a good man."

"Undress me," said Niki, making no move to reach for his own clothing.

Copley's hands shook as he reached for the hem of Niki's shirt, distantly wondering if and when Max was going to join them. He could hardly focus when he lifted the fabric and caught a glimpse of Niki's stomach.

Nikita wasn't overly hairy, but there was enough there that Copley could comb his fingers through it as he pushed his shirt higher. He paused to look as he revealed another tattoo, tracing the outline with his fingertip. Niki's skin prickled beneath him, and he shuddered under the touch.

"What do they all mean?" he wondered aloud, exposing another tattoo and tracing over it as well. Some he had found the meanings for online, but others remained a mystery. They seemed to come alive as he moved, the chains on his ribs clinking together silently with each breath.

"Some of them are my past," said Niki, touching the manacles at his wrists, "and some are my present." He touched the tiger at his throat. "A few, I hope, are my future." He tapped the hooded figure along his chest, just at the level of his heart. The figure was kneeling in a submissive pose, their features in shadow with their eyes downcast.

"They're beautiful," said Copley, smiling as he spotted a patchy-looking alley cat hidden along Niki's side. He'd never noticed it before, which was probably for the better. The outline alone looked like a two-year-old had sketched it. Thank goodness it was small. "Okay, *most* of them are beautiful."

Niki chuckled, petting down the cat's back in a way that would have made a live one purr. "One of my first prison tattoos. I lifted sixty packs of smokes in a week, so rumors started that I was a master thief. The man I did it for died a week later." His smile dimmed for a moment before it went soft.

Tugging Niki's shirt the rest of the way off, Copley tossed it toward his own before continuing to explore. Niki was as soft as he was hard, his muscling smooth yet rigid in perfect proportions.

The belt buckle was calling him. He dropped his hands to it, prying the buckle open before tugging it through the loops. It was leather and heavier than it looked with the pure shine of simple polish. It was broader than the one Maxim had used on him, the thick surface almost too wide for the loops.

Niki's erection was straining at his seam as Copley tugged the button wide and eased his pants down to his thighs. His mouth watered as he stared, hoping and wondering at the same time.

"Can I suck you? I think I deserve it." He gave Niki a winning smile as he tugged his boxers down, gasping as his cock sprang free. He pushed his pants all the way free, discarding them like the rest.

One muscle clenched in Niki's thigh as he shifted, showing off the pure and powerful girth. They were almost like tree trunks, if tree trunks had sex appeal and a touch of hair. One thigh was spotless while the other had a scar running along the inside only a few centimeters away from his throbbing pulse.

"What happened here?" asked Copley, tracing over the thick scar. He couldn't imagine enduring such pain in a delicate area. A bee sting sometimes brought him to his knees.

"Hazard of the job," said Niki, without humor. "There's a bullet wound here as well, and here." He pointed to two circular wounds that were faded and pale pink. "Luckily, it was the splatter of a shotgun and not a single bullet or it would have taken my kidney."

Copley kissed them, probing them with his tongue before pulling away. Among the tattoos, the scars were especially difficult to see.

"How are you feeling?" asked Niki, sliding a hand through Copley's hair and tugging softly. He waited for Copley's 'green' before he continued. "I'm going to give you a choice today. Did you want to come over and over until you can't anymore? Or do you want me to edge you until you lose your mind before I let you come?"

Copley shuddered, dropping his hands to his own body and settling on his belly. That choice wasn't a choice at all. Both were torture—the most exquisite torture in the world. "Can we do both?"

"Anything for you." Niki gave him a smile that was beyond predatory. "Did you touch as much as you want? Your hands will be full for the rest of the night."

Could it ever be enough? If he had two hours per day set aside just for touching Niki, it would never be enough. It would be a full-time job before he ever got his fill. Niki seemed to understand with the way his eyes went dark, and he grabbed Copley's wrists, moving until they were touching him again.

"There will always be time to touch me, baby. You're so good for me." He pulled Copley's hands away, tipping him back and dragging him to the top of the bed.

Copley gasped at the rough treatment, kicking his legs and squealing as Niki straddled him. Niki had always been so gentle, never showing off his raw power. Copley couldn't have resisted if he wanted to.

"I'm going to restrain you," said Niki, pinning Copley's wrists to the bed. His eyes burned into Copley's, pinning him more than his hands. "I'll need you to check in with me more than usual. If anything hurts or starts to tingle, I need you to tell me right away. This is serious, Copley, and I need you to listen. Can you do that for me?"

"Yes," said Copley, squeezing his hands as Niki applied more pressure. His grip was tight, pushing on the delicate tendons and nerves. "That's too tight, Niki."

Nikita's grip eased immediately, and a smile lit his lips. "Good boy. I needed to make sure you could listen to me. I knew you could do it. Sit in the middle of the bed now. Put your arms behind your back, but only where they're comfortable. Don't strain yourself, or you'll be feeling it for a long time."

He let Copley up, standing from the beds and moving to the closet. Pulling a tote out of the closet, he opened the lid, grabbing a length of red rope. "I think red will be best so we can turn you into a slut for Maxim. He'll love that."

Copley flushed as he settled in the middle, rolling his shoulders as he tried to find a comfortable position. The nights on the floor had taken their toll, and there weren't many positions that didn't pull his neck or shoulders.

"Okay?" Niki tossed the rope on the bed, the thick, coiled strands even more intimidating up close.

"Just a little sore from sleeping on the floor," said Copley, rubbing at his left shoulder that strained a touch more than the right. It pulled tight at the slightest movement, zinging painfully when he tried to move his arm back.

"Let me see," said Niki, climbing back on the bed. His cock was still hard and bobbing with every movement, but he acted as if it were soft and had no bearing on his actions. *If only I had that kind of self-control.*

Copley melted into the first touch against his skin. Niki was so warm, his hands sending a wave of heat that made his toes curl and his cock twitch. He let out a moan as Niki kneaded his shoulders, digging straight into the pinched nerves. "Fuck. Oh God, that's good."

"So fucking tight," said Niki, his voice dropping as if he were talking about something else entirely. "Let me get you loosened up." He pushed Copley gently on his front, straddling his thighs and hovering over him. As he leaned forward, his cock dragged over Copley's crack.

Copley let out a gasp, arching his back, despite the twinge, and pushing his ass into Niki's cock. Pre-cum painted his ass cheek, leaving a path of fire and ice. Shuffling his legs, he tried to get his ass higher in the air, desperate to feel Niki closer.

"How am I supposed to give you a massage when you're wiggling around everywhere?" asked Niki lightly, chuckling when Copley wiggled his ass back and forth, slapping his cock with every sideways pass.

"I told you I'm not a good listener," said Copley, sighing as Niki dug in deeper, his shoulders going numb as endorphins flooded his system. He moaned, hardly able to move as his mind was blown.

No man had ever touched him this way. In fact, he often used his work benefits to book massages that he really didn't need. Paying someone to rub his back for half an hour had always seemed easier than asking his previous partners to do it. The times that he had asked, they'd always let out a sigh before giving him two half-hearted touches that left him tighter than before.

But Niki put every bit of effort into it, touching him like he actually wanted to, with a hard cock to boot. He'd never felt so wanted before. His thoughts were already drifting, and he was forgetting about the things he'd been so worried about.

"Stay just like that."

Copley couldn't have moved if he'd tried. His body was limp, every dry pass pushing him farther into the bed. The only thing that would have made it better would have been massage oil.

The familiar sound of a cap had him perking up. He looked over his shoulder, letting out a deep groan. Niki was lubing up his cock and stroking it from base to tip with slow, measured strokes. Copley spread his legs wider, inviting him in.

"No, baby. Just like you were." Niki pushed his legs tight together again, slicking between Copley's thighs.

Oh, God. He clenched his legs tighter together as Niki hovered over him again, this time pushing his cock between the slippery tunnel of his thighs.

"That's nice." Niki let out a hiss, easing some of his weight onto Copley. He wanted more. He wanted everything that Niki had to give him. He didn't care if he got completely squished into the bed or if he couldn't breathe.

Grabbing Niki by the ass, he pulled him down until his full weight settled on him. It was a lot, but at the same time, it was calming, not to mention it made him feel like he was about to come. His cock throbbed against the bed where it was trapped.

"Am I too much?" Niki lifted himself in a half push up before dropping again slowly and moving his cock through the tunnel of Copley's thighs with his movements.

Copley shook his head, biting his lip. If anything, it wasn't enough.

"I need a verbal answer, Copley. What's your color?"

"Green." His word turned into a groan as Niki settled back. "I like when you crush me like that. I like feeling trapped beneath you — like I couldn't escape if I tried."

Niki let out a chuckle, his breath whispering over the back of his neck. "You can try if you want. Trust me, you won't escape. Between Maxim and me, we own this fucking town. There's not a place you could run that we wouldn't find you. There's not a wall I wouldn't fuck you against or a desk I wouldn't bend you over. You're *mine*."

Copley's body went tight as his orgasm rushed at him, crashing into him as he bucked into the bed and rutted, Niki's cock sliding against his balls as he emptied himself into the sheets. "I'm yours."

"That's right." Niki nibbled his shoulder once before pulling back as Copley went lax and his orgasm drained away. He closed his eyes, taking a deep breath as the chill of the room tickled his exposed skin.

"Put your arms above your head. Does that feel okay? Any soreness?"

Copley stretched his fingers and extended his arms. He was still like jelly from the massage and his orgasm. A train wouldn't have hurt him at that moment. "Green."

Cool rope slithered against his wrist as Niki wrapped a length around it. He made a complicated-looking knot before looping it around his other wrist, binding his arms above his head. The loops weren't tight enough to hurt, but they were enough that he couldn't slip free of them.

A second set of loops bound him at mid-forearm, then at the sensitive crease of his elbow. Every one was secured with a knot that Niki tied in seconds. The final set was at the level of his biceps, tucking under his chin so he had to lean his head back a bit. Niki helped him to his knees, his bound arms in front of him.

"How does that feel?" Niki tucked the stray end into the last loop, leaving a seamless tie behind. It was beautiful, especially the contrast of red against his flushed skin. The tension of it pulled at his shoulders just a touch, but not nearly enough to hurt.

"It's interesting." He flexed his hands before tugging against the ropes, testing the strength. It was like pushing against a brick wall, so secure that he had no chance of moving. "Comforting, actually. I never thought…"

He trailed off. He'd never thought he would have anything to do with the kink scene. A few months ago, his idea of taboo had been fucking with the lights on.

"Think you can touch my cock like that?" asked Niki with a soft smile. "You can touch it as much as you want. You can even try to make me come…if you think you can do it."

I do love a good challenge. Shuffling forward, he closed the distance between them, reaching for Niki's cock with both hands. The first pump gave him the clue for Niki's smirk. The binds tightened if he tried to bend his arms, so he had to move them together, straight up and down, to give Niki any friction. It was slow and difficult, and worse than any torture his Doms had imagined for him.

He sent Niki a glower, biting his lip in determination.

"Still feel good?"

"Still green," he said, maybe just a touch sharper than he had intended. Niki seemed to ignore his tone, letting out a sigh as Copley worked him.

"Up on your knees then. I'm going to get under you so you can fuck my face." Niki scooted under him, picking him up by the hips before dropping him so his cock slid straight into the warmth of Niki's welcoming mouth.

He had nowhere to put his hands except on the bed between Niki's legs, unless he wanted to keel over. At the first suck, he almost fell over anyway, his half-hard cock waking up and going fully hard again. He sank into Niki's mouth as much as he thought he could get away with, spreading his legs as Niki grasped his hips, tugging him down even farther.

"Do you not have a gag reflex?" Copley spluttered as Niki dragged him all the way down, until his groin pressed him into the bed, then farther still. Fuck, it was good, the suction alone enough to put him right on the edge. He was still sensitive from his first orgasm, and he shouldn't have been able to come again so soon. But Niki had proven him wrong before.

Niki pushed him up with brute strength alone, taking a few deep breaths. "I told you to fuck my face, baby. Any time now." His voice was scratchy and thick as he brought Copley down again.

"Oh my God," Copley whispered, tipping forward and resting his face on the lattice of rope. If he lined up just right, he might just be able to feed Niki's cock through the loops so he could at least return the favor. Humping down, he dove at Niki's cock with his mouth, trying to keep his arms straight and his balance at the same time.

Every muscle strained tight, his arms and back most of all. It only pushed him higher, until he was flooding Niki's mouth with an orgasm that felt like it was pulled directly from his balls. He couldn't move away, only bury himself deep and try to keep his teeth behind his lips as he cried out. Niki lifted him off with one push, tossing him on his back on the bed.

Flailing did not fucking work with his hands basically hog-tied. He shot Niki a second glare, who sent him a soft smile that melted his insides to a warm goo.

"How are the arms and shoulders?" asked Niki, slipping a finger beneath the rope at Copley's wrists.

"Starting to get a bit sore," said Copley, shrugging his shoulders to ease some of the strain. "I can hardly feel it, really. I don't feel like myself right now." He blinked slowly, tugging his wrists so they strained at the rope. An ache slipped through the fog, something that he knew he would feel later. "But probably a yellow."

Niki untucked the end of the rope, pulling something that made it unravel so much faster than it had taken to put together. Copley cursed as he pulled his arms apart, the ache hitting him ten-fold. His cock twitched, somehow still interested as he grimaced.

"Here, baby. You did so fucking good for me. You held so still and listened so well." Niki grabbed his left arm, kneading Copley's muscles the same way he had his back, easing the tension as it hit a peak. Copley let out a groan, sinking onto the bed and letting his eyes fall shut as he gave in.

"So good." Niki moved to the right, kissing each palm as he finished. "Maxim is back from taking care of a bit of business. Did you want him to join us, or did you want me to head out for a bit?"

"Don't go." Copley sat up, reaching for Niki and grabbing his hand tight before he could slip from the bed. "Unless that's a limit for you? I know he's your brother, but it's not like you guys are fucking. I don't think you'd be into that." *A guy can dream.*

Niki grimaced as he looked to the door. A cupboard slammed in the distance, along with the clink of glasses. "It's almost a limit. I don't want to leave you, even if I know you're in safe hands. But you can't expect anything between Maxim and me. It's off the table one hundred percent. Maxim might even think up a punishment if you even ask him about it. I don't mind watching, listening or participating…to an extent."

Scratching the back of his neck, Copley nodded. "I think I get it. It's kind of a double standard, too. I mean, some straight men dream about having a threesome with twin women but think it's too weird for me to be with both of you, not to mention any names." *Sauble.* "But I would never ask for you to do that."

A knock at the door pulled both of their gazes and Copley grasped Niki's hand tighter, just in case he decided to change his mind. Maxim poked his head through the crack. It must've been snowing harder because his hair was full of water droplets that nestled on his eyelashes as well. His cheeks were flushed pink, along with the tip of his nose. *So cute.*

"You guys done fucking or do I have to listen to you for the next two hours?" Maxim drawled, throwing the door wide and pulling his hoodie over his head.

Slightly less cute.

"You want to join in and make a subby sandwich?" Niki asked, leaning against the headboard and dragging Copley into his lap. His cock poked along the seam of his ass before finding its way to nudge Copley's balls. "I was thinking of holding him on my cock while I get some reading done, and I thought maybe you wanted to blow him to see how many times you could make him come. Twice already, but we were just getting started."

Copley burned as Maxim's gaze pierced into him, flitting from his semi-hard cock to the thin red lines on his arms that were already fading. Maxim crossed his arms, his biceps flexing against his T-shirt like they had something to prove.

"I'm in, but I don't want you slipping and getting too close to my mouth. No-fucking-thank-you."

Niki shrugged, looping an arm across Copley's chest. "Like I said, I just want something to keep my cock warm while I read. I can take his mouth if you prefer. A hole is a hole."

Holy fuck. Niki was right, he wasn't a soft Dom in the least. From what Copley understood, soft Doms steered away from humiliation and objectification, but maybe that had just been a part of their dynamic that they'd been missing out on with all the restrictions.

"Nah, you can have his ass. That way, I can fuck his mouth if I need to burn off some energy." Maxim pulled his T-shirt over his head, fumbling with his belt before tugging it free and tossing it to his side of the room. It landed with a thump, bouncing once before it hit the wall. His jeans went next, leaving him bare with nothing on underneath.

"What are you waiting for?" asked Maxim, crossing his arms and kneeling on the end of the bed.

Copley glanced at Nikita, only to find him staring back at him. *Oh, wait.* "Y-you want me to?" He touched Niki's cock, the remaining lube making it feel tacky and even bigger than it was.

"Well, it's not going to get in there itself," said Niki, letting out a sigh as he grabbed his book.

Copley glanced at the book, going even hotter as he saw the title. *Pride and Prejudice.* How could he even read a book like that during something like...like? He bit his lip. *The lube. Where the hell is the lube?*

"Is it broken?" asked Maxim, crawling another step toward them. His cock was already hard, bobbing with every movement. Everything about him was distracting, from his tattoos to his strength.

Niki shrugged a second time, taking his bookmark out before settling to read. "Give it a minute to figure it out. It's not used to a cock like mine, so I'm not surprised it's slow."

I am not fucking slow. Bratting finally made sense, especially when his Doms seemed to be feeding off each other. He could take a cock, though, and they fucking knew it, even if they needed a reminder.

After grabbing the lube from the bed, he slicked up three fingers, jamming them deep in his ass as he poured another stream of slick over Nikita's cock. He didn't linger but stretched himself brutally until the ache turned into a zing that went straight up his spine.

He would have lots of time to adjust, though. Niki said that he wasn't even going to move.

Pulling out his fingers, he moved closer to Niki's lap. Turning so his back was to Niki's chest, he hovered for a moment as his confidence wavered. *Yeah, it's gonna hurt, but it's gonna be so fucking worth it.* He bit his lip, sinking down on Niki's cock.

The head popped past his rim with a sensation akin to fire, but he bit back his yelp and forced himself to take Niki deeper. He didn't get far before Niki grabbed his hip, halting him from going farther.

Copley sent a glare over his shoulder. "Is your cock cold or not?"

Niki's brows nearly hit the ceiling, but he let go, turning back to his book, even as his breathing stuttered. Copley pushed himself all the way down, groaning at the fullness and the stretch that was almost too much to take.

"Better?" Copley asked, his voice just above a squeak. *That smarts.* He definitely should have opened himself up more, but Niki's panting made it all worth it. It wasn't often that he could catch his Doms off guard, so when he had the opportunity, he had to take it.

"Damn, baby," said Maxim, pumping his own cock a few times. "You must have been looser than I thought."

"He's really not," hissed Niki, his grip going tight on the book as Copley managed to take the last inch, rocking as he settled.

Maxim snickered before closing the distance, dipping down and kissing Copley's cock once. "Two orgasms you say? Fucking pathetic. Don't know how you let this guy get away with that, baby."

One last smirk and Copley was hitting the back of Maxim's throat, the suction and warmth going straight to his balls and stripping the rest of the pain away. He rocked into Maxim's mouth, nudging deeper until Maxim swallowed around him.

"Stay still," said Niki, bracing his hip as he rocked again. "This is a good part." He turned back to the book, seemingly lost in the pages a moment later. The paper scratched as he turned the page, the yellowed lettering looking well-loved.

When it came to sex, Copley had never had to use his imagination before, but it was like the floodgates had been opened and he was ready to go balls to the wall. He clamped down on Niki's cock, using every ass muscle at his disposal and reveling in Niki's hiss.

"I'm still," he said, shooting Niki an innocent smile as he looked up from his book. "I'm not moving at all." He held his hands out, clamping down as Maxim sucked him deep. His eyes rolled back in his head as he almost lost it, his goal of driving Niki wild slipping away momentarily.

"You know, I don't usually like brats, but I think I'll make an exception for you." Niki grabbed Copley's arms with a growl, twisting them behind his back before pinning them with one hand. "That okay?" he asked softly, his voice so much softer than his grip.

"Green," Copley breathed, tilting forward to give his arms more room. Niki tugged him back by the wrists, his cock sliding deeper and skimming over his prostate. Maxim chose that moment to cup his balls, massaging them with one hand as he continued to suck.

Copley couldn't have held on if Niki had ordered him to stop. He came into Maxim's waiting mouth, his hips twitching as he emptied himself. Niki groaned as Copley clamped down again, this time completely against his will.

The first two orgasms had been fun, the second pushing him only a tad past over-sensitive. The third was brutal, spots dancing behind his eyes and he gasped, and his body trembling as the pleasure peaked and stretched. He blacked out for a second, slumping ahead only to have Niki tug him back. The manhandling pushed him higher.

He couldn't stop trembling as Maxim kissed his belly, licking the furry trail between his abs and dipping into his belly button. He seemed completely unfazed and so did Niki, who had returned to his book the moment Copley could see again.

"I don't think I can do another one," said Copley, his voice shaky even to his own ears. He squeaked as Maxim touched his cock, the sensitive flesh still swollen and partially hard. Maxim tugged his balls in response, sending him a smirk that spoke a thousand words.

"I didn't ask you," said Maxim, tugging Copley's balls a second time before stretching them down until it *pulled*. "But if someone asked *me*, then I'd tell them you can do two more."

At some point over the next hour, Copley's brain went offline. Niki stayed hard in his ass, pressing against his prostate in the most painful way while hardly making a single thrust, even with how his breathing became hoarse and he emptied himself inside.

Copley wailed and groaned, managing to get his hands free as Nikita came. He desperately tried to pry Maxim off his groin, but in the end, it was no use. Niki let out a low laugh, grabbing Copley in a hold that left him nearly paralyzed as Maxim continued to work on him past the point in which he must've had a sore jaw.

So he floated, giving in to his Doms and only resurfacing when Niki whispered into his ear, prodding Copley until he managed to answer with a stuttered 'green'. It was harder each time as he lost himself and lost count until the pleasure and pain were everything he knew.

The best part—even better than any orgasm he'd ever had—was the comforting safety in Niki's arms and the way that he knew there was no reason to be embarrassed as Max drank in every sound and twitch.

His cheeks were damp when they stopped, Max pulling away at the same time Niki released Copley's arms and started to massage them. Niki's cock slipped free next with a sound that should have been more embarrassing than the fountain of cum that was dripping from Copley's hole.

Copley turned into Max's chest as they lay on the bed, spreading his legs and trying to answer as Niki cleaned him and checked him over. Eventually, he stopped trying, drifting in a state that was so close to sleep but filled with a euphoria that he could almost taste.

He reached for Max or Niki—he wasn't sure who anymore—burying his face and breathing deep. It must've been Maxim. There was the slight smokiness of cigarettes to his skin, along with the sweat and musk from so much sex.

"Did you come?" asked Copley. Somehow it mattered, even when he was out of his mind.

"Fuck, baby, you couldn't have stopped me. You're so fucking hot."

Warmth touched his chest, spreading outward until every part of him was filled to the brim. He was *good*.

Chapter Twenty-Four

Copley

"You come here glowing like that, and you won't tell me a single detail?" Sweetie squawked, waving her cigarette in dismissal as a john tried to get her attention. "Give me something, honey...anything. I gotta know, are they hung like beasts?"

Copley shuffled his feet, kicking up a bit of snow as he knocked a rock out onto the road. He'd started to flush the moment Sweetie had pointed out the hickey on his neck, and it had only gotten worse when she'd noticed his limp. He hadn't exactly been fucked hard enough to hurt, but his whole body was sore in that nice way that made him want to stretch out somewhere warm and just rest.

"No details," he whispered, conscious of the others around them at the bus stop. An old lady that he didn't recognize looked particularly invested in their conversation.

"Six inches?" Sweetie whispered. "Seven? Fuck, tell me. I can't take it. How much dick do you get to double-dip?" Her eyes sparkled as she laughed, licking the lipstick off her teeth. "Say that one three times fast."

"I don't know," said Copley, even quieter. He took a quick peek through his lashes before staring at his shoes. The bracelet on his wrist hung heavy as a reminder of exactly who he belonged to.

He'd cried when Maxim had brought it home, dropping to one knee and wrapping it around Copley's wrist. It was solid black and made of some kind of metal that Copley had never heard of. The links were sturdy enough that he didn't have to worry about breaking them, and Niki had already used it to tie him to the bed. No amount of pulling had broken it yet, and Maxim had only smirked when he'd tried.

The two medallions hanging from it were his favorite part. Shaped like tiger heads, both were gold and gleamed against the black like stars. They were carved with the Cyrillic version of Maxim and Nikita's names apparently, not that Copley could read them.

He touched the medallions, fiddling with them beneath his coat. He wasn't really embarrassed about sharing things with Sweetie, but he wondered how they would feel. They knew that he was friends with her, and Niki seemed to have *some* respect for her, but they were still her bosses in a way.

Ah, fuck it. The punishment would be worth it.

"Honestly, imagine one of those big dildos at an adult store — the kind you get for when you're feeling really brave. You know the ones, right? They're usually some stupid color like pink or baby blue." Copley knew because he used to have a few in his collection. Just another casualty of his past relationship.

"Yep," said Sweetie, her eyes starting to glow. She licked her lips, smearing her lipstick as she leaned in.

"Yeah, they're bigger."

Sweetie's mouth dropped open before she slapped him on the arm. "I always knew you were a size queen. And you're just a little guy, too. You must do some kind of yoga just to get down on those things."

Chuckling, Copley leaned into her, resting his head on her shoulder. She was finally wearing a winter coat, even if it was open at the front to show off her assets. The fishnet stockings looked lined, too, probably to get all the Santas out there hot and bothered.

"I'm joking," said Copley, snickering as she swatted him. "They're above average, but they're still just men. Besides, who says I don't fuck them?"

"I can see it now, honey," said Sweetie, smacking her lips as he pulled away. "You'd treat them so good that their little Dommy brains would just explode."

Copley rolled his eyes. He wasn't sure how Sweetie's Dom handled her, to be honest. She always seemed to be the one who listened to no one. If he hadn't seen her submit with his own eyes, he never would have believed it were possible.

Sweetie went quiet, turning her head to the side. The laugh dropped from her lips as she froze, her cigarette slipping from her hand.

Copley turned, his stomach clenching into a ball of ice. He recognized the man standing on the corner with a smoke between his fingers, but he'd only met him one time. It was the only time he'd seen Niki truly angry, and the only time he'd seen him with a gun.

Maxim and Nikita had whispered his name a few times between them when they'd thought Copley had been asleep. He was bad news if he worried the Twin Tigers.

Dimitri.

Dimitri wasn't a huge man by any means, but there was a look about him that had Copley instantly terrified. Maybe it was the dark circles under his eyes, his gaunt cheeks or the way his yellowed teeth shone in the light. Or maybe it was the tattooed dagger through his neck that dripped with vermillion.

Copley took a step back, bumping into Sweetie as he did. Dimitri's eyes settled on him, and he nearly puked. *This* was an evil man, not Nikita or Maxim. As much as he loved the adrenalin rush, they'd never terrified him before.

"Lookie here," said Dimitri, tossing his smoke and snubbing it out with his boot. "Must be a two-for-one deal. Buy one bitch and get the second free." Something shone at his hip as he moved. There was a silver gun tucked into his pants, catching on his coat as he swaggered toward them.

Sweetie stepped between them before Copley could say a thing. It was probably for the best. His tongue was lodged on the roof of his mouth, and he couldn't budge it, no matter how hard he tried. He wanted to scream and run at the same time, but despite his pounding heart, he couldn't move an inch.

"Hey, Dimitri, I haven't seen you, honey. You find some other girl? If you're trying to make me jealous, it's working." Sweetie cocked one hip, pulling her coat wide and thrusting her chest out.

How did she even do that? His respect for Sweetie doubled, then tripled. He had seen the fear on her face, but she was flirting with Dimitri as if it were nothing.

She was one step away from being a Hollywood actress.

Dimitri grunted, looking over her shoulder to stare at Copley. Copley tried not to take a step back, but he did it anyway, his back striking the sign for the bus stop. A bus wouldn't be along for another half hour at least, and there would be no cops in helping distance in the next century.

"What about you, subbie? You like what you see?" Dimitri licked his lips, letting out a dark laugh as he dragged his gaze over Copley's form.

His chest went tight as his blood ran cold. Maxim had called him subbie a time or two, and he'd taken it as an endearment because a submissive was who he was. But Dimitri rubbed it in his face as if it were a bad thing.

"I've been watching you, boy," said Dimitri, pushing Sweetie to the side before closing the distance between them. "Why do you stay with two murderers who don't even treat you right? I could open up your world to so many things. You would never want to say no."

"Ew." The word slipped out of his mouth before he could help it. The thought of it was just...gross. Yellow teeth and cigarette breath were not his things, and neither was the meth-addict murderer look. At least with Maxim, he smoked outside and brushed his teeth right after. Nikita wouldn't even let him sit on the couch without washing his hands, either.

Sweetie snorted as Dimitri glowered, his lips curling back into a snarl.

"I mean, no thank you," Copley rushed to say, swallowing as his throat clogged. *'Cause I was raised to be polite.* Sweat dripped down his back, the signpost an impenetrable barrier behind him.

Dimitri put his hand on the post above Copley's head, wrapping his fingers around the freezing metal. The stench of cigarettes was overpowering with something else almost rancid underneath. "What's wrong? Afraid that you might like it?"

Screwing up his face, Copley ducked beneath Dimitri's arm, twisting so he didn't put his back to him. He caught sight of Sweetie's cell phone as she texted behind her back.

Copley's cell was under two layers of clothing, but he wasn't unarmed. He touched the lump in his pocket that Maxim had made him bring with him after he'd found out where Copley was headed. After their altercation with Sauble, they seemed to trust him even less.

"Not the issue," said Copley, letting some of his natural attitude bleed into his voice. There were two people in the world that he submitted to — and Dimitri wasn't one of them. "I'm afraid that I might get lung cancer if you get too close. And when was the last time you had a shower? Did you need money for a place to go? I know a few places that will let you stay for next to nothing for a few nights. One of them isn't the greatest, but it doesn't look like you've seen better."

Sweetie looked at him with wide eyes before mouthing *'are you insane?'*. Even *she* wouldn't push that far apparently.

Probably. I'm probably going to get myself killed. After pulling the canister of pepper spray from his pocket, Copley swiveled it until it sat just right in his hand. He was pretty sure even having it was against the law, but it was better than the gun that Maxim had first offered.

Nikita had given Maxim a look at that, before he'd grabbed the gun and put it back in their safe. *I probably couldn't even figure out how to fire it.* Television had only taught him so much.

"You're going to pay for that," Dimitri hissed, grabbing for Copley with one wiry hand. There were tattoos across his knuckles that probably spelled 'bad news' in greenish ink.

Copley raised the pepper spray, squinting his eyes shut as he tucked his finger under the flap and jammed the button. Sweetie let out a squawk, and it sounded as if she stumbled backward a few steps as Dimitri roared.

Copley's face was on fire as if he'd just spent hours exfoliating, and it seeped into the seams of his eyelids and his nose. The taste was beyond description, making him want to puke and drink a gallon of milk at the same time. Dimitri went silent except for his shout and a low hiss of pain.

Turning away, Copley squinted his eyes, searching for Sweetie in the fiery haze. He grabbed her hand, taking off at a run as she stumbled over her heels. A few steps away and he could finally breathe, his lungs still tingling as he coughed. He could only imagine how much it hurt to get a shot of it directly in the face.

"Fuck. Warn a girl," said Sweetie as she rubbed her reddened eyes, dragging Copley to a stop halfway down the block. They turned back and her grip tightened as she started to laugh. "Every time I think I have you figured out, you manage to surprise me."

Dimitri was on his knees, clawing at his face as tears streamed down his cheeks. He flopped to the side, trembling as he let out a yell. His whole face was bright red, his ink standing out in vivid lines.

Fuck. Copley rubbed his eyes as the tingling worsened. The wind must have pushed some back into his face and it fucking *burned.* It was like the one and only time he'd tried Chicken Vindaloo, except the burning was in his eyeballs and nose, not on his tongue.

"Now I feel bad," said Copley, frowning as Dimitri's gun came loose and tumbled away on the sidewalk. Copley grabbed a handful of snow, hoping that a dog hadn't been by as he thrust it into his face.

A car door slammed beside them, and before Copley could look, arms were around him, jerking him into a familiar chest. He drank in the clean and masculine scent, shuddering as his eyes filled with tears. He clung to Niki's shirt, pulling him closer as the melted snow dripped down his face.

"Where's your coat?" he asked, refusing to let go when Niki tried to turn him. A moment later Copley understood why and looked away himself, his stomach flopping uncomfortably.

Maxim's hands were covered in blood as he leaned over Dimitri's prone form, the sound of his fists making impact over and over, turning Copley's stomach.

"Don't," said Copley, shaking his head as the burning resumed.

Niki pulled him tighter, leading him to the car and helping him into the back seat. Niki followed him in, cradling him tight and pulling the car door shut to cut off the sounds. They started again for a moment as Sweetie slid in the opposite side, hugging Copley tight.

"Dimitri came here to hurt you, honey," said Sweetie, putting a wet kiss on his forehead even as Niki scowled. "Let your boy do his thing. Let him take care of you in the best way he knows."

Niki nodded to her, tugging Copley into his lap as Sweetie stepped back out of the car. She sent them a little wave before putting her hands on her hips. "I'll get the girls off the street for tonight, boss."

"Thanks, Veronica. I owe you one," said Niki, his voice soft and deep enough to help soothe the fierce ache of Copley's face and lungs.

"Make it two, boss, and we'll call it even." She shot him a wink before she slammed the car door shut.

"You okay, baby?" asked Niki the second the door was shut.

Copley pulled back, staring into Niki's face. His beautiful eyes looked so full of worry and a touch of fear that went straight to Copley's heart. He glanced out of the window to where Maxim was standing, his hands now somehow clean, and his chest heaving as his breath misted the air.

Maxim turned, their gazes meeting. The rage melted away in a moment, leaving behind the man that Copley knew and loved. He certainly wasn't innocent, and neither was Nikita. *But does it change how I feel about them?*

"I'm fine. Thank you for coming." He turned to Nikita. *It doesn't change a thing. I still love them.* "When Maxim is done, let's go home. I think I'll mail the rest of my Christmas cards."

Nikita chuckled, bringing their foreheads together. "Anything for you, Copley."

Chapter Twenty-Five

A few months later
Maxim

February for him was usually dry hands, cracked knuckles and finally giving in to the peer pressure of wearing a coat. It was hard not to when the temperature dipped well below freezing with a wind that could knock someone over.

Niki had always read through the dismal month of February while Maxim had to hit reality head-on. He'd picked up one book in the last year, and he'd immediately set it back down with a snort. He didn't need any fantasy world to try to whisk him away from his life.

He fucking loved his life and his job, even if it put him in danger from time to time. Nestor had been lenient lately, too, which was more concerning than not. That man didn't know the meaning of mercy.

But Maxim had never expected the freezing and shortened month to actually be *nice*. Usually there was nothing to celebrate other than losing five pounds from shivering, and everyone was always fucking grumpy.

But he'd never had Copley before, either. Maybe that was why the cold didn't feel half so bad as he gave up his coat to wrap around Copley's already-covered shoulders, opening the door to the restaurant for him so they could get inside the warmth. And maybe that was why he shot a smirk over his shoulder as he let the door close in Niki's face, who almost ran into the glass face-first.

You deserve it. Niki should have given his coat up first. Only having a T-shirt underneath was a piss-poor excuse. Maxim was wearing a T-shirt, too, and he couldn't feel his fingers all that well, but he'd given Copley his coat, regardless.

"Seriously, Max, I'm sweating to death in here," said Copley, peeking out of the multiple hoods that Maxim had pulled tight. "Like, I can't even really breathe, and my hair is all messed up now."

"But you're warm," said Max, shooting him a smile as he slowly started to undress his sub. He ignored his budding nervousness as Copley's clothes were revealed. "Your hair still looks good, too, so no worries." He leaned in, placing a single kiss on Copley's forehead.

Copley's shirt had started as a simple black T-shirt, until Nikita had purchased a Cricut and had gone to town. Cyrillic letters covered the shirt now with words that almost made Maxim blush. The best part was the collar at his neck, two tiger medallions hanging from it that matched the one on his wrist.

Would Copley blush if he knew exactly what his shirt said? *On my knees. I submit to them. Fuck me. Take me.* The back was even better. *Hold me. Praise me. Tell me I'm a good boy, and I'll blow your mind.*

Hopefully, no one could read fucking Russian, because Maxim would have to gouge their eyes out. Those words were for Nikita and him alone.

He shook his head. He'd never thought he would ever find love, let alone share that person with his brother of all people. Somehow it worked. They dated separately or together, and the same with their scenes. Maxim was getting better and hardly needed Nikita's advice anymore.

It worked. And with the two of them, it kept Copley protected.

"This place looks so nice," said Copley, peeking out from beneath Maxim's arm before looking back for Niki. The door opened a second time and Niki stepped in with a whirlwind of snow.

Maxim hardly cast a glance around the restaurant. Why would he when the only thing of any interest was in front of him? Someone had done some decorations, though, and the tinkling of laughter was always nice, too.

"Sorry. I forgot to lock the car." Niki brushed the snow from his coat and hair, sending most of it to the ground. Pulling his coat from his shoulders, he grabbed Copley and Maxim's before finding a coat check off to the side.

Copley had started to retreat in the way he always did when he was nervous. He chewed his lip, staring pointedly at the ground, and even refused to look up to Maxim when he cleared his throat.

"What if I embarrass you?" Copley poked the ground with his toes. "I've never been to a munch before. What if I mess up?"

Oh, baby. Maxim was almost disgusted by the pure love that wrapped its claws around his heart. *Almost.* Tossing his arm over Copley's shoulders, he dragged them past the little foyer and into the main part of the restaurant.

"The better question is, what will you do when I embarrass *you*," said Maxim, shooting his sub a grin. "I wasn't sure about it when Nikita told us that Clint had invited us to this munch, but I appreciate the loophole. This isn't for you or me, baby. It's for Niki."

He glanced back at Nikita, who had taken on a new light as soon as he'd stepped through the doors. Clint had said that he couldn't come back to the club because of his record, but an off-site munch was a whole different ballgame.

"Don't let them look at me," said Copley, his nerves obviously getting to him.

News flash. Every eye in the place was looking at them, both nervous and intrigued. *They should be nervous.* Maxim hadn't fucked Copley for three days, and his patience was about to expire. His desire to treat his sub right was the only thing keeping him from throwing him over his shoulder and stomping off to a storage closet.

There were a few people among the tables that he recognized, and some he wouldn't mind knowing. There was one standing against the wall with his arms crossed, a thick chain collar at his throat with an engraved *H* dangling from it on a paw-shaped tag. Maxim had to take a second glance. The man looked like a Dom through and through, until a much shorter man grabbed him by the collar, dragging him willingly to his knees.

"So, we can't fuck at these things?" asked Maxim, probably a touch too loud from a few smiles that were sent his way. It was a legitimate fucking question.

Nikita shrugged, nodding to a man with some of the thickest biceps that Maxim had ever seen. *This whole place is fucking eye candy.* He dropped his gaze to Copley. *And I've got the fucking pie.*

"Munches are like informal meets — a kind of get-together. It's a good place to talk kink and meet fellow Doms or match with subs, but there's usually no playtime — not that there aren't thirty things in this room that would make our boy come."

"Huh, I was thinking the same thing. Fabric napkins to tie his wrists, and that candlestick looks an awful lot like one of those toys you picked up for him."

Copley shivered next to him, his face flushing for a whole different reason. He lowered his voice. "You'll be fine, baby. And if worse comes to worst, tap my leg three times and I'll find a nice place to fuck you. Your hungry hole misses my cock." He patted Copley on the ass before following Niki through the crowd.

It was bound to be a good night.

An hour later, after a glass of wine, of all things, and a heated conversation with someone named Henley over the best brand of handgun, he felt the signal he'd been waiting for. Three slow taps on his thigh.

He launched from the table, spooking Henley, who nearly keeled off his chair. His much-taller sub tensed, reaching for something at his waist that wasn't there. Maxim sent him a wink. "We have to finish this conversation later. Your Norinco can blow me. I'll take a Glock any day."

"We're headed out of town in a few hours, but I'll catch up with you when we swing by next," said

Henley, grasping Maxim's outstretched hand in a shake.

"Where are you going?" Nikita turned to Max, completely oblivious to the entire conversation. He'd been droning on about rope bunnies for the last thirty minutes.

"Copley needs a good fuck and so do I. The restroom is off-limits for the next...make it an hour." Maxim smirked as Copley choked, turning redder than the napkins. Henley chuckled, turning to another Dom as he plunged his hand into his sub's hair.

"Come on, baby. Don't keep me waiting," said Maxim.

Copley sent him a secret smile, his budding love for humiliation probably making him hard as fuck. "I won't."

Want to see more from this author? Here's a taster for you to enjoy!

It's a Kink Thing: Getting Kinky
M.C. Roth

Coming March 2023

Excerpt

"That was amazing, baby." Hunter rolled to the side, nuzzling into the pillow as he let out a breath. There was cum leaking from his ass and dripping between his thighs in pale rivulets. Elliot reached for it, smearing it until the slickness turned tacky. It clung to his fingers, thick and smelling almost purely of him.

"Ew, gross. Why would you do that?" Hunter turned his head, making a face as he shuffled away.

Letting out a sigh, Elliot bit back the urge to growl out exactly why he wanted to see his husband marked with his cum. Instead, he pressed his dirtied fingers together, watching the cum slowly start to flake away.

There were two reasons really, and he knew Hunter didn't want to hear either of them. He had tried to tell him before, stuttering through his answers before Hunter had turned his nose up.

Turning on his back, Elliot stared at the ceiling and the small silver fan making slow laps in an attempt to dry the sweat from his soaked skin. His flesh prickled as his heart started beating normally again, his thighs still burning from the workout.

"You okay?" asked Hunter, reaching for the cloth by the nightstand that he'd put there in advance. It was dark and probably cold, still ready to wipe away every trace of their love in a few quick strokes.

Always the planner.

Hunter wasn't one to let them sit and just *steam* after sex. He seemed to hate the feeling of cum on his skin or inside him. Most days he asked Elliot to use a condom, treating it like going bare was some kind of special occasion.

Elliot let out a grunt, rolling to watch his husband. Hunter started with the cloth between his thighs, where the smeared layer was mostly dry. In a few moments, there was no evidence except the slight redness to his hole and a softness that Elliot longed to reach out and touch.

He wondered if he could slide right back in there, soft cock and all. *Too bad it's off-limits.*

Hunter leveled him with a look, his dark hair sticking to his skin. A few strands had come loose in their lovemaking, lost in the bedsheets, only to tickle them later. "What is it? Was it not good? I thought it was great—your best yet—and that's saying something."

What is this? A pep rally? Elliot really didn't want to be one of those guys who said 'it is what it is', but that was the only thing that came to mind. He wasn't boasting when he said he had the stamina of a champ. And he always made sure he kept up his two-to-one ratio—for every orgasm he had, he made sure Hunter had two.

"Uh…yeah." Elliot looked to the side. There was a picture of them on the nightstand from their last trip to

Disney. Their smiles had been brighter than the fireworks that night, and he'd felt like a kid again for the first time in years. They'd made love on the balcony of their room when darkness had fallen, the stars and the creepy guy two floors up, their only company.

"Wow, thanks," Hunter deadpanned, dropping his feet to the ground and marching to the bathroom. "I don't think I've ever had such a rave review before. If you weren't in the mood, you could have just said so."

The funny thing was, Elliot *had* been in the mood, almost voraciously so. He couldn't seem to get enough, and no matter how many times he came, he always craved more.

But each time he thrust home with Hunter beneath him or riding him, the joy and expected pleasure dulled to a faded whisp of something that never quite lived up to what it was supposed to be.

"It's not you, Hunt. You're beautiful and amazing. I just…" He couldn't say it. Their sex life was active, if not a touch on the boring side, but it lacked everything that he wanted and needed. "Maybe you could top next time?" *And every time after?*

Hunter made a face from the doorway to the bathroom before running a hand through his messy hair. It only looked wilder when he was done, sticking up in directions that defied physics. He really was the most beautiful man Elliot had ever seen.

He often wondered why Hunter hadn't taken the modeling gig he'd been offered years before when they had just been starting a life together. He belonged on the cover of magazines, not working from home and hidden away in an expensive condo.

"You know I'm not really into that," said Hunter, shrugging his naked shoulders. There was a love bite on his pec that was quickly turning from red to purple, a vivid reminder of what was left of their passion. "I have a hard time topping you, baby. Even thinking about it gives me weird vibes. I can try, though."

Elliot's stomach sank like it so often did after they were intimate. Hunter didn't have to explain the weird vibes because it was the same thing he felt every time. It wasn't supposed to be a chore, but that was exactly what sex had become. Yet, somehow, he craved it.

"I don't want to push you to do something you aren't comfortable with." Elliot turned away as his chest went tight, trying to hide his face. The truth was, Hunter topping him was only the tip of the iceberg of his sexual desires.

The sheets rustled and the bed dipped as Hunter returned, leaning over and placing a kiss on Elliot's cheek. "Tell me what's bugging you, baby. I can't help if you won't tell me. It's you and me against the world, right?"

"Yeah." Threading their fingers together, Elliot closed his eyes, forcing his tears back. He was tall and built, and some guys mistook him for a gym rat, but he was really a huge softie. The simplest insult could ruin his month, and Hunter had been the only steady thing throughout his adult life. Hunter had picked up the pieces so many times he'd lost count.

He owed him everything.

"I need more," said Elliot, biting his lip as everything threatened to come pouring out of his mouth. He could barely hold it back. It had been building for so long, that he was surprised it hadn't burst free already. The images were there, though, plaguing him at night when he was supposed to be sleeping.

"Okay? Like more sex? We can do that, baby. As much as you need." Hunter placed another kiss on his cheek, and Elliot fought the urge to flinch. There was no warmth to the touch, only bleak helplessness.

"No, not like that. I need *you* more. Some days I just need you to just take over and look after things. You know what I mean?" *God*, he wasn't saying anything right, but he couldn't make sense when everything was a jumble in his mind.

Hunter paused, flexing his hand. Elliot could only wonder what he was thinking and what the look on his face was. Disgust? Confusion? Or the '*no*' that he really feared? None of it would be new. They'd gone down this path a dozen times, Elliot testing the waters and Hunter screaming 'shark' before they'd even put a toe in.

"Like the banking and stuff? I can do that, too. I know you have a lot more responsibilities at work than I do, so I can definitely take care of some extra things around the house. If you need more free time or 'you' time, then I can help you with that."

We are getting nowhere. He gritted his teeth in frustration, wishing he had something to bite down on. It was almost terrifying how quickly the rage came on lately. "I need you to take control," said Elliot, his voice almost a growl. "In sex…in everything."

He blinked his eyes open as he felt Hunter pull away. When he turned his head, he met Hunter's confused and hurt gaze. The beautiful blue he'd fallen in love with was there, distorted beneath the fresh glaze of tears.

He'd promised himself never to hurt Hunter or be the cause of any pain, but it was plain as day in front of him.

"Never mind." He forced a smile on his face, pulling the covers up to his chin. He was exposed and naked, suddenly afraid of what Hunter would see if he looked too hard. "Forget I said anything. I'll make breakfast if you do the dishes."

"You sure?" Hunter scratched at a flake of something on his stomach that he'd obviously missed. His relief was almost palpable.

Sitting up, Elliot brought their lips together in a brief kiss. "I'm sure. Sorry… I shouldn't have brought that up. You're perfect, Hunt. A man wouldn't ask for more unless he were crazy."

There was that cute flush across Hunter's cheeks that made him look ten years younger. Sometimes, he still looked the same as he did during their college days. It was only when he smiled that Elliot could really track the differences.

"Can I have French toast?" Hunter perked up, grabbing his robe and throwing it over his shoulders. The front draped open, showing off his abs and his perfectly soft cock.

Elliot's cock stirred again, and he pressed the heel of his hand to his groin, squishing it into submission as he rolled out of bed. He grabbed boxers and jeans, jamming his cock up along the waistband so Hunter wouldn't see. If they rolled back into bed now, they'd get nothing done all day.

He swept his hands inside Hunter's robe one last time, trailing down his smooth skin that had him fully hard in moments. Letting out a shuddering breath, he placed a kiss against the side of his neck, licking the sweat that was still lingering there. Hunter let out a giggle, squirming in his hold.

"I'll make you whatever you want as long as I can have this," said Elliot as he grasped the robe's tie and tugged it free before tossing it on the bed. "You get the juice and I'll get the rest."

It was domestic bliss at its finest, even with a gaping hole in his gut and an unsatisfied arousal that thrummed beneath his skin. Hunter lounged on one of the stools at the end of the kitchen island, his housecoat open and his naked ass on the leather surface. He scrolled through his phone as Elliot gathered ingredients and started up the stove.

The kitchen was small for the two of them, especially since the price tag of the condo had been so large, but Elliot secretly loved it. There was no elbow room to speak of and some of the cupboards didn't open because the handles would have run into an adjacent drawer, but it kept everyone in the kitchen close. He only had to reach out and he'd be able to touch Hunter, who would send him a smile with every caress.

He cracked an egg into a bowl, grumbling at the shell that escaped and slipped right to the bottom. He dragged his nail against it, but it foiled him until he promptly gave up. *Nothing a little cinnamon won't fix.*

Hunter made a choking sound behind him, the chair squelching as he shifted. "Oh my God. Look at this, baby. Can you believe it?"

He spun his phone to Elliot who grabbed it, turning the stove down a touch before he looked to the screen. His jaw almost hit the floor as his heart came to a brief stop. *This is… It's…*

"Some kind of swingers club or something? Alice sent me an invite to the open house." Hunter chuckled, leaning his cheek on his hand. "I don't understand how people are into that kind of thing. All that leather and skin, and people getting spanked and stuff? How humiliating."

The crackling of the toast in the pan dimmed to a quiet haze as Elliot stared at the invite on the screen.

His palms were suddenly slick, fresh sweat breaking out along his spine. It was no swingers club.

Unkinked. Of course, he recognized the name of the place hosting the open house. The dim picture of a white unmarked door that Alice had included didn't do the place justice from what he'd heard.

He'd been dreaming about it for the last year — everything from the supposed leather attire, mysterious rooms and the people within its soundproofed walls. When he closed his eyes, he could almost imagine the smell and the taste that would roll across his tongue.

He'd learned about the kink club almost by accident when a co-worker had mentioned that they were into BDSM after they'd gotten a little tipsy at an office party. One Google search had left him hard and wanting, fresh dreams haunting him about the kind of life and dynamic that he'd never have.

The hole in his chest was suddenly gaping, its maw open wide and ready to swallow him whole. His mouth was dry, his eyes burning as he struggled to look away. There was no information — not really — only a time and a date, when he craved so much more.

"We should go." The words were out of his mouth before he even knew he was saying them. Elliot flushed, dropping the phone on the table before turning to the fridge and grabbing a few more slices of bread. "It sounds fun, I mean. They have a dress code and everything. It would be like Halloween."

He was sure that if a kinkster ever heard him say that, they'd be insulted. If their thoughts were anything like his, it wasn't so much dressing up as revealing a part of themselves that they'd kept hidden at their nine-to-five. He'd figured that out when he'd splurged on a pair of leather underwear. He still had them, hidden at the bottom of his filing cabinet beneath their old mortgage papers.

Hunter stared at him, his jaw slack and his eyes wide. His cheeks had flushed, the rosy blush creeping down his neck. "You want to go to a sex party?"

Oh fuck. "It's not a sex party, and look... It says that the public is welcome for one night only, and they have a demonstration about Dominance and submission. You're always looking to try new things, so why not go out on a limb?" *Please, please, please.*

Hunter leveled him with a look, pulling his lips back over his teeth. He could probably see right through Elliot's lie. Elliot was the one who was always on the search for new things, like his tropical garden, which he'd moved to his office after Hunter had complained.

"I mean, I like new foods and stuff. I'm in love with that Indonesian restaurant we found, but I don't know if we're going to fit in with this kind of crowd. It doesn't seem exactly natural." Hunter took his phone back, squinting down at the screen.

Elliot had heard that one before more times than he could count, but never from Hunter. It stung, lancing into the coolness of his chest like an open wound.

"You're sounding a lot like your mom there," said Elliot, his heart sinking even lower. "It hasn't been that long since your family considered you and me 'unnatural'. Hell, some of them still do, even if we get a Christmas invite. It's like they think I woke up one morning and said 'hey, I want to be homosexual now so people can tell jokes about me and threaten me with bodily harm'." Elliot shook his head, trying not to grit his teeth. At the rate he was going, he would wear them down. "I love you, and you happen to have a penis." *Penises are the best.*

Hunter flushed, biting his lip. "I'm sorry. I really didn't mean it that way, and that was terrible of me. If you want to go, we can absolutely go. I'll even dress up."

Elliot looked up as something on the stove started to burn, black smoke puffing into the air. Grabbing the spatula, he flipped the toast out of the pan, the charcoaled side landing face-up on the counter. *Shit.*

"When is it? I didn't even look." His heart pounded, his hands shaking as he pulled a few paper towels free from the roll to clean up his mess. Egg and cinnamon swirled under his hand as he tried to wipe them away.

"This Friday. Oh, don't you have that work thing?" asked Hunter, seeming almost relieved.

"Nope. That's next Friday." *It's absolutely this Friday.* He could miss one meeting without any sort of penalty, especially when it was an after-hours one. It was one benefit of being one of the best in the company.

"Oh." Hunter's face fell and he clutched at the edge of the robe, tightening it across his chest. "I guess we can go then."

"We don't have to." Elliot cracked a fresh egg into the French toast mix, not even trying to retrieve the shell this time. His hands were so unsteady that he wouldn't have been able to pull it out, even if he managed to trap the tiny piece against the wall of the bowl.

"No, I want to. I'm really excited," said Hunter with the enthusiasm of someone marching to their doom. Running his hand through his hair, he let out a long sigh. "Just help me pick out something to wear. I'm terrible at that kind of thing."

Chuckling, Elliot placed a fresh piece of bread into the pan, the egg mixture sizzling as it hit the surface.

The sharp scent of cinnamon and vanilla almost covered the burnt charcoal still clinging to the air.

"You are right about that," said Elliot, his smile real for the first time in ages. "You wore a plain gray T-shirt to a concert. I mean, come on, it's a concert! It's the only time you can wear all black with a spiky collar and do your hair in a pink mohawk and people don't give you a second look."

Hunter stuck his tongue out, shifting on the chair with another wet sound. His ass must've still been leaking. Luckily the chair would wipe clean easily, not that Elliot really cared. As far as he was concerned, he was okay with a bit of cum on every surface except for the table, and even that could be bargained for.

"Or, you could just wear this," said Elliot, sliding his hands back into Hunter's robe. "Put on a little G-string and maybe tape some Xs over your titties." He pinched Hunter's nipples, grinning at his squeak. "Sounds like a perfect dress code to me."

Hunter slapped him playfully on the hand when he pinched him a second time. "You are insatiable, baby. Maybe a sex party is exactly what you need."

Elliot wasn't going to bother correcting him again, not when he was finally going to Unkinked in the near future. "Oh, but I have you all to myself until Friday. What am I going to do with all that time?"

He mouthed at Hunter's neck, sucking a bruise in the same spot he had before breakfast. Hunter shivered, no longer trying to push him away.

"I think your toast is burning," Hunter whispered, tilting his head back to give him better access.

"No, it's not—oh shit." Elliot lunged for the pan, dousing it under cold water as smoke rolled from it. He sent Hunter a wink, trying to play off every bit of nervousness. "Saved by the pan."

About the Author

M.C. Roth lives in Canada and loves every season, even the dreaded Canadian winter. She graduated with honours from the Associate Diploma Program in Veterinary Technology at the University of Guelph before choosing a different career path.

Between caring for her young son, spending time with her husband, and feeding treats to her menagerie of animals, she still spends every spare second devoted to her passion for writing.

She loves growing peppers that are hot enough to make grown men cry, but she doesn't like spicy food herself. Her favourite thing, other than writing of course, is to find a quiet place in the wilderness and listen to the birds while dreaming about the gorgeous men in her head.

M.C. Roth loves to hear from readers. You can find her contact information, website details and author profile page at https://www.pride-publishing.com

PUBLISHING

Sign up for our newsletter and find out about all our romance book releases, eBook sales and promotions, sneak peeks and FREE romance books!